ISCARIOT

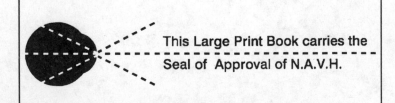

This Large Print Book carries the
Seal of Approval of N.A.V.H.

ISCARIOT

TOSCA LEE

THORNDIKE PRESS

A part of Gale, Cengage Learning

GALE
CENGAGE Learning·

Detroit • New York • San Francisco • New Haven, Conn • Waterville, Maine • London

GALE
CENGAGE Learning®

Thorndike Press® Large Print Basic.
The text of this Large Print edition is unabridged.
Other aspects of the book may vary from the original edition.
Set in 16 pt. Plantin.

LIBRARY OF CONGRESS CATALOGING-IN-PUBLICATION DATA

Lee, Tosca Moon.
  Iscariot / by Tosca Lee.
    pages ; cm. — (Thorndike Press large print basic)
  ISBN-13: 978-1-4104-5691-5 (hardcover)
  ISBN-10: 1-4104-5691-9 (hardcover)
  1. Judas Iscariot—Fiction. 2. Large type books. I. Title.
PS3612.E3487I83 2013
813'.6—dc23   2013000022

Published in 2013 by arrangement with Howard Books, a division of Simon & Schuster, Inc.

Printed in the United States of America
1 2 3 4 5 6 7 17 16 15 14 13

For my parents.

EPILOGUE

A dog chokes by the side of the road in Capernaum. He is rabid and manged. He is foul and unloved.

He is more worthy to live than I.

If only I had never left Jerusalem as a child. If only Herod had never died. If only I had never laid eyes on the gaunt man by the side of the Jordan.

The Nazarene.

They will say that I betrayed him, that I reduced his price to thirty silver shekels. That I turned against my master.

They do not know me.

They will not ask themselves if they might have done the same. To even think it is to court the possibility that we may not be so different. It takes away the right to condemn, the comfort in saying, "At least I am not like him!"

My master taught a parable about that, once.

7

But if they do not know me, neither did they know him. And so the truth goes with me to the abyss.

Judas. It was once a good name, a strong name, the name of our people: Judah. It is the dwelling place of the Temple, which is the dwelling place of the Lord.

I cannot see the Temple from here in the valley, the marble and gold of her face, or the smoke of her altar, dying at the end of the day. There is only the smolder of trash, the bulging of my eyes . . .

The cut of the noose.

The sun is setting. Sound has left my ears, but I can feel the wind rushing through the valley and past me like a stolen breath, east toward the wilderness as though borne on cloven hooves.

There. The dark light.

And now I am afraid. Because I know that in Sheol no one praises God but ruminates forever on what might have been.

The dark light again. Someone is coming. It is a boy.

It is me.

■ ■ ■ ■

PERDITION

■ ■ ■ ■

1

I was six years old the day we fled Jerusalem, and Caesar Augustus was emperor.

I had known nothing but Jerusalem all my life. It was the home of the Temple and navel of the world. Even infected with Roman soldiers and Herod's stadium, God's house was in Jerusalem, and no good man of Israel ever wanted to leave it.

And so I was stunned the day my father, a devout man, announced that we were leaving.

Especially now. Just that morning Father had come bursting into the house with the news that Herod, our king, was dead. I had thought it the happiest day of my life, if only because I had never seen Father so jubilant. He sang that day, one of the hymns of David, as my mother clapped her hands and my older brother Joshua and I went shouting and dancing into the street. We weren't the only ones. Soon all Jerusalem would erupt with joy.

We were still celebrating when Father's friend Aaron came hurrying toward the house. "Where's your father? Simon!" he shouted. "They're taking the eagle down!"

Father came out to meet him but Aaron was too excited to even kiss him in greeting. "They've gone to take Herod's eagle off the Temple!"

Even at the age of six I had heard plenty about this abomination affixed to the great Temple gate, this golden kiss of our king to the buttock of Rome. It was everything a Jew must hate: a graven image, which was an affront to God's law, and the symbol of Rome.

"Boys, get inside," Father said. And then he left for the Temple.

For hours, I imagined him on the shoulders of others, tearing the eagle free to the sound of cheers. But when he returned, his jaw was tight beneath his beard.

"Pack what you can carry. Quickly," he said. "We're leaving."

We left that night, bribing the guard to let us out the small door in the city gate.

All the next day we traveled in silence, my mother's hand viselike around mine, my brother pale and pensive as he cast furtive glances at my father.

12

I didn't know what had happened — only that Jerusalem was somehow unsafe and the lines had deepened around Father's eyes. I knew better than to press him with questions; I would ask Joshua to explain it all to me later. He was brilliant, my ten-year-old brother. Even then everyone knew he would become a great teacher of the law. And for that reason I wanted to become one, too.

But a few hours later, when I realized I was the farthest from Jerusalem I had ever been, I began to worry.

"Father," I said. "Will we be home in time for Passover?"

It was my favorite holiday, a time when Joshua and I went with him to buy our lamb and bring it to the Temple priests.

"No, Judas," he said. "Jerusalem is a tinderbox and God calls us to Galilee."

"But why —"

"No more now."

That night, in the dank lower room of an inn, my brother lay in troubled silence beside me.

I leaned up on my elbow. A lone lamp somewhere on the floor above cast a dull glow across the stairwell; I could just make out Joshua's profile staring up at the ceiling.

"Herod isn't dead," he said finally. "I

13

heard Father talking with one of the men we traveled with today. It was a rumor. The king's sick, but he's alive."

"But Father said —"

"He was wrong. They all were. The rumor gave men the courage to take the eagle down. Until Herod's soldiers arrived." He turned and looked at me. "Aaron was arrested."

I stared at him in the darkness.

"It was the teachers Judas and Matthias who led the charge to the Temple with their students."

Father and Aaron both had been students of the famous teacher Judas bar Seppho-raeus. It was partially for him — and for Judas Maccabee, the warrior called the Hammer — that I had been named. The lower room was suddenly far too cold.

"I heard Father say that when they got there Aaron pushed right through the mob. He climbed up on the shoulders of one of the students to help pull the eagle down. But Father couldn't get through the crowd. So he stood back to watch — he said he wanted witness for his sons what would surely become known as the first day of the Lord's coming. They had just gotten the eagle off when the soldiers came. No one heard him trying to warn them through the cheering."

"Then he didn't do it!" But even as I said it, I was afraid.

Joshua was silent.

"Will they arrest Father?"

"No. But that's why we left."

"What'll happen to the others?"

"I don't know."

"But what if —"

"Mother's coming. Go to sleep."

But I couldn't sleep. Only after Father came down did I even close my eyes, but not before wishing we had traveled through the night. For the first time since leaving Jerusalem, I wished we were a league away.

I dreamed of soldiers. I was used to seeing them throughout the Holy City, coming in and out of the Antonia Fortress or working along the walls and aqueducts, but that night they came to the room where we slept and dragged my father away. I woke up screaming.

"What's this, Judas? Hush," Father said, drawing me next to him. I could smell the heat of day lingering on his skin. "All is well. Sleep now."

I curled beneath the weight of his arm, my eyes open in the dark, until the soldiers became as fleeting as ghosts and there was

15

only the low rumble of his breath beside me.

We were fifteen miles from the Sea of Galilee by the time we stopped in Scythopolis. It was nearly Purim, the spring feast before Passover.

Scythopolis was the largest city we had come to since Jericho and there was construction everywhere, including a wide street being paved in perfect basalt squares. We passed a building that looked like a temple and I gaped at the statue of a nude man in front of it, the finely chiseled face and full lips — the naked sex dangling between his thighs like a cluster of grapes. I had seen few graven images and I had never seen an uncircumcised penis.

"Look away," Father said. "This is not the Lord's."

I did look away, but I was already reconstructing the images in my mind — of the nude man and wreath-headed others dancing in naked relief across the temple face behind him.

We found an inn run by Jews and that evening, after changing into clean clothing, began our fast and went to the synagogue.

Right in the middle of the reading of the scroll, my stomach began to growl. Joshua leaned over and whispered, "Maybe our fast will bring God's kingdom that much more quickly."

I nodded. I didn't know exactly what the coming kingdom would look like except that there would be no Romans or Gentiles or Samaritans in it.

Most important, Aaron would not be arrested and Father would be safe.

That night we stayed up late on the roof with the other guests beneath the full moon. At home, my cousins would play games into the night and sleep late the next day, shortening the time until sundown when they could eat at last. But here there were no games, and the little children had already eaten and fallen asleep beside their mothers.

I was by then miserable with hunger, my stomach twisting into a fist. But I knew I must learn to fast if I hoped to be an important teacher like my brother, who listened in on the men's conversation as though he were one of them already. But as the night wore on I began to pray for the comfort of sleep.

"Herod's moved all those they rounded up to Jericho," I heard the innkeeper say. "A merchant brought the news two days ago."

Joshua nudged me and I realized they were talking about the men who had been arrested. Suddenly I was very awake.

Another man, who had walked with us from the inn to the synagogue earlier, shook his head. "There'll be no good end for them. Why must they martyr themselves when, in a few more days, Herod will be dead? May the Lord make it so!"

A round of assenting murmurs.

I stared at Joshua, my heart hammering. I didn't know what a martyr was, but I saw the roundness of my brother's eyes, the grim line of Father's mouth as all the men began speaking at once.

"The Romans will still be here."

"I'd take the Romans over Herod. His own family isn't even safe from him. Caesar said it right that he'd rather be Herod's pig than his son."

"I wouldn't put it past that whoreson to eat a pig."

I rolled forward, arms clutched around my middle.

"Come, Judas," Joshua whispered, motioning me to follow him downstairs. I uncurled in agony to follow him.

He led me to his roll near our things in one of the inn's back rooms. After rummaging around, Joshua took my hand and laid a

18

stale piece of bread in it. "Here. If you don't eat, you'll be sick like last time."

I looked from him to the bread, thinking. I should give it back. I should throw it down.

"You are very zealous," Joshua said. "But you are young and not expected to go without food."

"But the coming kingdom —"

"A piece of bread will not make the Romans leave or Herod die any faster. I'm your older brother, aren't I?"

I nodded, tears welling stupidly in my eyes. I ate the bread in quick bites as I followed Joshua back up to the roof.

I was just swallowing the last of it when a surprised shout broke the night — followed quickly by another and the shrill sound of a woman's voice.

We ran back to the roof to find everyone on their feet staring at the sky. And then I saw why: The moon, so full and white when we had gone down into the house, was partially sheathed in shadow.

"It's an omen!" someone said. "A sign!"

I blinked at the sky, at the moon half-covered as though with a black lid. Would it go out? What evil could do that?

And then I knew.

I began to tremble, my skin having gone cold and then hot at once. A wail filled my ears. It came from my throat.

"Shush, Judas!" My mother pulled me to her. But as she did, my stomach lurched and I doubled over and vomited at her feet. It was only a little amount, the bread having come out in pale bits shamefully illuminated by the light of the disappearing moon. I began to cry, the acrid taste in my mouth and nostrils, as my mother gathered me up and carried me past the mess to the corner. I was by now beside myself, shaking, hot tears tracking down my face.

"It's my fault!" I cried.

"What?" My mother said.

"The moon — I did it." As Eve with her fruit, I had ruined the moon for the sky.

"Ah, my dove, no you did not — what is a little bread to God? I told Joshua to give it to you so you wouldn't get sick. Hush now," she said, starting to clean my face. "This is not about you, Judas."

But as shouts sounded from other rooftops and the men began to argue about what it meant, I knew better. The world could be ruined by the smallest of actions. For striking a rock, Moses had never entered the Promised Land. And now I had been the sky's undoing.

I jerked away from my mother, ran to the clot of men, and found my father. I grabbed

20

his sleeve.

"Judas! What's this?"

I fell down to my knees, and he hauled me up under my arms.

"It's my fault!"

"This? No, Judas, it's a portent, a sign. Don't be afraid. The Lord winks at us. See?"

I cried harder, hiccupping now. He didn't know the grievousness of my sin. "I ate and see what happened!" I wouldn't blame my mother or Joshua — I alone had eaten the bread.

He blinked at me in the darkness, and then chuckled. It had not bothered me so much that my mother did not understand, but hearing this from my father — and in the face of such obvious disaster — I felt more alone than I had ever felt in my life.

"Do you think you've caused this, little Judas? But there — see? The moon is emerging again."

I followed the line of his finger. Sure enough, the shadow had moved a little bit away. I watched as it began to retreat, my fear subsiding the tiniest increment.

He patted my back. "The Lord won't reject you for being a hungry boy. But if it will make you feel better, we will immerse tomorrow."

The next day I immersed in the synagogue

mikva three times to the bafflement of my father and the empathetic observance of my brother. Not until the third time did I feel any measure of relief, and even then not until I went outside that evening and saw that the moon was whole once more.

The news came before we left Scythopolis: Herod had died the night of the eclipse — but not before burning two of Jerusalem's great teachers and forty of their students at the stake in Jericho. My father broke out with a great cry and tore his clothes. Joshua did likewise.

I simply cried.

The students who said they had not instigated the taking down of the eagle survived, and I hated them for it. I hated them because I knew Aaron was not among them — Aaron who would have condemned Herod until the last of his life for sheer love of the law. And then I cried harder because I wished he had not loved the law so much.

For nights to come I shivered beneath my blanket and dreamed of the students burning in the fires.

Though I thought I shouldn't love Sepphoris, I did. I shouldn't, because it was far from Jerusalem, and her fortress seemed to inhabit a world that knew no such thing as the holy Temple. And I should not love it because it was Herod's, and even though Herod was dead, his sons were eagle-kissers just like him who wanted everything Roman — down to the scraps of power the empire threw them like crusts to dogs.

But I loved it because Father was safe. Nothing could touch us here.

I came to know Sepphoris by its sounds. Voices of children my own age wafted up from farther down the hill where the farmers kept their houses and tended their vineyards. Roosters crowed throughout the day. At times I could hear one of the distant shepherds playing a flute. And always there was birdsong.

That spring when it rained, water trickled from the roof into the channels of the cisterns below. It was a good sound, the sound of water. Moss clung to the stones of the houses, so that even on sunny days the air near any house seemed to smell of rain as pines rustled overhead.

We stayed with my father's cousin, Eleazar — a priest who helped place Joshua and me with a teacher who was so impressed with Joshua's early abilities that he called him "little rabbi."

I saw how everyone looked at him with

23

ready fascination, as though such a boy might be proof that God had not forgotten us, but planted in the soil of this generation the mustard seed of a greatness unknown by the last. And though I knew I would never be Joshua's equal, I didn't care. People would say, "There goes the brother of Joshua bar Simon. What is his name? Ah, that's right — Judas." And that would be enough.

That year was the first that I did not go to the Temple for Passover. Instead, we watched the families that left together, my heart full of jagged envy as they sang their psalms out the city gate.

Eleazar had fallen ill weeks before and been unable to leave with the rest of the priests. I saw the way his wife, old Zipporah, covered her face with her hands when she thought no one was looking. It made me afraid for Eleazar, whom I had grown fond of, and I prayed for him. I immersed so often that my brother got angry with me and told me that even the Pharisees didn't wash that much, nor the Essenes, who were so extreme as to not move their bowels on the Sabbath. Was I going to keep from that as well?

I did briefly consider it, but I knew better than to rely on my stomach to do what it was told.

We celebrated Passover in the synagogue and at the home of Eleazar, who had recovered in what seemed like a miracle, claiming it was Mother and Zipporah's good lamb stew.

Then, a few days later, the first pilgrims began to return.

Too early.

We had just gathered for the evening meal when Eleazar's nephew came into the house, tearing at his hair.

"They slaughtered them with their sacrifices!" he shouted.

"What's this?" Eleazar demanded, rising from his seat.

"The new king sent his guard to the Temple the day before the feast — a guard of foreign mercenaries. Some of the pilgrims started throwing stones at them in protest. The king retaliated by sending in his army. They massacred the people. Pilgrims — men, women, children. Thousands dead!"

Father staggered, the color gone from his face. The house that night was filled with Mother's and Zipporah's weeping and the groans of Eleazar, who sounded less like a weathered old priest than just a broken old man.

Three thousand died in the massacre that

Passover. The tinderbox had exploded. It was only the beginning.

2

With Herod dead and his son Archelaus barely on the throne, rebellions sprang up across the country. That summer, news about the movement of soldiers came like lightning strikes, closer and closer together: Romans, arriving on the coast. Legions, marching down from Syria . . . Soldiers camped outside Jerusalem itself.

We tried to ask Father about it, but he was often gone on some new business and we might not see him for days. When he returned, he was silent, tense, and tired.

Eleazar was by then miraculously healthy. So when his priestly course was selected for Pentecost duties in the Temple, he left for Jerusalem with another priest and a local carpet-maker who wore the tefillin of the Pharisees strapped so tightly to his forehead and arm that they seemed practically embedded in his skin.

With Eleazar gone, I noticed my father's

increased absences more keenly than ever and began to cling to Joshua. He was eleven now, nearly a man, and interested in the latest news to the point of obsession. I felt completely deserted, and scowled at him one afternoon when he came running into our teacher's house after having been missing all morning. But instead of sliding into his seat in the courtyard, he shouted, "Jericho is burning! A rebel named Simon has proclaimed himself king!"

We raced together to the market.

It was there, in the bustle of the stalls, that I first saw him: a broad-shouldered man moving through the crowd. He was tall, which was what first caught my eye. But it was the way he passed among the people like water that caused me to stare. His mantle was up over his head so I knew nothing about his face, but I saw the way others responded to him with silent nods and tilts of their heads. Was he a teacher? Men noted his movement with their eyes as though standing aside for him without moving. And several vendors he passed pressed food or even a small jug of wine into his hand, and turned away as though the transaction was done before they had accepted payment.

"Who's that?" I said, my gaze fixed on him.

Joshua pulled me to the edge of the street. "Never say to anyone what I'm going to tell you. And stop staring."

I nodded, desperate to gain back my brother's confidence, which felt so recently removed from me. When I tried to locate the man again, he was gone.

"That . . . was Judas bar Hezekiah," he said with a strange smile.

Judas son of Hezekiah?

Joshua waited a beat and then said, as though I should have known: "His father was the most famous bandit in Galilee. Come." He tugged me toward home, his need for news apparently satisfied. But I noted that he glanced back, once, over his shoulder.

That evening Father prepared to leave with some men who came to the door to fetch him. When Joshua asked to go with him, he hesitated before nodding and motioning for him to hurry. I leapt up as well, but Father shook his head.

"No, Judas."

I was hurt as he crouched down in front of me. "Joshua is eleven, nearly a man. It's fitting he should go. But you — keep your mother and Zipporah company. Enjoy your

29

boyhood, Judas, while you have it."

I turned and ran into the other room.

Sometime that night I felt Joshua lie down beside me, but instead of curling against him as I often did, I pretended to be asleep. When he said, very softly in the darkness, "Judas?" I refused to answer.

I woke with a hard shake that rattled my teeth. "Judas!"

Mother.

She tugged me up along with the mantle covering me. In the distance, thunderous sounds. The faint smell of fire wafted through the house from somewhere outside.

I clung to her as she carried me out the back room and down the steps carved into the bedrock beneath the house. Joshua came after us with a lamp, the flame seeming to bob in the darkness.

Zipporah was the last one down. I could barely make out her wiry form as she stood with Mother on the narrow stair, pulling something across the opening, encasing us in darkness. Cold.

"Joshua?" My voice sounded too loud in the man-made cavern.

"Quiet!" Zipporah hissed from the stairwell.

"I'm here," he whispered. I reached for him, accidentally knocking the lamp in his hand so that the wick came out of it and sputtered on the dank floor.

"What's happening? Where's Father?"

Joshua started to speak, but Mother said, "Hush now. Your father is seeing to things."

That night, Judas bar Hezekiah took Sepphoris.

"His bandits have taken the palace and looted the armory!" Joshua cried, running into the house the next morning. I felt I should be excited, but all I could say was, "Where's Father?"

"He's at the palace."

"With Judas bar Hezekiah?" I said, confused.

"No, Judas has gone on already to Jerusalem." His eyes were alight. "Don't you see? If he controls the capital here, he controls western Galilee. And now he's going to the Holy City."

He came and laid his arm over my shoulders. "Judas bar Hezekiah is the Messiah and our father is a hero!"

My heart sailed with pride for my father. Of course he was a hero. I had known all along — even as I felt desperate jealousy at the realization that Joshua had known what was happening and shared something with Father that I had not.

Father returned the next night before the

coming in of Sabbath, somber and silent, so that I did not throw myself at him or even ask him questions. But he was there, which was enough, though he had brought with him something I had never seen on him before: a sword. He put it away from us in the corner of the front room, his gaze warning us to let it be.

Late in the day, as Zipporah and Mother fixed the Sabbath meal, he drew me onto his lap so that I felt the strong circle of his arms.

"I know these days have been hard for you, Judas," he said, his beard against my cheek smelling of fire. "I will explain everything in time and these things will all make sense. But for now, remember that I love you, and what I have done, I have done for you and Joshua, and for your sons, so that one day they may be free."

We celebrated Pentecost at the synagogue. It was the first time Mother and I had ventured out in days. All of Sepphoris was on nervous edge, like a cage of doves shaken on the way to market.

"When Eleazar returns, we should think of leaving," I overheard Father say a few nights later. I was in bed with Joshua in the next room, unable to sleep. By the sound of

32

his breathing, I knew he was awake, too.

Mother's voice registered alarm. "What? Why have we come if only to leave again? Unless you mean we'll return to Jerusalem . . . ?"

"No. Every army, would-be king, and messiah is on his way to the Holy City. It'll be a miracle if the city withstands the day."

"Then we should stay. We are safe in Sepphoris and you are a man of importance here. Now that Judas bar Hezekiah has taken the city —"

"Judas bar Hezekiah has lived too long in the hills. Men flock to him for his zeal and because his father was a hero. But he doesn't know how to run a city or to protect it!"

"He has men like you!"

"Men like me are not enough. I fear what may happen to us here. I've only exchanged one tinderbox for another!" His voice broke and in the ensuing silence I knew Mother had taken him into her arms.

I had never heard Father like that before. But when I pushed up from my mat to go to him, Joshua grabbed me by the arm and held me back.

That night I lay awake long after my parents ceased their quiet and strained coupling in the next room and the sound of

33

Father's — and Zipporah's — snores had filled the dark house.

I didn't like the idea of leaving, even if Sepphoris wasn't as safe as Father had thought — especially now that the soldiers and tax collectors were gone.

But what disturbed me more than the thought of leaving was the crack in his voice. The brokenness of it. I didn't want to hear that in my father, whom I regarded as greater than any bandit king.

Within days pilgrims began to return from Pentecost, all telling the story: fighting in the streets. Blood in Jerusalem's gutters. Fire in the Temple so that even the marble burned. The Temple nearly destroyed.

After hearing the news, something happened to Joshua. He barely spoke, but I knew by the tight pull of his brows that there was no quiet inside his mind. When I tried to talk to him he just shook his head, as though he couldn't hear me through the din.

"Joshua," I said, shaking him. "What is it?"

His eyes darted to me, wide and wild, as though my words were a jackal in the house. "What does it mean," he said strangely, "if the Lord resides in the Temple, and the

34

Temple burns down? Why does the Lord not defend his own house? What does it mean? Has God abandoned us?"

I didn't know what was more alarming — the line of these questions, or that they came from him. Something shuddered inside me.

"But no, Judas. Don't remember I said that. It is our sin that allowed the Romans to exile us in our own land, as it allowed Israel to be exiled to Babylonia — the prophets said it. We will repent and God will restore us."

He threw his hands up over his face. As he prayed the Shema, I didn't need to see his expression to know that it was twisted beneath his fingers.

Hear, O Israel, the Lord is One . . .

But as I recited the words with him, I was shaken.

Joshua was the best boy that I knew. I could never hope to be as good or perfect as him. He would grow up to be a better man, even, than Father. If Joshua should worry about repentance, what did that mean for me? For all the rest of Israel?

The next day, Malachi, the priest who had gone up to Jerusalem with Eleazar, came to the house, his face streaked and dirty, his tunic ripped. At the sight of him Zipporah dropped a vessel of oil on the floor and fell to her knees. A great moan escaped her as though it were her very life.

"There was such a fire," Malachi cried. "Eleazar stayed back to usher as many as he could out the gate. But before he could come out, a beam from the portico crashed down on him when the balcony gave way."

After a few more days, we stopped looking for returnees from Jerusalem, and no more came.

We were forbidden from going to the city gate or the marketplace, but no one could contain the news that came next. It was practically shouted in the streets: The Jews had attacked the Romans.

Jews attacking Romans! This was the end of Roman rule, some said. Others feared retaliation, swift and decisive, and blamed the Samaritans for joining with the Romans against us, calling them dogs and sons of whores. Varus, the Syrian governor, was gathering a new force, one man said. Soon he would return with legions of soldiers to quell every outburst in Judea, where a common cry had risen in Jerusalem: Freedom for Israel! Death to Rome.

"We're leaving," Father said a few days later. "We're going to Kerioth, to the house of your mother's sister." It was midsummer and we had been in Sepphoris just over three months. The city had swollen in population as people came from every hamlet and village to seek shelter. Everyone was afraid.

Mother pleaded with Zipporah to come with us, but she was like the tree that grows up through the courtyard of a house and becomes a part of it. She had seemed old to me before, but in the days since Eleazer's death, she had grown ancient.

I had no roots in this place, but I did not want to leave either. The Jerusalem I had loved no longer existed. Here, my father was known as a conspirator of Judas bar Hezekiah, who called himelf king and others called Messiah. I saw the way other men nodded at him, the way they stood aside and inclined their heads.

Even as we packed our things I prayed to God to keep us here, to delay us even a little while.

That evening Judas bar Hezekiah returned to the city. The first thing he did was send for Father. By the time he came home the next afternoon, he was more haggard than I had ever seen him.

"Good," he said, looking around at the things packed and ready to leave. "Tomorrow Judas is going out of the city again. I have promised to stay until he returns."

"What?" Mother cried.

"Only until then. And then we will go."

He lay down on his mat and fell asleep, his arm over his eyes.

As Joshua continued to struggle with those questions only he was wise or tortured enough to ask and as Zipporah grew ever more silent, I begged God again that we would not have to leave.

I would regret that prayer the rest of my life.

3

"Come, Judas."

Mother hoisted her water jar. She had already brought around Zipporah's donkey. It was nearly the coming in of Sabbath, two days past the time that Judas bar Hezekiah was to have returned to Sepphoris.

I hated going with Mother to the spring at the bottom of the hill. This was woman's work and though I was younger than Joshua, I certainly was not a girl.

"Judas," she said again. I didn't move.

Mother sighed and glanced at my brother, who immediately got to his feet. I felt shamed by his dutiful looks, the way he got to his feet without protest, his conciliatory smile at me. His very goodness. Something broke within me.

"No, I'll go." I bounded up. I didn't want to, but I did it to best him. And I really didn't want to stay with Zipporah, who seemed less and less present in this world each day. She had taken lately to searching all the stone vessels in the house, saying she was looking for the good wine, when everyone knew that wine wasn't kept in such jars and that she was really looking for nothing.

"You can't lift the water up onto the ass," Joshua said, getting up.

I spun on him and spat at his feet. "I can too! And I'd rather go with Mother than stay here with you!"

I didn't mean it. I was jealous that he had been included so much in Father's business while I remained behind. I was hurt by his preoccupied absence even when he sat beside me. I even felt betrayed by the strange depression that seemed to have seized him, so that in some ways he seemed closer to Zipporah than he did to me.

I will never forget Joshua's look in that moment, sad and downcast. Because I knew that he missed our times together, too, and that this separation between the world of the boy and that of the young man was hard on him.

His shoulders drooped and for an instant he looked like only a boy, betrayed by his best friend.

Outside in the narrow alley, Mother said, "You will apologize to your brother when we get back." I nodded, miserable.

After we passed the city gate, no longer manned by true soldiers but rough-looking men who watched Mother so openly that I pressed closer against her side, I began to look for interesting stones along the path. On occasion one might find a shard of Roman glass or even a small coin washed up by a recent rain. If I found one, I would use it to make my peace with Joshua. I should not have spit at him. I had seen a boy do it once and had been fascinated and horrified by what a terrible person he must be to have done such a thing.

I did not want to be a terrible person.

Somewhere in the distance, flute song rose on the breeze. I used to hear it on my way to the synagogue coming from somewhere farther down the hill, or from one of the hills nearby. I wondered, as I had before, who it belonged to.

We came nearly to the bottom of the hill path — I could see the spring from here, the girls like graceful willows bent over it with their water jars.

That's when I noticed the flute song had stopped.

Mother halted. She must have noticed it, too. She squinted in the direction of the northern fields where some of the farmers had their small houses. I could barely make them out; they were obscured by a dusty haze that seemed to have risen out of nowhere.

A crescendo of rumbling thunder to the north.

I looked up at Mother at the same time that a barrage of shouts rang out over the valley, high from the city gate.

"Romans!"

I had seen soldiers all my life. But there was something about that cry that put me in a fear I had never known.

Mother grabbed me by the arm.

Screams. Alarm from the gatehouse. The crash of breaking pottery as girls abandoned their water jars. They came running up the path, clawing hems away from feet made clumsy by fear, a few of them dragging their animals with them. Mother pulled me back against the hillside.

An older woman had been picking her way down the path behind us and now lay pressed against the hillside beside me. But when Mother jerked me up by the wrist and made to follow the river of others fleeing uphill, she grabbed Mother by the shoulder and me by the arm.

"Don't go back!" she said. "They're going to their deaths! Don't go back. Run!" She was unbearably strong, and I remember in the confusion thinking that she was hurting me.

"My son is in the city. My husband," Mother cried, trying to pry free, but the woman held her fast. She let go of my arm instead and pointed north along the valley. Now I saw them, coming through the fields as blood wells over the edge of a cut. I knew the crimson of those shields.

Romans. Thousands of them. Soldiers on horseback and infantry carrying javelins and wearing swords. The earth shuddered beneath them, spewing dust in their wake.

"Return to the city and you go to your death. Run! And pray your son and husband escape to join you!"

My mother grabbed me by the arm, but then hesitated.

"Go!" the woman shouted. And then her lips pulled back from her teeth so far that the gape of her mouth seemed unnaturally long when she screamed, *"RUN!"*

My mother seized me up though I was by then too big for her to carry properly and tore down the path, jarring me with every step, the beating of her feet against the ground sounding inside my skull. She skidded, nearly went down, and then reaching the bottom of the hill, she ran. South, away from the incoming legion, toward the hills.

She fell once, dropping me, nearly landing on top of me. Her breath came in great, wheezing gasps. Her veil slipped down her hair. And then she yanked me up by the arm and we ran, legs churning against the grass, stumbling over stones and shrub. I looked back to see if the old woman was following, if she were able, impossibly, to keep up with us. But there was no sign of the woman — only the Romans filling the northern valley, once the drying brown of summer barley, now swelling with red.

The caves of the southern hills were shallow, some of them barely pocks in the limestone. I knew this place. Hadn't Joshua and I explored this very hill before? It had seemed very far away at the time, and yet Mother and I had reached it in a few desperate heartbeats.

We crept through trees and crawled inside the mouth of the deepest cave we found. My mother's arms came around me then, and I heard the thudding of her heart — a heart that should never beat in fear.

I wondered where Father was, if he had run home or hurried to the gate and down the path to shout for us. If Joshua, stuck with crazy old Zipporah, had learned what was happening and knew to hide.

"What about Father? Joshua? How will

they find us?"

Mother shook her head, squeezed shut her eyes. She was saying something, and I thought at first it was to me, but then I realized she was praying, rocking with each word.

Eventually her rocking stopped, though her whispered prayer seemed to continue for an hour.

Beyond the cave the valley was full of sounds: the jingle of tack and equipment, the shouts of soldiers as a legion set up camp.

After some time, her prayers died to nothing though I could still feel the frantic beat of her heart through her chest, indistinguishable from the pounding in my own ears.

"What about Father and Joshua?" I whispered again, the sound too loud inside this stone space.

"I don't know," she said, her eyes wide, staring at nothing. She reminded me in that moment of Zipporah, and somehow that frightened me most of all.

The sun slanted across the entrance of the cave. Sabbath was coming. We moved farther back against the limestone wall. That's when I finally noticed the smaller openings carved into the interior face of the cave.

Four in all, two of them still covered with stones.

We were in a grave.

I curled in Mother's lap and squeezed my eyes shut as the light fled the day. She held me tight as the words poured from her lips:

When the wicked advance against me to devour me, it is my enemies and my foes who will stumble and fall. Though an army besiege me, my heart will not fear.

When it was fully dark, Mother crept out of the cave. After what seemed like a very long time and I had begun to panic, crying out for her in hoarse whispers, she finally returned and drew me into her arms.

"Can we go back?" I said.

"No, my cub. The Romans have camped outside the city."

And even I, being a boy, understood: They intended to take the city and everything inside it.

That night, I promised the Lord I would never spit at my brother again, that I would be the best teacher of the law, that I would be zealous and pure all my days if only Joshua and Father — and Zipporah, too — could escape or, better yet, that this might all be a dream.

But the only dreams in those days from Jerusalem to Syria were nightmares.

I woke up alone.

"Momma?"

I scrambled to the mouth of the cave, near-skidding out of it, desperate to be away from the dead within it.

Mother grabbed me as I came running out and pulled me down beside her.

Below us in the valley, an entire legion had arrayed itself overnight, precise, mechanical as the Roman machine itself, exacting a new and visceral fear in me. There was a line set up near the path we had come down just the day before, and tall wooden machines I had never seen before.

And there, in front of it all: the standard, the eagle. As though it had followed us from Jerusalem.

We crouched like animals, watching the activity of the camp, looking for any sign of people coming out from the city. But there were none.

We scraped for anything to eat, digging up roots and peeling apart the fat leaves of a cactus. We had realized by then that we were not the only ones hiding in the hills; we had seen a woman creeping through the trees farther down. Mother tried to call to her, but she dared not do it loudly and the woman didn't seem to hear. At times throughout the day we heard a faint strain of prayer carried up by the hot breeze along the hill, as if it came from the air itself.

We lay on the floor of the tomb a second night, listening to the sounds of the Roman camp as the smell of their fires wafted into the hills. Occasionally we could even hear soldiers' laughter in the darkness.

It was there, in that tomb, that I had a horrible thought.

I had prayed to stay in Sepphoris. I had prayed for it, and God had granted my request.

I began to shake. In wanting to enjoy the esteem of others, I had become a satan to my family.

Mother tried to comfort me, but her comforts could not right the horror of my wrong. It was my fault. It was all my fault.

She brought me what few seeds and roots she could find — I retched up most of them, and flies came to lap at the swelter of my vomit there on the limestone floor.

I fell asleep to the rhythmic sound of Mother's prayers, entombed in guilt. I wondered if Sheol was like this.

Black smoke wafted into the hills. We shrank

back as far as we might from the nightmare swelling around the city — the screams and the fire, the intermittent, thundering crash of city walls.

Sepphoris was under siege.

I covered my ears and screwed shut my eyes in the darkness of the cave. But I could not shut out the smell of fire.

That night I found a sharp shard of stone. Creeping to the wall, I carved, as best I could in the dark, my name.

Judas.

I carved Joshua's beside it. Hot tears streamed down my cheek.

I had wanted to be a great teacher, to sit in a seat of honor. Now I only wanted to have my father and brother back, in any obscurity we could be together.

4

The Romans were in the forest.

The fall of axes rang out from the grove for half a day, their rhythm a dull thud in the ears. We dozed to the strike of axes, the shouts, the laughter. Always the axes. Always the laughter.

My mother and I lay curled together in the darkness of the cave until we could no longer tell waking from sleeping, nightmare from delirium.

My mother, I think, might have lain in that grave and gone directly to Sheol, were it not for me. I knew it by her eyes, dull and lifeless, staring at nothing in this world as though already fixed on the next. When she closed them, only the slow beat of her heart and the occasional sound of her breath let me know she lived.

Sometimes I thought I heard voices crying out in the darkness, reciting even, part of the Shema or a hymn. Sometimes I heard them cry out before falling into groans.

By the eighth day, the hammer-falls and ruckus of the Roman camp transformed into the machinelike grinding of a legion on the move. We lay in the stupor of hunger and dehydration as they passed along the west side of our hill, south into the Galilean countryside.

Finally, my mother stirred against me.

"Come," she said. Her voice was hoarse. I heard her try to swallow.

She took my hand and together we went down the hill on weak and unsteady legs. Now in the sun I saw that her hair was coated with dust, her face covered in grime, as were her clothes. She looked as though she had come out of Sheol itself. In a way, I suppose we had.

Distantly, I thought: We have missed Sabbath, which occurred our first night and next day in hiding. And then I realized: It is Sabbath again.

We paused halfway down the hill. Where the grove of pines had stood, there were now mostly stumps.

My mother moved woodenly, the smooth, girlish step that had never ceased to cause men and women alike to watch her, gone.

We came to the bottom of the hill.

51

The road was lined on both sides with crosses.

Mother's knees buckled and she stumbled, yanking me nearly to the ground. Her breath came like a serrated knife. Her hand was crushing mine, shaking all the way up her arm so that it seemed her shoulders had seized up.

A keen escaped my lips and I sagged but she jerked me upright, with what strength I don't know.

We walked onto the road. Through the gruesome corridor, past the bodies of ten. Twenty. Fifty. I lost count.

I had seen the crucified from a distance in Jerusalem — nearly every day someone went to hang on a tree for something. It was the Roman execution reserved for noncitizens, devised specifically to be as lengthy, painful, and humiliating as possible. They crucified them naked and we always took care not to look at them, at the crude shame of them suffering their way to Sheol.

But now I stared at the bodies wracked in such gruesome display, every one of them a signpost to Roman power, a warning to anyone who had not submitted himself to the cross of Roman occupation in life.

The air was saturated with blood and excrement, rank with bodies already decaying in the stifling afternoon heat. Some of them stared down at us with flat eyes as though having realized upon the moment of death that the next life was not what they expected. The mask of that horror remained on their faces like the shed scales of a lizard, a thing bearing only the imprint of the life that once wore it. Ravens came and went with a flap of dark wings, settling on the corpses to jab at their faces. No calls, no cawing. Just the flutter of wings and intermittent silence as they pecked at wounds and genitals, lips and eyeballs.

I became aware of the dazed milling of others like us, of their cries in the putrid air. Farther ahead, a woman had all but collapsed at the foot of one of the crosses. Another man, standing in the middle of the road in the rough tunic of a peasant, clasped his head, turning one way and then the other, making no other sound but the slap of his palms against his stricken face.

A few people had surrounded a cross near the end of the vulgar passage, two women and an old man, trying to take down a body. Every so often one of the women let out a terrible wail. Whenever she did, an answering whimper came from one of the stakes nearby. The man on it was still alive.

And then Mother stopped. Her back was

poker-straight. When I lifted my head to look up at her, her expression was terrible and void.

I followed the line of her vision to a form I did not recognize. A body turned into a single contortion of agony, the legs broken at perverse angles.

This time Mother spun me away, hard, her fingers digging into my shoulder as she doubled over, retching.

I pulled free of her, ran back — and then skidded to my knees in the stony dirt.

I knew that face, twisted toward the sky.

Father.

A horrible sound filled my ears. Only when my mother clasped me to her at last, smothering it, did I realize it had come from me. I wailed and thrashed and tore my hair — not because it was proper to do, but because I could do nothing else.

I wanted to go to him, cling to him, but I was as horrified as I was desperate for him. Gone was the serenity of that embrace, of the skin smelling of sun, the beard, even when it smelled of fire. He was covered in gore and flies.

Mother gripped me by the shoulders.

"Do not see your father's nakedness," she said, her voice hoarse.

I tried to tear my gaze away but couldn't

until she pulled me hard against her, burying my face against the stained linen of her tunic.

There at my father's feet, I died. My name was written in the grave already. Though we had crawled from its mouth just an hour before, a part of me, I knew, would never emerge.

The city walls were broken into black and craggy teeth. This was no longer Sepphoris. These were the smoldering remains of Gomorrah.

Past the rubble of the city gates, bodies littered the street, swarming with flies. One of them, an old man still clutching his staff.

We covered our noses with the fronts of our tunics, and I struggled to keep up as Mother's step quickened past the debris of houses and storefronts, past the smoldering remains of what had been the synagogue. We stumbled past upturned carts, broken pottery, toppled buildings. Above us, the fort that had presided over the entire hill had crumbled in one spot, the limestone blackened all along the face.

Once we reached the residential area, we ran.

At the burnt lintel to Eleazar's house, mother gestured me back.

"Stay here," she said, her face already turned toward the dark front room. It smelled like smoke. Smoke, and something else. She covered her nose and picked her way into the darkness.

I waited, heard her gasp and stifle a cry somewhere inside.

"Momma?" I cried into the silence. "Momma?"

I fled into the house and nearly tripped over a blackened form on the ground.

Zipporah. I recognized her only by her singed hair and feet — the only part of her that had not burned.

I backed away, choking at the sight as much as the smell. I could hear Mother moving in the lower level, her broken cries of "Joshua! Joshua!" echoing up along the stair.

I held very still, looking around at the charred remains of Eleazar's house, at this nightmare version that had replaced the home I'd known.

When Mother returned to the front room her face was streaked with tears and grime. She blinked at me as though only just remembering I was there, and then took me by the hand.

I don't know how many houses we went into after that. Each of them told the same tale: fire, looting. Everywhere we went, Mother called Joshua's name. By the time we had made our way halfway through the residential quarter, she was screaming it.

We saw a few others coming into the area, stumbling their way through the streets in a daze. But when Mother cried out, "Where are the rest?" their gazes fell away from her to stare at the burnt shells of the houses, of bodies covered with insects on the street.

After searching the entire city, we left.

On the road there was a woman propped up against the foot of a cross. Several strands of her hair were stuck in the dirt of the toes of the man upon it. Mother went to her, bent down to look her in her face, which was so bruised and swollen that had it been my own mother I could not have recognized her. Twin milk spots stained the front of her tunic.

"Where are the others?" Mother whispered. The woman gazed dully at her and Mother shook her until she whimpered. "Where are the others? There were thousands here the day the Romans came!"

The woman's voice gurgled — no, it was her tongue. She opened her mouth and I saw that she had none, and that her teeth were broken and her tongue had been cut out. Mother's eyes were stark as the woman took one of her own wrists in her other hand as though it were a shackle — the same I had seen on the slaves sold at market in Jerusalem.

Mother sank to her knees.

They were gone. The ones who stood grisly sentry over this pass and those sprawled in the streets were all older men and women. The rest — those younger and more able-bodied — had all been taken for slaves.

I would never see my brother again.

5

Some of the peasants who came to stagger at the sight of the crosses, who had taken down the man still alive, helped us take Father down and carry him to the hillside cave where we had sheltered just days before.

I carved his name into the rock above Joshua's and mine. We had no spices to anoint him, but piled whatever stones we could find before the mouth of the cave. We had no monument for his burial except our own survival. The words of our prayers seemed stolen by the air.

That night one of the peasants took pity on us and brought us to his house where his wife fed us bread and olives and gave Mother a veil to cover her hair.

The next day, we left.

Those were not safe days. They were not safe for a mother traveling with a child. They were not safe for any man. Soldiers and bandits roamed the hills, the soldiers gathering up men to crucify or sell into slavery to satisfy their Roman masters, the bandits preying on anyone they found.

We came to Scythopolis, where we had stayed the mystical night of the eclipse. Now that we were back, I was frightened of the pagan temple, of the wide Roman street . . .

. . . of the soldiers within the city.

At the sight of their crimson my bowels loosened on the spot. I soiled myself, shamefully, before Mother could get me to the public toilet.

Mother sat with her hand out near the city gate, but there were many beggars in worse condition than us. When, by the end of the day, she had acquired only a few small coins and those not even enough for bread, she took me to an inn.

It was small and dirty, and the innkeeper looked Mother up and down in a way I had never seen a man look at a woman.

"That boy stinks!" he said. "You can't bring him in here."

Mother took me outside and went back in to speak to the innkeeper in tones I couldn't hear from the street. I didn't know what she was saying but I didn't trust him to talk to her honorably. I should take her away by the arm and shake my fist at the man. But I was in the throes, by then, of the summer fever, stupefied by grief and fatigue.

A few minutes later she came for me and we went in and a skinny servant girl brought us some water to bathe and, wrinkling her nose, told Mother she would take and wash my tunic.

Finally clean and having been fed a few spoonfuls of lentils, I fell asleep on some straw in a back room. That night, when the street outside was the quietest it had been since our arrival, Mother got up.

"Go back to sleep," she said, covering me with her veil. And then she went out. She came back a little while later but just when I started to sit up, to say I was thirsty, I realized she was not alone. I could hear the heavier step of another entering our tiny room behind her. I could smell him.

I huddled under the too-thin fabric of her veil in the dark, mouth dry, heart pounding. I screwed shut my eyes against the rustling of clothing, the hot stink of him in the stale air. Against the strained grunts of this man who was not my father, who did not talk to her in low tones as Father had, but got up as soon as he was finished, tugging his tunic on the way out as though he had just used the toilet.

I lay still long after he left, until the sound

of Mother's quiet weeping subsided and I was sure she had fallen asleep. I stayed silent so she would not know that I had seen what he had done to her, or what she had allowed him to do.

We stayed there for weeks, waiting for the countryside to be safe, listening to reports of Romans, Syrians, and Arabs overrunning the region — all under the standard of Rome. Of Jews nailed to crosses still warm from those crucified before them. The new king was in Rome pleading, it was said, for his crown.

I recovered from the fever and took up with a band of wild boys in the city. We would rough up our faces and beg copper quadrans off of foreigners near the pagan temple. Sometimes we would steal. But when I pointed out that the boy who was our leader had not divided the coins evenly, they beat me up, called my mother a whore, and took every coin I had.

I stayed away after that, and could not bring myself to look my mother in the eye.

By the time we left Scythopolis late that summer, it was said that two thousand Jews had been crucified for the rebellions throughout Israel, so that the stench of bodies lining the roads to the Holy City rose higher than the smoke of the Temple itself.

I cried when we came to Kerioth, but not in the same way that my mother did, falling into her sister's and her aunt's arms. I cried because although I immersed in the mikva and fasted for the first time without incident, I knew it changed nothing. It would not return my brother from slavery or my father from Sheol. Nor would it restore my mother's honor or take away the bastard already growing in her belly.

I went to work writing letters for others in the village and studied in the synagogue. By the time I turned twelve I could read in Aramaic, Hebrew, and Greek. I recited my brother's best rhetoric and amazed my teachers. But their praise was hollow in my ears, because I knew I didn't deserve it and that I was as false as a coin struck from bad metal. I stayed away from lessons for a while after that and got into trouble so that my mother threw up her hands, not knowing what to do with me.

I harbored little hope by now of becoming a sage. The others might not know about the uncleanness we had all suffered, but I did, bearing it like leprosy beneath my skin.

By the time I turned sixteen, Herod's son Archelaus failed utterly as king. Despite setting several captives free — several well-known brigands among them — and promising to lower taxes, he proved as ruthless as his father. He was banished and Judea came under direct Roman rule while his brothers, Philip and Antipas, retained Galilee and the northeast reaches of Israel.

There was an uprising that year — the first of any real note since that terrible year a decade before — in response to the new procurator's call for a census so that Rome might inventory Judea in order to tax it. That year, Judas bar Hezekiah came out of hiding. All this time, I hadn't known whether he lived or died.

This time, Judas did not wage war, but began to teach that to pay taxes to an emperor worshipped as *Divi filius* — the son of God — was tantamount to idolatry.

Hearing this, something stirred in me for the first time in years. That evening, the Shema was renewed to me in a way it had not been since I had watched Joshua pray it in Galilee. *Hear O Israel!* I was now a man with a mother and a younger brother to provide for yet I knew that I must go to join them. But by the time I had made preparations to leave my mother in the protection of her uncle just a few days later, word came that the revolt was already over and that Judas bar Hezekiah had been killed.

It was then I realized that not only did I

not mourn Judas bar Hezekiah, but that I despised him. I despised him as much for squandering the hope of a bleeding nation as for his failure. Because in failing he had proven again that it was impossible to stand up to the satan that was Rome, and that the lives of men like my father had been spent cheaply.

The next day I went to accept an offer of betrothal from the father of a girl in our village. And then I wrote to my father's former patron, Nicodemus, in the Holy City.

That winter, I moved my bride, my mother, and my brother Nathan to Jerusalem.

I will never forget the day we entered the city gate. Walking through the streets, I imagined that I breathed for the first time in years. That I was finally home.

But I was not truly home until I came to stand before the Temple. As I emerged from the mikva and put on my clean tunic to enter her gates, I felt that I had woken up from a years-long sleep . . . from a years-long nightmare.

It was not the same Temple I had known — the burn marks of that Pentecost still scorched the upper reaches of her porticoes. But neither was I the same.

Standing in the inner court, I inhaled the

smoke of the holy altar and knew that my life before had passed away and that a new one had begun at last.

That day, I set aside dreams of messiahs and rededicated myself to the keeping of God's law.

I knew a kind of peace after that for many years.

And then, shortly after Purim in my thirty-eighth year, that peace shattered.

■ ■ ■ ■ ■

IMMERSION

■ ■ ■ ■

6

I loved the Holy City best at two times of day: at dawn and at the going out of day.

Jerusalem in the morning was a city full of promise. When even the streets most rank with urine seemed on the verge of renewal, the stones of the oldest city gates set in tension as much as mortar, as though waiting, in silence, for something.

And there was nothing more stupendous than the moment just before sunrise, when the Temple, hulking over the upper city, seemed to stir. When the first rays of morning struck the stone so that it glowed ruddy as skin. It gave me pause whenever I saw it, as though it had nearly assumed human flesh . . . before the sanctuary became the gleaming white of the most beautiful building on earth. And then again, at sunset, that glimpse of russet stone, as though the blood that ran from the great altar's drains to the Kidron Valley was not the blood of animals, but the blood of the Temple itself, poured out for the lush life beyond the city.

My steps fell smartly on the southern stair as I ascended to the Temple. They were proud and purposeful and with good reason: My wife, Susanna, was pregnant and soon to deliver what the midwife was certain would be a boy.

My hope soared. This was the longest Susanna had carried a child in years since the two that had never come to term and the daughter we had lost while she was still in swaddling. And a son! The Lord had remembered me, and the day would come when I would see the covenant carved into the flesh of my flesh by circumcision. Though I had been a man since the age of thirteen and studied Torah all my life, I felt for the first time that I was on the cusp of some promise, some mystery between the Lord and me alone.

I arrived early to be among those waiting when the great doors opened. To hear the first singing of the Levites as the morning offering was brought to the altar — including the first of two daily sacrifices on behalf of the Roman emperor's welfare. I watched the smoke of it coil into a formerly flawless sky.

"We sacrifice for those who enslave us," a

familiar voice murmured behind me.

Simon. My closest friend. On his way, no doubt, to sit at the feet of his teacher in the porticoes.

I turned, brows lifted. "Ah, but perhaps today is the day that the Lord, moved by our keeping of the law, drives them from our land."

"I fasted yesterday. If today isn't the day, it must be your sin holding us back," he said, straight-faced.

"Well now you have an opportunity to pray for Rome."

His droll expression slipped away. "For Rome! When did you go mad?"

"Haven't you read the scrolls? Even in exile our forefathers were commanded to pray for those who enslaved them."

Not that I had any intention of praying for Rome. No, never. But Simon, I knew, relied on me to give him what he loved best: a good debate.

He argued why we must not pray for Rome in low tones as we passed through the outer court. The place was in chaos since the High Priest Caiaphas had brought in several vendors from the market outside the city. The Pharisees had condemned the move, as offended by the smell of dung as by the commerce within the Temple courts.

71

Simon ranted about it regularly and I, too, bristled every time I saw — and smelled — it. But today nothing could touch me.

Finally I said with a laugh, "Enough! What can I say to you? You are the best of us."

Simon stopped, frowned. "Will you let me go so easily? You disappoint me, Judas."

I gestured across the courtyard. "Do you see those workers coming in? Not all of us can spend the day debating the law and dining with Pharisees. Some of us have to work."

"Yes, you go work. I will be zealous for the both of us. Again." He kissed me and left. Simon the Zealot.

In a small subterranean room off the Wood Chamber, I prepared for the day. For nearly a decade I had overseen the payment of stonecutters, carpenters, and artisans beneath the auspices of the treasury and an old Levite named Elias. The Temple not only employed the most skilled workers of all kinds, but was the most steady and best employer in the city. The most steady, because it was perpetually under construction all these years since its near-destruction the year of Herod's death. The best, because it paid well and at each day's end.

I, too, had been paid well all the years I had worked in my office off the Wood

Chamber, but as soon as my son was born I would leave my work here. Susanna's family owned an olive press and had recently begun importing olives from Perea. It was not a big venture, but successful enough for me to help her father turn additional profit with the making of several loans at interest — something I had learned from the transactions of the Temple itself. It was not something we were open about, as many considered it thievery. But it would become a good living for us both — and one day for my son.

I was content.

By mid-morning the workers were dispatched with the tokens by which they would claim their wages. The outer court was full of Jews and non-Jews alike, pilgrims buying the best animals they could afford to sacrifice, tourists simply gawking at the beauty of Herod's Temple.

I turned and looked up at the dressed stones of the sanctuary, gleaming white in the mid-morning sun. *See the gold spikes along the top?* I would say to my son one day. *See the gold vines adorning the columns of the Temple porch?* Right then I decided that as soon as my son was born I would buy a gold leaf in the market to be hung over the entrance to the sanctuary. Then, one day when he was old enough, I would point out which one was his and he would know he was a part of the most beautiful building in the world.

I fetched my mantle, ready to go home — less for the midday meal than to seek out my wife, if only to bare her shoulders and caress her swelling breasts. I would ask nothing of her in this last month of her pregnancy, and immerse later, if I must.

I had just emerged into the outer court when my young friends Isaac and Levi came striding toward me. I knew the purposeful tread of that gait and groaned inwardly.

Levi grabbed my hand and kissed it — the greeting one gave a rabbi. "Blessed is the womb that bore you, Judas." I laughed and pushed him away.

Isaac kissed me in the usual way, eyes shining with the kind of zeal that only comes with youth. "Judas, you must advise us," he said.

"I must?"

"Yes," he said. "You are the most learned of all of us."

"Don't tell me. You want to know whether it's lawful to divorce your wife."

"What? No!"

"The school of Hillel says yes. The school of Shammai says no. You are a student of

74

Shammai, so that means no for you."

Levi grinned.

Isaac sputtered, "But that's not what we want to ask you."

"It's not? And I just got those two points straight. Well then, what is it? Make it quick. I have a particularly beautiful wife to get home to."

"Tell us, Judas. What must we do to bring the coming kingdom? What must we do to be saved?"

A strange anxiety sliced through me. I glanced back at the gate — it had worn a golden eagle once. Looking back now, I half-expected to see one there again, gleaming in the sun.

Isaac pressed the question before I could respond. "Indulge us. One teacher says one thing, another something else. But what do you say, Judas? How are we to rid ourselves of Rome and be saved?"

He was staring at me, the sun ripening the fruit of his cheeks, keen light in his eyes. I wondered what they would say if they knew that I resided a full week once in a grave. That my father bore the curse of one who hangs on a tree. What my mother had done to keep shelter over my head and food in my mouth. Or that she lay with a strange discharge now for months, requiring me to immerse daily so that I might be pure enough to come into the Temple at all. It was the reason I had moved us to a house with a mikva.

My whole life, bathed in impurity — I, who had once wanted to be a teacher of God's law and whom they looked to almost as the sage I had always hoped to be. I glanced down, pretended to adjust my mantle.

"Well?" Isaac said.

"You know the law as well as I. What does the Shema say?"

"That you will love the Lord with all your heart, soul, and might."

"What do the sages say?"

"To keep the law, but —"

"You see? You know as much as I." I forced an apologetic smile. "Now, if you will forgive me, my friends, I am far too distracted by thoughts of my wife, waiting for me."

I hurried home, but my desire had left me.

I returned to the Temple after eating to work through the afternoon. The last sacrifices of the day were on the fire when I left for home again that evening.

I was so absorbed in my thoughts that I didn't notice the figure that fell into step with me until he clasped me by the arm.

Startled, I found myself looking up into the face of Levi for the second time that day. His mantle was up over his head, and though I had known him for years, there was an unfamiliar air about him.

"Come with me, Judas."

"Thank you friend, but I must get home."

"It won't take long. Please."

Now curious, I followed Levi to his house where his young daughters, Huldah and Mary, came running to meet him. I watched the way he scooped them up, their faces pressed against his cheek, little Mary's hair curling in his beard as he kissed her.

"Tell your mother we have a guest, that the man from Kerioth is visiting," he said.

He did not lead me up to the roof even though it was still warm enough, but into one of the back rooms where his wife brought us wine and olives. Though beautiful, she seemed somehow wasting compared to Susanna, so lush with life even to the tips of her swollen toes. At the thought of Susanna, the desire that deserted me earlier returned.

I determined to make this visit brief.

But then, something strange: Levi got to his feet and prayed. It was not the typical prayer for wine, but the Amidah, which we prayed three times a day.

Sound the great shofar for our freedom . . .
May all the enemies of Your people be
destroyed . . . Blessed are You, Lord, who
causes salvation to flourish.

For an instant I recalled the face of Isaac
wavering before me earlier that day. *How
must we be saved?*

"Judas, what I am going to tell you must
remain between us. You must agree to this
now before I speak."

"So solemn, Levi? Are you luring me into
debate? Or do you mean to scold me for
teasing Isaac?"

"No," he said quietly. "No debate, and
Isaac is the purest of any of us. Men like
him will bring the favor of the Lord long
after men like you and me are gone. No,
what I'm about to tell you I could be killed
for. Even hung on a tree."

I hesitated.

"Then perhaps you should not say it."

"I must. We have more in common than
you can know. Swear, Judas, to keep this
between us. I'm placing my life in your
hands."

Curiosity. The same unrest that had
gripped me earlier . . . either of these might
have compelled me to answer as I did.

"I swear."

He nodded.

"What is this about?"

"A confession."

"A confession of what?"

"Judas . . . I knew you — of you — before we were friends."

"My reputation precedes me?" I said with an uneasy laugh.

He chuckled. "Yes, there is that. You are known for your scholar's mind, and even more so because you aren't affiliated with any school. You should have been a Pharisee or a teacher. What an anomaly you are! But I mean something else."

"I'm afraid you'll have to be more plain, my friend."

"Then here it is. They might call you the man from Kerioth, but I know that you came from Sepphoris before that. And that your father conspired with Judas bar Hezekiah."

Anything. He might have said anything and I would have expected it. Anything — but that.

Was he an informant of Herod's son Antipas? Of the High Priest, or the Sadducees? I stared at him, the familiar angles of his face suddenly those of a stranger.

"My father was a man of God," I said,

trying to control the sudden tremor in my hands.

"I know he was."

A rivulet of sweat slipped down the inside of my tunic.

"I know, because I belong to a brotherhood born of the legacy of men like your father."

"What?"

He leaned forward, peered intently into my face. "Listen to me. The Essenes believe we are closer now to the ultimate stage of history than ever. And we believe it, too, Judas. We believe Rome's days in Israel to be numbered. We are committed to it. The time is coming."

"Who is this 'we'?"

"The Sons of the Teacher."

"Which teacher?"

Fire sparked in his eyes. "The one for whom strict adherence to the law requires rebellion. 'No Lord but God.' "

No Lord but God. It had been the war cry of Judas bar Hezekiah in his last rebellion — the same one I had meant to join so many years ago. The philosophy had been called a school. And because of it, Judas bar Hezekiah had been called in the years before his death, "Teacher."

Levi himself was a Galilean, only recently

come to study in Jerusalem. It all came into place.

"The teaching lives on, Judas. In many men."

"How many rebels are there? Who is your leader?"

Levi shook his head. "That I could not tell you even if you laid a sword against my throat. None of us knows more than a few others among us — namely, the one we immediately report to. But I dare not even tell you his name, for his protection as much as yours. But I will tell you there are key figures among us, I do know that. This is the brotherhood that will complete the work of men like Judas bar Hezekiah, and of your father. The time is nearly here. Join us, Judas!"

I sat back and tried to calm myself. To digest Levi's revelation along with the wine that had since soured in my stomach.

"You're right. What you say could get us both killed," I said. "What makes you think I welcome this knowledge?"

"Don't you think I've seen the way you look toward the Temple, always? The way you break your back keeping the law, praying for the day that Israel is free? But there are those of us who are willing to do more than pray for it. Your father was such a man.

We, too, are committed to the coming Day of the Lord. Join us, Judas, and together we will see Israel free from Rome!"

I had never spoken of my boyhood since laying foot in Jerusalem nearly twenty years ago. Now, to have it all laid bare by a man I had known only a few short years, to have it brought to me like dung from the side of the road, like a thing flayed open to reveal the maggots inside . . .

I was trembling as I said, very quietly, "My father was killed for this cause, my brother hauled away to the slave block. That life is behind me. And now I have a son of my own on the way. I won't consign him to the same fatherless fate!"

"Judas —"

I got to my feet, cut him short with a gesture. "I will keep your secret. But never speak to me of this again."

On the walk to my house, did the shadows turn to stare, did they chase me down the alleyway?

At home, I bolted the door. Fell back against it, sucked in a long and steady breath.

7

Now it all made sense to me: The way Amos, another student, clasped Levi's shoulder. The way they parted in the courtyard, not looking back. The unspoken language of sedition disguised in plain sight. I simply had not had eyes to see it. Or, rather, I had not chosen to. Now I realized that a part of me had known and even sought its ubiquitous presence here in the Temple, even as I claimed to have relinquished the messianic dream.

Freedom for Israel. Death to Rome.

It fired my imagination and left me restless. At night, I lay awake, wondering: What if the Essenes were right, and the Day of the Lord was soon to come?

No. Such thoughts only brought death. The Lord himself must bring it to bear. I was soon to be a father.

I did better than not reveal Levi's identity; I avoided him altogether. What's more, I announced to Elias that I would leave my position in the treasury with the start of Passover. The ancient Levite wept, as sentimental as a woman in his old age. I clasped him and thanked him and promised to come to his house to announce the birth of my son, but I was relieved.

The day I left my job at the Temple I saw Levi from a distance. He was walking through the columns of the porticoes. His last glance at me was a smile, but one of sadness.

Passover was less than two weeks away when my mother received word from Kerioth that her sister was dying.

As a boy I had looked forward to Passover — from the place at the table left open for Elijah, the prophet who would return before the coming Messiah, to the flooding of Jerusalem's streets and valleys and neighboring hills as her population swelled from thirty thousand to three times that number.

But the years since Sepphoris had cemented the violent symbolism of Passover for me: the slaughter, the blood amidst the hope of freedom — first from Egypt, now from Rome.

This year I wanted only to celebrate it in quiet, in remembrance of the past and in hope of a different kind of future. But when the letter came, I reconciled myself to the journey south to Kerioth.

My brother Nathan and I set our mother on a donkey and left with his wife, daughter, and son born last winter. Susanna would not make the trip so close to her time. I hated to leave her — with a house of holiday guests to tend, no less — but I would not make Nathan, known as a boy of questioned birth in Kerioth, take Mother there alone.

Two days after our arrival, my aunt died in her bed.

That afternoon, as Mother bathed the body, a man came running into the village, shouting.

"Pilate has seized the Temple treasury!"

I had been making arrangements for my aunt's burial. Hearing the man, I hurried out toward him. "What's this? Speak plainly. What's happened?"

"The Roman procurator Pilate sent his soldiers into the Temple to seize the treasury!"

He clapped himself on the head and cried out: "Aiee! What have we come to? Like Antiochus of old he has looted the treasury!"

"Quiet!" I said to the man. "This is a dangerous thing you say. A dangerous comparison you make." Everyone knew that

Antiochus had done more than steal from the treasury — he had profaned the altar by sacrificing a pig on it.

The man hissed through several missing teeth, "Isn't it true? Doesn't Rome profane our altar with sacrifice on behalf of their emperor, who calls himself the son of God? Where is our Maccabee to put him down and chase out Rome? Where is our Messiah to cleanse our Temple? Come, Elijah! Come, son of David!"

Judas Maccabee. I had been named in part for the warrior hero and reared on tales of his cleansing of the Temple. My skin prickled at his words.

"Stop!" I said. But he had already begun to gather an alarmed crowd. Soon he would incite a panic. Fear had already lodged like a bone in my throat — for the Levites working in the Temple treasury. For the students in the porticoes, the pilgrims in the courts.

But then a terrible thought occurred to me: If a man was saying this here in Kerioth, what was being said in Jerusalem? What kind of outrage would this act of Pilate provoke there, among the city's swollen numbers?

Tinderbox.

As I hurried back to my aunt's house, there was only one face before my mind:

Susanna.

With swift goodbyes, I left my mother in the care of my brother and headed north, to Jerusalem.

The Holy City was in the throes of holiday chaos. Pilgrims camped on the hills as thick as the knots of a carpet, flooding the Kidron Valley all the way to Bethany. The smoke of their fires and colorful strew of their tents was everywhere from the hillside to the rooftops even of the synagogues. Only the Valley of Hinnom, where the city's garbage continuously burned, was devoid of pilgrims' tents.

But Jerusalem was in the throes of something else as well: rage in her streets, outcry over one more violation at the hands of Rome and her prefect, Pilate.

Entering the city, I joined the crowds flooding the streets, swarming in the direction of the Temple. I would gauge the outrage there firsthand, and then get home and collect Susanna, take her from the city if I must.

But to enter the Temple, I had first to immerse. The dust of travel was on my feet and I could not enter without immersing, especially on this day of all days. I made for the mikvot on the southern end of the Temple. The lines wound all the way down the street! I briefly considered the mikva at a nearby inn . . .

And then I stopped.

I had been in the same house with my dead aunt. I bore corpse uncleanness. Immersing would not cleanse me of that today.

I could not enter the Temple.

"Judas bar Simon!" A familiar voice rang out over the throng.

I twisted at the sound of my name and stared at Isaac. I will never forget the sight of his face. Shining. Strangely beatific.

"Have you come to join us? Come!" He reached across the chest of another man, to pull me toward him. I clasped his hand, pushed my way between two other men moving crossways against me.

"Tell me what happened!" I said.

"Pilate seized the Corban."

The Corban. The monies set aside for public works — I myself had paid out wages from the Corban to laborers paving streets or repairing gutters.

"Come with us!"

My first thought was, *to where?* And then I thought of Susanna. I had all but decided to forget the Temple, which I could not enter, and go directly home to her, make certain that my bride and unborn son were safe.

Still, I shouted after him, "Where?"

My fingers slipped free of his and the shouts around us drowned him out. And then I realized that all around me a protest was forming.

"Isaac!" I shouted.

He was gone. The crowd was surging toward the northwest corner of the Temple, and I got caught up and carried along with it, trying all the while to pull free of that inexorable human current. I saw Isaac once more a moment later and then he was gone, like the head that bobs above the surface of a wave before going under for the last time. Then I was swept along, past the western wall of the Temple, toward the Antonia Fortress.

And there, on a platform built out from the fortress steps I saw the man himself. A figure anyone would know by sight alone.

Pilate.

He sat on a simple seat in the purple equestrian stripe of his rank. His hands were folded in his lap, his head tilted as though he listened to an invisible someone standing before him — but there was something about the set of his jaw, the cast of his eyes as they dropped like shadows upon the shoulders of those clamoring below.

Something was wrong. The guards at the

entrance to the fortress behind him seemed too still. And there were none at the platform's edge in front of him, between the procurator and the growing throng.

Shouts filled the air: "He steals from her treasury! Give back to the Lord what is His!"

Something landed on the platform an arm's length from Pilate's sandaled foot. A rotten piece of fruit. He flicked a glance at it, but did not move even as a few of those closest to the platform began to grasp at the scaffolding.

"We stand by while Rome desecrates our holy place!" someone shouted. "Send Pilate back to Rome!"

Someone else picked up the refrain. Within seconds it echoed throughout the crowd. "Pilate back to Rome!" Fists pounded at the air.

Pilate sat unmoving. Not a scowl, not a dogged look of guilt. Nothing but the impassive face of a statue. And then he stood, gathered the hem of his toga, and calmly walked into the building.

There was a momentary cheer from a few of those behind me, as though Pilate had indeed fled to Rome. But it was cut short by a sudden cry, farther up, as a group surged back from the steps. It took me only a moment to realize that either a riot had broken out, or that the crowd was under attack — but by whom? I had seen no Romans in the crowd.

Melee on all sides — the pushing of the throng. A woman ahead of me went down, and when the man with her tried to haul her up, the mob rushed over him like water flowing to fill a hole in the mud. A man brought a club down onto the head of another to my right. It caved like a summer melon, splaying blood in my eyes. I stumbled backward, almost falling to the stones in shock.

The man who had done it wore the clothing and beard of a Jew.

Shouts. Screams from the steps of the Temple.

Where before I had fought my way toward the Temple, I was now swept along with the rush of those running away from it. I stumbled to stay aloft, grabbing the shoulders of those beside me. I leapt up on a cart tipped over in the street and searched for a way around the sea of people.

Violence. Death. Chaos in every direction.

"Judas!"

I glanced down to see Simon, his face flushed.

"I have to get home!"

"Come!" He frantically motioned me. "Hurry!"

I got down and followed him, shoving through the crowd, heart thudding in my ears, ice in my gut. Past the Ephraim Gate. Together, we broke into a run.

"Isaac is dead!" he said. "Bludgeoned to death against the western wall."

Innocent and fresh-faced Isaac! I ran faster.

"By whom?" I had seen only Jews in the crowd.

"Samaritans," Simon said, his lips peeled back.

Revulsion rose up in me. Samaritan soldiers passing as Jews. Samaritan auxiliaries, doing the dirty work of Rome.

Until that day I had forgotten to be vigilant, the rhythm of my life having lulled me into the belief that Jerusalem was a safe place.

It was not.

We ran down the street. Almost home.

"Susanna!" I shouted, bursting into my house.

Her mother came into the front room. "Judas! Back so soon? What of your aunt — is that blood on your face?"

"Where's Susanna?" I demanded.

"She's gone to market for some things for

the feast — Judas!"

I was already tearing out of the house, Simon on my heels, back through the gate toward the pavilions, shoving by those fleeing the riot, coming at me now like crazed and wild-eyed animals.

I could see it from a hundred paces off: the market in shambles, baskets of spices and produce upturned, amphorae of wine and oil smashed to the ground, looters grabbing anything they could as merchants quickly packed up whatever they could save.

We ran into the middle of the pavilions, turning, looking all around.

"Susanna!" I shouted, tearing at my hair, running down a small side street filled with the toppled stalls of vendors. I spun around, started to run back —

And saw the form crumpled against an overturned table. A woman, lying in a heap like debris on a riverbank after a hard rain. I knew the embroidery on that mantle. The foot in that sandal. The dark wool of that uncovered hair.

No. It must be someone else wrapped in Susanna's mantle, wearing her tunic over a broad, swollen belly . . . staring with her lifeless eyes.

Simon came into the side street just as I fell to my knees beside her, gathered her into my arms, and slapped her cheeks.

"Susanna! Susanna —"

That's when I felt the blood in her hair, thick and sticky, coming from a place at the back of her head where it caved, soft as a bruised fruit.

She was still warm.

"Help me get her to the midwife!" I cried. "Help me!"

Simon stared at me, face as ashen as the stones beneath his feet.

"The midwife! Now!"

Simon ran up the street ahead of me, back toward the New City. Weeping, I hefted my wife's lifeless body into my arms and staggered after him.

Nightmare slow, those moments. Morbid and intimate, the form of my wife in my arms, the precious bulge of our son between us.

Simon and the midwife came rushing out to help me. The midwife felt for Susanna's pulse, shook her head, told us to hurry.

We laid her on the floor of the courtyard. I groaned and tore at my beard as the midwife cut open her belly, the blood pooling on the earth.

"A son," she said, as she put the boy in my arms.

I fell to my knees, cradling the tiny form.

He was too small, the tiny eyes already fringed with Susanna's lashes so delicately closed, having never had a chance to open.

The first time I died I was a boy staring up at his father on a tree. The second was that day, as a man, kneeling beside the gaping body of my wife, cradling my dead son.

I did not bathe. I hardly ate though my mother brought me dates and olives, and Nathan's wife poured me honeyed wine. I could stomach none of them, dreaming at night of Susanna in Sheol with our lost children. It haunted me, thinking of her there, four starving babies gnawing at her shrunken breasts.

I combed the scrolls tirelessly. I tortured myself with thoughts of the Sadducees, who do not believe in the resurrection of the soul. I writhed with the need to know that I would see my family again. I thought of going to the porticoes, to the great teacher Shammai himself, to beg to know for certain. I wanted assurances. I wanted promises.

What else should there be for Susanna, a woman of honor? For my brother, who was perfect, my father, who deserved better than the shame of a cross? Isaac, earnest to the end.

They had all loved the law and kept it all the days of their lives.

It eluded me, the thing that had kept Mother's head lifted in the middle of her disgrace. That had sustained Father through the tortured hours on the cross. That had overcome Joshua's doubts.

How then are we to be saved?

I read and reread the story of Job. My mother could not pry the scroll from my hands. I cried out at night when the rest of my household slept and stood for hours in the cold water of the mikva. But I heard only silence. Not even a still quiet voice to answer me.

I had pursued the law with all my heart and it had gained me nothing. It had not sped the kingdom or called out to God, or struck the false, Roman-appointed priests dead within the sanctuary of the Temple.

By the time my month of mourning was over I knew only one thing: I was tired of being holy. The great warrior hero Judas Maccabee had not been so holy, after all, waging his wars on the Sabbath.

Neither could we afford to be.

That evening, I went to the house of Levi.

"Come inside, Judas," he said.

That night, I stepped into the dark waters of the mikva, galvanized by new promise:

the revolt to come at the hands of these secret Sons of Abba, which was the name for "father" but also given to teachers . . .

These Bar-Abbas.

And then, that fall, the voice of Zion came.

8

People had been talking about the Baptizer for weeks.

Pilgrims who'd come to the Holy City for the Feast of Tabernacles brought stories about his fanatical preaching and obsession with immersion in the living water of the Jordan.

They brought stories, too, about his open condemnation of Herod Antipas, who had married his brother's wife in violation of Torah. For these things alone I would have wanted to see him myself.

But it was the whispers of those who had come from the river that raised the hair on my arms.

Elijah.

He is Elijah!

Elijah. Who was to return before the coming One.

"I wonder if he really could be a prophet?" Simon said the day I persuaded him to travel from Jerusalem to find this Baptizer. We had gone out with a group of students, Amos and Levi among them.

"No prophet has been seen in four hundred years," Levi said. "No, my friend. He's an Essene for his love of washing or a madman. But an interesting madman."

"Who says he's a madman?" Amos said.

"Who else would speak out publicly against the king? But for that we love him. And so we brave scorpion and jackal to look upon this madman before Herod's men come to kill him. Come to think of it, any mouth Herod would silence must be the mouth of a prophet indeed. We should hear what he has to say before he dies."

I chuckled, but the sound was hollow. He couldn't know the disquiet his words evoked in me, or that I felt the serrated edge of them all the way to the river. Something had returned to life in me, larger and more ravenous than before. And though I feared disappointment in this madman, this Baptizer, I feared hope even more.

By mid-afternoon we came to a small scarp overlooking the Jordan — and gaped at the sight before us.

Lean-tos and tents covered the scrub in a colorful swath all up and down both sides of the river. There must have been three hundred people sitting on the banks or going into and coming up out of the water. Laborers, their skin like dried brick, rich men in fine linen, and children in rags. Women spread garments to dry on the grass and nursed babies beneath the shade of acacia trees.

And then I saw him — out in the middle of the river, like the eye of a gathering storm.

He was as sun-dark, nearly, as a Nubian. His hair fell in ropes past his waist, over sinewy shoulders the skin of which looked as though it had baked to the wiry muscles beneath. His beard fell in a black stream to the middle of his chest. But it was his voice, carrying up from the river to our vantage on the scarp, that made him seem feral as a thing uncaged. It was not the voice of the elder who read the scrolls in synagogue, or the scholar debating in the porticoes. But of the man who runs to the village warning of coming disaster.

"The time is coming! Hear what I say: Repent now! The kingdom is near!"

A part of me instantly recoiled. Recoiled because they were the words I had hoped all my life to hear. And from outrage. How dare he arouse false hope! How many times had I heard such promises only to find death?

Compulsion swallowed me and I knew I had to see him closer, if only to tell him to stop his wild and empty talk.

"Judas!"

I hardly heard Simon's call behind me; I was hurrying down the stony slope, skidding most of the way, tearing toward the bank, the crowd thick before me. Rather than fight my way through them, I surged into the river's shallows. The water was cold in contrast to the hot fall sun that had sent sweat dripping down my back on our day-long journey.

My robes tangled around my legs as I pushed upriver toward the source of that voice, past an outcrop of reeds.

I emerged from the reeds panting, up to my knees in the muddy river. And then only one man stood before me, not twenty paces away.

The Baptizer.

He turned to look at me and I caught myself. His were not the eyes of a madman.

"Welcome," he said, holding out his hand to me, seeming not at all surprised by my appearance.

I did not take his hand. I dared not. Because his eyes were not only *not* mad, but filled with a clarity I had never seen. They were *too* lucid — the eyes of someone who had seen more than eyes should see. And now they were looking at me.

For an instant, I felt laid utterly bare.

I fell back, suddenly desperate for the cover of others, for the very crowd I had fought to break free from just a moment ago.

"The time is coming. I tell you today, one more powerful than I will come," he said, and I realized he was no longer shouting, but speaking directly to me. His voice dropped. "One whose sandal *I* am not fit to carry."

There was a moment, strange and uncanny, in which I thought he took my measure as much as I took his. But then he turned to the shore and cried, "Come! Today I baptize you with water, but he will baptize you with fire!"

They came, surging into the water, and I allowed their number to swallow me, grateful to escape the brunt of that gaze.

All around me I heard the whispers of those praying like a swarm of locusts, confessing wrongdoing. Beside me a man murmured that he had stolen from his neighbor, and another that he had broken the Sabbath.

And then they began to immerse, lowering themselves into the chilly water, more people on the banks shedding outer garments and some of them stripping down even to their loincloths, some of the women going farther off to a bend in the river.

Feeling foolish, I turned and sloshed through the water, desperate to escape, staggering up onto the bank. I was looking around for Simon and Levi when a young man came alongside me and shed his tunic.

"Will you immerse? Come, we'll go together."

I shook my head.

"It's living water — it's the living water of the Lord, for the forgiveness of sins!" he said.

"Forgiveness of sins?" Simon had found me and stepped forward. "Nonsense. This Baptizer is no priest and this is not the Temple."

"The Temple is impure and in need of cleansing!" the man replied. "You as well, my friend. Immerse and tell everyone that Elijah has returned."

"Leave us," Simon said. "And be careful you don't blaspheme. The Temple is the dwelling place of the Lord!" The man gave Simon a parting look, and then moved on, undaunted.

Simon took my arm and tried to draw me away. "They are overzealous. These radical teachers!"

But I stood rooted, watching the young man as he waded into the shallows toward one of the Baptizer's disciples. They seemed to speak, and then to pray. And then he was sinking beneath the surface at the hands of the other man.

I watched until he burst from the water, his hair and beard like a shroud about his head. The look on his face was sublime.

Next to me Simon muttered, "Mark me: This will become a dangerous place."

Were it not too late, Simon would have insisted we go back to Jerusalem that same day. But it had been nearly seven hours' walk coming here, and we couldn't leave now until daybreak. I was secretly glad, wanting to unravel the mystery of this man, of the strange clarity of his eyes.

That night, Levi and I gathered as close as we could to the fire where the Baptizer, whose name we learned was John, was sitting with some others. Even at this hour, the crowd was so thick around him that we couldn't hear what he was saying, and I felt a strange surge of envy for his disciples sitting within that innermost circle.

"Did you notice," Levi murmured, "that he is wearing a camel shirt?"

"Yes," I said, understanding his meaning:

so had Elijah.

"What is he saying?" I said to the group in front of us.

One of the men said, "There's a tax collector up there, asking what he should do. John is telling him not to collect more than required."

Next to us, someone snorted. It was common knowledge that those who owned the collection franchises collected as much as they possibly could, keeping anything above the amount owed Rome for themselves.

"There's a tax collector up there?" Levi said with a frown. "Why would he allow a tax collector to immerse?"

"Someone asked if he is the Messiah," another man said.

Messiah. The Anointed One. Gooseflesh sped up my arms.

"And what does he say?" But even as I asked it, I berated myself. I had renounced would-be messiahs and thrown my lot in with the Sons of the Teacher. If there was to be a Messiah, we would be it — though we would not shun the help of a man able to raise an army when needed.

That was the true reason Levi and I had come.

"He says he's not the One," the man said.

I did not know what was stronger, my

disappointment or my relief.

I woke before dawn with a stiff neck and growing frustration — a sense of stymie that sat like something sour in my gut. By morning light, the Baptizer was stalking along the bank nearest us, already teaching. The crowd was smaller than yesterday and I found myself unnervingly near him.

His words knew no end! Again and again, he called for repentance and announced the coming kingdom until my frustration grew so great that I leapt to my feet.

"Where? Where is the Lord?" I cried.

The Baptizer's eyes turned and caught mine, his gaze a snare. This time I did not melt backward.

"He's coming! I tell you, he is coming, and the kingdom with him." He walked up to me. "Come. I will baptize you."

I did not need a messiah. I did not want to see the death of yet another anointed one come to march Israel deeper into the clutches of Rome.

But how I craved cleansing! How I longed for it, mourned every time that the waters of the mikva fell away from my skin, knowing my peace, too fleeting, would soon follow.

My throat tightened. I was keenly aware of every eye upon me as he turned and walked into the water. Months ago, I had buried one hope to retrieve the ember of another. The Judas of last spring would not have followed the Baptizer into the Jordan.

But the Judas of this fall would.

Impulsively, I took off my sandals and pulled my tunic over my head, ignoring Simon's surprise behind me. Clad in only a loincloth, I staggered after the Baptizer into the water.

The silt of the Jordan slipped between my toes, and the hair stood up on my arms. The sun was just rising over the far bank as I came to stand before John — and then, as I lifted my eyes, it crested and I was overcome with light.

I covered my face and whispered every unclean thing I could think of. From my anger at God himself for the death of Susanna, to the day I spat at Joshua . . . to the fears, plaguing me still, that the Lord had left us forever — or worse yet, never existed. That, too, I whispered, my words falling to the water like so many insects skittering on its surface.

I uncovered my face, and spread my arms wide. The hands of the Baptizer were on my head. He pressed me back. My knees buckled beneath me. Dark enveloped me, cool on my chest and over my face, which was oticky already with tears. And then I was sinking into the chill of the river rushing past me, the light pervading that darkness so that it was not nearly as dark as it should have been in those muddy waters.

So like the womb. Like that moment before birth where there is no awareness of wrong or evil or pain or hope or anything but that still voice that whispers merely: *I am.*

I stayed there for as long as I could, until I thought that if I wanted to, I might actually breathe that murky light in along with the cold unconsciousness of it, the unknowing innocence of soul unmarred by skin or blood or life.

And then I was rising up. My knees straightened and my back lifted and my face came through the surface of the water. I could hear John as though from a distance as the sun broke on my face, every droplet of water a prism of refracted miracles, a thousand voices singing the language of light, and I thought: *I am made anew. At last. At last.*

The Lord had not left me. The Lord had not left Israel. I believed it and knew it to be true.

If only for a moment.

9

Levi arrived at my house before the city gates had even opened for the day.

"I'm leaving," he said.

"For the Jordan?" It was early winter, the hills verdant with the rain of the season, and we had spent every day we could at the river with the Baptizer. "I'll go with you, but let me see to some food for us —"

"No. I mean I'm leaving. To follow John."

Now I saw the pack he carried over his shoulder, the simple tunic he wore in place of the usual linen . . . the lines missing from his forehead . . . the smile playing about his mouth.

Until now, I had never seen it be anything but sardonic.

"I've come to tell you that you'll soon correspond with my contact directly. As will I, from wherever I am."

"Leaving! So suddenly?"

"No, not so sudden. I've long been restless Now I finally realize that I am meant to be out there." He jutted his chin eastward. "Not here, sheltered in the porticoes of the Temple engaged in meaningless debate. We inflate ourselves with our knowledge, honing the fine points of the law while people die beneath the burden of Rome, for hunger — not for the law, but for hope! They are dying, Judas, of despair that God has forgotten them or that we will ever be free." There was fire in his eyes.

"But when did you come to this decision?"

"Yesterday I heard the students of Gamliel denouncing John as a blasphemer. Don't you see? They'll fan the ire of the Pharisees against him. John needs men like us who can smooth the way between him and them until more men have had time to join us. I *believe,* Judas. The kingdom is coming. And the eyes of our brotherhood need to be there. So I'm going. Will you tell Simon goodbye?"

I had not seen Simon in weeks, Levi and I having been more united in our mutual fascination with the Baptizer who only offended Simon's Pharisee friends.

All I could think to say was, "Are you sure?"

"I have never been so sure of anything.

Give me your blessing and assurance that I will see you soon there."

I kissed him numbly and stared at the door long after he had left.

A moment before his arrival I had been thinking of going to the river as well. I thought myself impatient for the kingdom, but now in the face of Levi's going out to usher it in, I realized I had been far too content to rest in the cleansing of the river as one escapes to an imaginary world.

But now Levi's commitment assaulted my conscience, jarring me from the false dream of inaction. In the days to come, I made my own preparations. I checked on the loans I had made on behalf of Susanna's family, that my portion of the accumulating interest would be set aside in the Temple depository for my mother.

I wrote to my new contact in the simple code Levi had shown me the night I went to his house. He had not needed to explain it; I knew it as the same cipher my brother had taught me once, learned from our father in what I had once thought was a game. It was a simple message, delivered to a name I did not recognize that was probably not even a real name, to an address in the upper city.

I am leaving after the Sabbath to follow John.

But the next night, before even the going out of Sabbath, a boy came to my door bearing a note. It read, simply: *Wait.*

Wait?

I stared at the wall of the front room, filled with frustration.

Levi had warned me once of the consequences of disobeying the Sons or betraying their initiatives. Would they threaten my mother or Nathan and his family if I disobeyed? Were I a man with no ties or family, I would have gone. But I was not.

And so I waited, telling myself that Mother and Nathan needed me.

The Sabbath went out, and the days stretched into weeks.

Every day the Temple warmed and cooled beneath the rising and setting sun, beautiful but impassive. Every day I went into her courts to pray, thinking all the while of the wilderness where John preached repentance and that one greater than he was coming. I was there at the Temple the day a delegation of Sadducees returned from the river to report on John.

The news was all throughout the porticoes: They had gone demanding answers

112

for their masters in the ruling houses — Hanan and Boethus in particular. I did not like any members of these families, and I cheered inwardly to hear that John had called them a brood of vipers. Could picture, even, the way he had flung out his arm over the river toward them as they stood on the low scarp overlooking the river in their linen robes.

Their report was rife with accusation.

How do you claim to forgive sins? Are you a priest? Give us an answer to take back to those who sent us.

— I am the son of a priest, but what is that to you? Who told you to flee the coming wrath?

Wrath? There is no wrath for us! We are the sons of Abraham!

— The ax is at the root of that tree. Those who don't produce fruit will be cut down and thrown into the fire! Or don't you know that God can raise up new children of Abraham from the very stones if he wants to?

You dare!

I knew then that the movement begun in the eddies of the Jordan had become a torrent. The Sadducees had not gone for answers but to gather evidence against him. To level killing accusation.

John and his disciples were in more danger

than they knew. They had to go north and leave Judea. I would observe the order to stay, but I felt compelled to at least warn them. And so I went up to the Jordan the very next day.

The crowd amased by the river had grown, teeming in the warmth of the valley. I noted the increased number of the lame and sick, of the painted, sinful women, even a few soldiers in uniform. What had this place become?

When I finally found Levi, he seemed a changed man. The sun had weathered and tanned his skin to a dark russet brown. His hair seemed to have grown longer in the scant weeks since I had seen him, lending him a wild quality not unlike his master. Though it was not a warm day, he stood in the river naked except for a loincloth, shouting the words I had heard so many times: "Repent! The kingdom of God is near!"

I waded out to see him.

"Judas!" He grinned, kissing me. "Blessed are the breasts that suckled you!"

"I've come to repent," I said with a smile. "Baptize me, Levi."

I released my complacency along with my envy over the waters of the Jordan before sinking beneath them. Too soon, I broke the surface, sound crashing around me like the shards of a thousand breaking pots.

"I must speak to John," I said, my beard still dripping.

Levi squinted without grinning, seeing, perhaps, the seriousness of my expression.

John was teaching farther upstream surrounded by pilgrims. I was disconcerted at the thought of speaking to him; what would he say to my warning?

But as we approached, he broke off, eyes fixed to the east. And then he surged forward, wading quickly toward the water's edge. It was not the self-possessed stride of a man accustomed to the river so much as a man stumbling through it, murmuring, eyes fixed on some thing — some one. We hurried after him.

I saw the object of his fascination then: a man — a very gaunt man — moving along the bank.

"Lamb of God!" John said, as though to himself. And then again, more loudly: "Behold, the lamb of God, who takes away the sin of the world!"

The man was so thin as to appear corpselike, unsteady on his feet. And now I could see that his skin was as dark as John's but patchy and peeling from overexposure to the sun and that his lips were blistered pink and bleeding in at least one place. John seemed to notice none of this as he took the man's hands and laid his arm around him, leading him gently toward the narrow bend in the river to the place where he kept his camp.

I turned to Levi, who was staring after them. "Who is that?"

"John's cousin, from Nazareth," he said strangely.

Nazareth. I remembered the tiny hamlet that resided on the toes of Sepphoris — a place I associated with the delirium of pain, hunger, shame. Could anything good come from there?

"By the look of him he's hardly had a morsel to eat since he was here last," Levi said.

"He was here?"

"A little over a month ago. He came to be baptized." Levi shook his head. "I'll never forget that day."

"What do you mean?"

"John didn't want to do it. Which is strange because John refuses no one. They seemed to get into an argument, and at one point John got down on his knees in the river, but his cousin grabbed him by the elbow and pulled him back up. John finally did baptize him . . ."

"And?"

"It was a cloudy day, but as John's cousin came up out of the water, the sun broke, and then John was staring at the sky as though he had seen Elijah in his chariot though none of us could see what he was looking at. People were saying 'Did you hear that thunder? Where's the storm?' But we heard no thunder."

I glanced upriver toward John's camp, but they had disappeared from sight. John didn't return to the river that day.

When evening came Levi touched my arm. "Come."

We made our way upriver past the other disciples' fires to the Baptizer's lean-to. There, John sat in somber conversation with the gaunt man, who was wrapped in several mantles against the evening chill and cupping a bowl of thin broth.

"Master," Levi said. "This is Judas bar Simon, who has brought us a warning."

The Baptizer looked up at me as Levi quickly repeated the warning I'd delivered to him earlier, and I was distracted again by the bluntness of that gaze.

"I baptized you," John said, after Levi had finished.

"Yes. More than once."

I tried not to stare at the husk of a man

huddled beside him, but it was impossible. The words echoed in my head:

Lamb of God.

When the Nazarene lifted his eyes to me, I could not look away. Where I had felt flayed open beneath John's gaze, I saw affinity in the Nazarene's — as though there lived within those sunken eyes mystery and pain to match my own.

That was the first day I saw him, the man who would become my greatest friend.

Two weeks later, John and his followers moved north. Meanwhile, stories came down from Galilee about his mysterious cousin.

Some said he worked a miracle at a wedding in Cana, though no one could agree on what it was. Others said he was nothing but a drunkard, a small-town hand-laborer accepting the favors of strangers and living off the celebrity of his cousin.

And then there were the others, who quietly called him something else.

Messiah.

As winter became spring, I found myself a man lost, without father or brother, wife or son, desperate for the hope I'd momentarily found by the banks of the river Jordan. Haunted by the eyes of the Nazarene.

A few weeks later, John was arrested by Herod. I worried for Levi. I was obsessed with the Nazarene. I could wait no longer.

I wrote to my contact:

I am going to Galilee, to learn about John's cousin, the Nazarene. I will learn his way and whether he may support ours.

And then I went to Simon's house.

"Come with me," I said.

He frowned, the shadows playing about his beard, darkening the hollows of his cheeks. His beloved teacher, the great Shammai, had recently died, throwing the porticoes into chaos. Since then, a new, slithering restlessness had taken up residence behind his eyes.

"And you think you will find peace or answers from a Galilean teacher?"

"My wife and son are dead. All that I have lived for — it isn't here, Simon. Please." I had not told him about my affiliation with the Sons, though one day I hoped to convince my contact to bring him to the cause.

He looked away, shook his head. "I'll go with you, but only until fall. We return for the Feast of Tabernacles."

"Yes, Tabernacles," I said, kissing him with relief.

Two days later, as Simon and I left the gate of the city behind us, the sky opened in a rare summer rain. It only lasted for a few moments, but I took it as a blessing.

With every Roman mile that we went farther down from Jerusalem, I felt a weight roll off my back like ballast thrown from a ship. I did not know what we would discover in this Nazarene, but for the first time in more than a year, I found myself re-acquainted with a freedom akin to hope.

I didn't know that I was leaving Jerusalem forever. That I would never return to dwell for more than a few nights within her walls again.

■ ■ ■ ■

ADORATION

■ ■ ■ ■

10

Had I ever seen the real hues of the Galilean countryside? The reds and purples that washed her horizon morning and evening . . . the lake that was the perfect mirror of the sky, so that you could fall into the clouds by merely standing on her shore . . . the wheat that swayed in her fields, grains pregnant on the stem . . .

The sheep that grazed her hills, bound with the harvest for imperial tables.

The closer we got to the cities and villages of Galilee, the more noticeable the stink of poverty became. Everywhere we turned, it seemed the true crop of Galilee was neither wheat nor barley nor even the grapes of the northern heights, but hunger and discontent, the burden of Rome's taxes seeding the soil like salt.

"I only hope you're not bitterly disappointed," Simon said. The words came out of his mouth by rote, like the words of a prayer uttered so often its syllables become devoid of meaning. He had always been a man of such belief — one who required only an anchor staunch enough to bear his zeal. He was adrift since the death of his teacher, and so I took no offense at this kind of censure from him.

The town of Magdala, on the west shore of the lake called the Sea of Galilee, stank of fish. Drying fish. Pickling fish. Rotting fish. Fish in the holding pools, several of them floating up along the surface, covered in flies. There were few boats this time of day, the fishermen working at the dock mending nets, securing them with fresh stone weights, repairing their boats with gopher or whatever wood they could come by.

We approached one of the elders near the city gate. He was thin, his knees bony through his worn tunic. There were only a small handful of men sitting with him, and I wondered why there weren't more in a town the size of Magdala.

"Sir," I said, "have you heard of a man preaching in Galilee, a Nazarene?"

"Ah, the healer."

Simon and I looked at one another.

"The one who preaches the words of the Baptizer?" the man asked us.

"Yes," I said. "The very one."

He waved north. "They've all gone outside the city to meet him."

We hurried past the docks, along the shore of the lake. It was the first time since leaving Jerusalem that I had seen even the spark of excitement in Simon, and I grinned.

North of the city, we ran through grass turned brown in the summer sun, past the occasional fisherman's hovel, anticipation as thick as the smell of drying fish around us.

What I saw gathered on that low plain utterly amazed me. Hundreds of people. I strained to see the gaunt man of my memory and dreams, but couldn't see past the children chasing one another around the edges of the throng, the men and women pressing closer to see and hear.

"Come!" I said, eager as a boy.

We pressed against the edge of the crowd. From here we could hear his voice but not make out his words over the murmur of those around us.

"What does he say?" I asked a man in front of us. He was dirty and reed thin, as though he hadn't had a meal in days.

"That the kingdom of God is like a pearl — one that a man sells all he has to acquire," he said, his eyes bright.

I glanced at Simon. It was the last thing I expected, having already heard in my mind the words of John: *Repent! The kingdom is at hand!*

I was about to ask him what else but before I could speak a surprised cry flew up from the gathering like a flock of startled birds. The crowd fell back, abruptly spreading out from the man at the center of it so that instead of standing at its fringe, as we had been, we found ourselves standing almost near the front of it.

And then, as those around us shrank farther away, I found myself staring through a lopsided corridor at the very man himself.

Could this be the same man who had come to the river Jordan, starving and baked by the sun? What a change in him! His hair was clean and glistened with oil, and his shoulders had some meat on them — I had not realized how wide they were before. But it was his face that seemed the most changed. It no longer had the sickly look of the starving and the dehydrated, but was full and alert as it had not been on that first day, when it had looked as drawn and haggard as though he had walked out of Sheol.

But I was struck, most of all, by how exceedingly ordinary he looked. The man whose gaze I had never forgotten — was it possible this was he?

The entire assembly had all but parted, some of the people stumbling even into the lake. Then I saw the reason why: A man had come to stand before the Nazarene, his twisted hands lifted before him, stunted fingers spread wide like the misshapen and missing points of a star.

A leper.

I took an involuntary step back.

The leper staggered forward on a foot that was the wrong color for flesh, his face obscured with warty growths so that it looked like the lichen-covered anchors we had passed on the docks. I felt, more than saw, Simon draw back at my side. Heard the strangled sound of his revulsion.

I had seen lepers before, but never in close proximity. They kept outside the city, living off the gifts and leavings of their family, impure beyond touching, required to announce themselves with shouts of "Unclean! Unclean!" They were a walking horror, a symbol of the displeasure of God.

This man was so covered in the disease as to be deformed, as to hardly look like a man at all. He had uncovered his face, the rest of him wrapped in the rags mandated by law. His skin had peeled away so that it was hard

127

to distinguish flesh from dirty cloth. And now I remembered why I used to think that lepers lived in tombs, because the man before me was truly no more than a walking corpse, his flesh dying on his bones while his soul perversely remained intact.

Mothers grabbed up their children, turned their faces against their breasts, while a few men angrily shouted for the leper to go away, couldn't he see there were people here? But it was not only anger that lent volume to their voices. It was fear. Every one of us had looked at some lesion in our flesh with dread at one time or another, worrying that a boil would rupture, that it would stay broken, giving too close of an access to the blood beneath, which was too holy to be spilled or touched. Every one of us feared broken flesh for what it signified — impurity and judgment . . . shunning from community and from the Temple. How great was this man's sin, that he had been struck so horribly, so disfigured by this disease — and how far were any of us from crossing that same threshold ourselves?

Surely the leper knew the law! And yet, even saying so, he staggered forward, his mouth gaping, lip-less and obscene.

"Please!" the leper cried, his voice cracking as though he had not spoken or cried out in a very long time. Now I could see the way his eyes darted this way and that, the way his hands with the stumps of fingers trembled like the flutter of a leaf. "Please!"

The Nazarene moved forward and one of his disciples said, "Teacher, he is unclean!" I blinked. I knew that man. Was that not Andrew, who had been a disciple of John?

The Nazarene lifted a hand to Andrew, his eyes on the leper before him. All around, the hundreds were silent. Somewhere in the crowd, a child wailed.

The leper lurched forward, closing the distance between him and the one man who had not moved since his appearance. He pitched to the ground, onto his knees, onto his face.

"Please!" he wailed in a hoarse voice that carried with terrible clarity. "Please, if you are willing, you can make me clean."

When the Nazarene sank to one knee and laid his hand upon the leper's shoulder, I staggered back as though struck. I stood fixed, acutely aware of the taut gaze of every person there, all fixed on one point like the gathered threads of a spider's web.

That hand on that shoulder.

The man on the ground lifted his head, his face contorted. His mouth gaped open in a low keen as though having gone so long without the touch of another human that it pained him to feel it at all. He lifted one starlike hand as though wanting to touch the clean hand upon his shoulder except that he didn't dare. He began to shake and his head dipped back down with the soundless moan of one who has suffered so long he cannot remember how to cry.

"I am willing."

I could not mistake the way his voice broke as he cupped the leper's face. As he said again: "I am willing."

His thumbs brushed over the boils of the leper's cheek, over the lesions rimming his mouth like the uneven stones lining a well in the desert. It was not the touch one gives an abomination, not the perfunctory graze of the physician . . . but the caress of one moved to weeping over the sight of something beautiful. The man dropped his head down into the Nazarene's palm, and sobbed.

"Be clean."

The man slowly lifted his head.

I staggered. The air left my lungs as Simon shoved past me, staring.

Where there had been lesions like boils, there was smooth skin, revealing for the first time wide-set eyes, a strong nose, and well-shaped mouth — a mouth for uttering prayers. A living being had emerged from

130

the flesh of the dead and for the first time since seeing him, I wondered what his name was.

He covered his face, his cries more primitive and profound than words. And when he lifted his shaking hands, ten well-formed fingers grasped for the sky.

I had seen many great teachers. I had heard many stories.

But I had never seen anything like this.

11

That night I lay wrapped in my mantle in an inn in Gennesaret, unable to sleep. I was thinking about the leper, of his return to his family. Of his return to the synagogue — to the Temple, from which he would have been barred all this time.

Of the way the Nazarene had cupped his face — as though the man were not a leper but his own brother or son or dearest friend.

How many years had the leper hoped for the day that he might be sprinkled with the blood of a bird by the priest and proclaimed clean? How many years had he dreamed of the eighth day after, when he might bring two lambs to sacrifice — and the hour that the priest would rub the blood of one lamb on his earlobe and his thumb and his largest toe and pronounce him clean? And how many months or years ago had he abandoned such hope — along with his earlobe, his thumb, his toe — in the limestone caves of Galilee?

What did it mean that a man could restore such hope to one lost?

Could this man do the same for a nation? *Messiah.*

I told myself not to think these thoughts. But then I thought them anyway.

It would be almost two days before we would see the Nazarene again. The teacher, someone said, had gone into the hills to pray. And so we stayed at the inn, waiting as many of those camping outside the city waited, to see him again. During that time, tales about him abounded, as numerous and unbelievable as so many Galilean fishing stories.

That he'd driven demons out of a woman from Magdala by simply commanding them to go. This, I knew to be impossible.

That the Magdalene woman now followed him wherever he went, even in his company as part of his circle. The mere idea was an affront to propriety.

That he had come to Galilee by way of Samaria. What good Jew traveled through that land of murderers? One man even said he had sat down at Jacob's own well and asked a woman for a drink. Simon declared this last bit rubbish and called the man a liar to his face. No respected teacher would speak to a woman who wasn't his wife — let alone ask a Samaritan woman for a drink. He would contract uncleanness by just touching her.

And yet, he had touched a leper . . .

"The teacher says that the kingdom of heaven is like a mustard seed," a local merchant who sold us some bread told us. "It's the smallest seed, but when it is grown, it is larger than all the plants in a garden and becomes a tree, and birds come to rest in its branches."

"Are you sure that's what he said?" I frowned.

"Heard it myself. I follow him every chance I get — have for months now. He also says the kingdom of heaven is like a net thrown into the sea that gathers all kinds of fish. And then when it's full, men pull it ashore and sort the good fish into containers, and throw away the bad ones."

"I don't like it," Simon murmured the second evening. "What teacher teaches with stories like these? How does one teach truth with fictions? It's a dangerous thing to toy with scriptures, to chance changing even one jot or tittle of the law!"

"He's speaking to common people, Simon. Not learned men like you."

"I heard someone say today that he doesn't even wash his hands before eating. What teacher ignores the purity laws?"

I did not tell him that I didn't think the Nazarene was interested in that form of purity. Nor did I remind him that the Maccabee himself had gone from town to town raising his army until the day that he was ready to march on Jerusalem and purify the Temple. I did not say that the day we arrived I had not seen just a throng of hungry peasants, but the beginnings of an army. I did not share any of this, though it sent my heart soaring in my chest and I knew I would report it to the Sons.

But Simon remained unconvinced.

"Someone told me they almost killed him when he went home to Nazareth. Because there he is only a hand-laborer and yet he claimed the scriptures were fulfilled in his being there. And because he does not teach by quoting the sages, but on his own word as though the scriptures were the commentary!"

"It's rumor and hearsay! What else have these peasants got to talk about?" I said.

"He didn't heal a leper or perform any sign there. Do you know the reason he gave? Because they did not believe. And so he couldn't perform it. Isn't that how conjurers work? Do you know what another man told me today? That he was in Egypt as a boy. Egypt — the land of magicians!"

"Don't be ridiculous."

"Judas, be careful. We will know the Messiah by his might, but we know a man of the Lord by the law and the company he keeps."

"To keep the company of the poor is not a sin."

"Why do you defend him? We're nearing the end of our funds. If we return now, we can get back to the city ahead of the pilgrims going up for the Feast."

"Simon, there's something happening here. Can't you tell? Can't you feel it? These men haven't come out to hear stories. They came for *hope*."

"Hope in what? I see a horde of peasants that will eventually get scattered when their leader gets put down like a dog! This is not the way, Judas."

Anger welled up in me like desperation.

"How do you know? Because they do not *wash*? Did you not see that leper come away with whole skin? Fingers — where there were no fingers? Can you not see the faces of those people, more desperate for what he has than they are even for food? There is something more simple and profound here

136

that even you and I, in our learning, can understand."

"You're infatuated with him!" he burst out. "You want so much for him to be this thing you desire, you overlook that he flouts the law!"

"He came from Egypt. You said it yourself. Andrew says he wasted away in the wilderness. For forty days. Forty — the number of years Moses himself wandered the wilderness. And then he returned and crossed the Jordan. Does this mean nothing to you? Didn't our forefathers do the same on their return from exile?" Even saying it raised gooseflesh on my arms.

"Bethlehem," I went on. "Did you hear that he wasn't born in Nazareth? He was born in Bethlehem. *Bethlehem,* Simon. The birthplace of David. And his parents were even of the line of David."

"So are a hundred other peasants every year. Someone whispers 'Messiah' and you go all crazy? Did anyone tell you he's also of questioned birth?"

I blinked. Of "questioned birth." Not quite a bastard, but not without a smudge on his lineage. My brother's birth had also been called "questionable," though in his case it was a kindness over calling him what he truly was. In small Kerioth, it had made finding a woman for him especially challenging. His wife, Rebecca, was of similarly questioned birth, her parents only betrothed at the time of her conception.

Why was everything we heard about this teacher troubling?

I pushed the thought away and closed the distance between us. "I am the last person to lose my mind over a so-called messiah. You have no idea what I have lost in the name of would-be messiahs!"

"Oh yes I do," he said, very quietly. "You are so presumptuous, thinking you are the only one who suffers, who has lost anything. I know very well what it is to see a brother put to the sword, a father hung on a cross! I do not need to tell you that these things have dire consequences. Herod's already seized the Baptizer that you rushed out to hear at the river. How long before he arrests his cousin, too?"

"He healed that leper," I said. "I saw it with my own eyes and so did you. That was no magician's trick."

His mouth was set, hardness in his eyes like a shield.

"A little longer," I said. "If the signs are not real, if you cannot say 'I see. I believe' with your own mouth, we will go back."

Even as I said it, I knew that I would not

go back, even if he turned and left me now.

"A little longer," he said, more quietly. "But think, Judas. Do you not see that maybe he is a very clever peasant with a grudge? With good cause, perhaps, but a grudge nonetheless — against the rich, the learned, the keepers of the law, every one of those who have seemingly deprived him of honorable place in this world? And so of course he appeals to peasants and landless workers. He is one of them. But he is not one of us."

The next day we got up early before the crowds could gather. The sun had barely tinged the sky when we came across a man I thought I'd seen with the Nazarene the first day — one close to him.

"Excuse me," I said, making for him. "Have you seen the teacher, the Nazarene they call Jesus?"

"He's resting," the man said in a thick Galilean accent. His face was dark from the sun and I assumed him to be another of John's disciples. "Don't worry, you'll see him soon enough. You can't miss him."

The disciple started down the path toward the docks and we quickly followed.

"And who are you?" I said.

The man glanced over at us as we came alongside him. "Simon bar Jonah," he said, his chin lifting a notch. "Though the teacher calls me Peter."

"He calls you 'Rock'?" Simon said with a queer look.

Peter knocked himself on the skull with a grin. His front teeth were crooked, one of them so much so that when he closed his mouth it seemed to almost stick out between his lips. "When it fits. Andrew is my brother."

"I don't remember seeing you at the river with the Baptizer," I said.

"I wasn't. With all the fishing tolls we need every able-bodied man in the family on the lake. No, Andrew was the wild one, telling tales of a man at the Jordan, baptizing any other madmen willing to go hear him." He flashed a wry smile at me. "We were secretly glad when John was imprisoned, because it meant that Andrew would come back."

I frowned.

"And yet, here you both are," Simon said, squinting at him, "following his cousin."

"Yes. Here we are. And I've pledged to follow him wherever he goes. I thought my brother was out of his mind the first time he came to tell me he had found the Messiah."

I glanced sharply at him. "Messiah?"

Peter lifted his chin. "If that's not a Messiah, then I don't know what is."

I noticed then that he had a sword at his side, partially obscured beneath his robe.

"Will you tell us where you're going?" I asked.

"Capernaum," a man said behind us. "Home."

We had come this far and now they were leaving for another village even farther away. These were all fishermen and peasants and farmers here. For an instant I wondered if Simon was right. We didn't belong.

I turned to the man who'd spoken behind me and my next question died on my lips.

Before me stood the Nazarene.

"Go on to the boat, Peter," he said.

Peter ducked his head and went ahead toward the dock.

"I've seen you before," the Nazarene said, turning to smile at me.

Was it possible he remembered me? Even now I remembered that first day, the gaze that had drawn me back to the river days later to look for him again.

"Yes," I said. "At the river. I came to warn John."

"What are you called?"

"Judas bar Simon. From Kerioth. Jerusalem, originally. And this is Simon bar Isaac, who studied under the great Shammai."

141

"Teacher," said Simon, who was nothing if not proper even in the face of doubt.

I couldn't gauge if the name of Shammai meant anything to the Nazarene. I knew only that the words he spoke next changed my life.

"Judas Ish-Kerioth. Simon bar Isaac," he said, looking at each of us. "Come with me."

"Now?" Simon said.

He chuckled. "Yes, now."

He went down to the pier where Peter was waving at us from the boat.

Exchanging a last look with Simon, we hurried after him and got in.

I desperately wanted to look into the Nazarene's face, to see if I could find in his expression a hint of the thing within him that had healed the leper, some secret in those too ordinary eyes. But he had pulled his mantle up over his head against the morning sun glancing off the water and I couldn't crane to see him without feeling like I might topple from my seat in the rocking of the boat.

Instead, I found myself staring at his feet, stretched out before him. At his simple sandals, and the worn and dirty toes. At the muddy hem of his tunic and his hands, dangling over his knees, fingers calloused and rough. They were not the hands of a

scholar but of the laborer who works with
stone, or in the field, or with wood when he
can get it — or at anything that will earn
him a day's dinar.

Introductions were made, but I hardly
heard them.

My mind was on the Nazarene.

Come.

And we had.

As we pulled away through the opening in
the breakwater I could see the crowd forming along the shoreline, following us.

"You look a little ill, city man," Peter said,
taking up one of the oars.

"It's my first time in a boat," I confessed.

Jesus chuckled, and Andrew joined with
him. And soon the others were laughing.

I didn't realize just then that in the short
distance of shoreline between Heptapegon
and Capernaum, I had begun the great
journey I had waited for all my life.

At that moment, with the sun lowering
against our backs, I knew only that the
world of the Temple, of Jerusalem, seemed
very far away. That here, beneath the Galilean sky, the coming kingdom might truly
be a seed taking root in the Golan hills or
even between the mismatched boards of a
fishing boat.

If only I had fallen overboard or drowned with a millstone around my neck.

12

Capernaum.

In the weeks and months to follow I would come to know her streets, her wine and oil presses, the basalt of her houses and synagogue. The winds that came down from the hills to the north, gusting through her streets on their way to the lake.

But the first Capernaum I knew was a tangled mass of faces, of arms and hands, all reaching for one man. Some came to lay eyes on him, others their hands, to touch him as one touches a relic or rubs the foot of an idol.

In such a crowd one cannot shy away from those noticeably deformed or ill. Cannot shirk the grasping of the desperate, the old, the mothers with their babies. The twisted faces of the weeping, the mesmerized, and the frantic.

They came to him as though he were wheat to feed the hungry, only to melt back into the press with beatific expressions. I didn't hear what he said to them, but I saw the way that Simon, standing closer by, stared at the teacher in the waning light of that day he'd called us to come with him. He was stunned, as though the sheer multitude had at last spoken mystery to him with the clamor of one voice.

I was still wary of his pronouncements of Jesus as a magician, however, and so did not ask him about it, even that night as we lay down to sleep.

It was still dark when I got up and went out to relieve myself around the side of Peter's house. His wife was already at work in the courtyard; I could hear the sound of sticks splintering as she broke them apart for the oven, the grinding of the hand-mill. The cook fires of the fishermen glowed orange on their boats in the distance. They would be back by morning, bringing the catch to market as they had yesterday, and a year ago, and a hundred years before that.

And yet today nothing was the same. Not the mist on the lake or the tiny dots of fire upon it. Not the thinning darkness of the eastern sky or the dogs coming to sniff at my feet.

Nothing.

146

And though I did not know how or what it meant, neither was I the same.

I pulled my mantle up around my shoulders and walked to the edge of town past the sleeping forms of those poor who had no other shelter than the sides of houses and shop fronts. The Shema was burning in my throat, and I knew today that I would not cover my eyes as I was accustomed, but that I would walk along the edge of the lake and sing the words with my soul: *Hear O Israel, the Lord is One.*

I had just come to a path outside the city when I heard the soft scrape of a step in front of me. I instinctively reached for my dagger. Some things about this world had not changed.

But even as the figure came toward me I sensed he was no bandit. He walked too simply, without a ghost of caution. It was by that uncanny ease that I knew it was Jesus.

And then there he was, an arm's reach from me: the man who had laughed in the boat and grasped the hands of the throng in the streets of Capernaum. Who had staggered to the back room of Peter's house last night to fall down, exhausted. I tried again to reconcile him with the gaunt man at the Jordan, John's cousin, wasted and skeletal as though he had not eaten once in the forty days of his absence.

His mantle lay draped around his neck. It was embroidered with blue thread, the tassels prescribed by law on each of their corners dangling together in front. He had been praying.

"Judas," he said, and I realized that I had stopped dead before him.

It was the first time I had found myself alone with him and could truly see him — not from a distance as an emaciated man, not through a crowd of others or the shield of his disciples, but standing directly before me. And here is the truth: He was so plain that I might not have known him from any one of the peasants or poor that surrounded him. His eyes were the brown of any man of Israel, his beard thin in spots, his face hinting at a slight lack of symmetry so that he might not even be called handsome.

I was looking for a sign of the miracle-worker, a glimpse of mystery or power. But I saw only the brown skin and creased eyes of a Galilean laborer, looking back at me.

"Teacher, the leper. How? How did you know you could heal him?"

He glanced past me toward the low wall of the town. "The same way I know I could repair that wall."

His gaze returned to rest on me.

"The thing you seek is not along this shore, or in the hills. But with me. Follow me."

Yes. I said it in my heart. I do not know if it made it to my lips.

It defied logic. He was a laborer and one of questionable birth and I was an educated businessman. But in that moment I felt I had found a thing, a person, worth the resurrection of my every hope. The thought terrified and exhilarated at once.

I meant to tell him that my father had been a hero. That I knew Torah and was considered as schooled as Simon or any student of Shammai.

But I said none of this. None of it mattered.

"Come with me where I am going, Judas," he said. "And you will find the thing you seek."

In that moment, I believed him. I believed him with all my heart.

We returned to town together, the crowd already gathering to greet him.

Simon was quiet all that day. But I didn't ask his thoughts or engage him. Something had happened to me. I felt part of something more profound than I had ever known before. Something greater than the schools of the porticoes or even the Sons of the Teacher. Greater, even, than the Baptizer . . .

. . . than the pain of a past that had brought me to this moment.

That day, I knew that God had spoken to me at last which way I was to go after so many missteps before.

In those first days, I was overwhelmed by the sheer number of people who came to see him. That came to be touched by him, complaining of ailments, who stayed to loiter near him as though he were a lantern, as surely as we, ourselves, did.

I didn't always hear what he said or see what he did in the jostle of those crowds. I only knew that some of them stayed and others went away, shouting. They came back with others until the crowds became so unmanageable that one of Jesus' followers, a fisherman named John, inevitably had to bring around a boat. It was the only way to accommodate them all, to not be caught in the crush as the people came in droves to hear Jesus tell his strange stories.

"A farmer went out to sow his seed," he would begin. I had heard this story, by now, several times. "As he was scattering the seed, some fell along the path, and the birds

150

came and ate it. Some fell on rocky places, where it didn't have soil. It sprang up quickly in that shallow soil."

It was not the language of the Pharisees or the sages but of farmers and day-laborers and yes, fishermen, too. And Simon would frown, because this was not the way the sages in the Temple or synagogues spoke.

A few days after our arrival in Capernaum, a few teachers from the synagogue came pressing through the crowd. One of them wore the tefillin of the Pharisee. I watched as people made way; Simon gave up his own seat for him.

Jesus seemed not to notice their arrival. "Listen!" he said. "Two men went up to the Temple to pray. One was a Pharisee and the other a tax collector. The Pharisee stood by himself and prayed, 'I thank you I am not like other people — robbers, evildoers, adulterers — or even like this tax collector.' "

At mention of the tax collector, a few people in the crowd hissed. Across from me, the Pharisee had an indulgent expression on his face, as one on the verge of receiving praise. It was, I thought, an expression I had seen often on the faces of many of the Pharisees I had known. They were, after all, men to be admired.

"But the tax collector stood at a distance. He would not even look up to heaven, but beat his breast and said, 'Have mercy on me, a sinner!' " A few smug nods in the crowd. Everyone knew no tax collector would ever say such a thing.

"I'm telling you that this man, rather than the other, went home justified before the Lord. All those who exalt themselves will be humbled, and those who humble themselves will be exalted."

The Pharisee looked around in confusion, red-faced at the perceived insult. "Why would he tell such a story?" he said, craning to look at one of the other teachers, and lastly at Simon, who appeared struck. "Why does he say these things?"

I stood stunned as the Pharisee gathered his robes around him and made his way past the other teachers through a crowd gone awkwardly quiet.

I was troubled that evening as we went with Jesus to the house of a well-known man in town. Nahum bar Saul was round-faced and beaming with pride at all the attention his house was receiving. Seeing him, it was as though I could read his thoughts: *I will be the talk of the town for this.*

The crowd had followed us, and when we had gone inside, their faces filled the windows, which were open to admit the afternoon breeze, though I thought they were also thrown extra wide so that anyone might see the company within.

As those few of us that the teacher had invited with him — Simon and me, the brothers John and James, the brothers Andrew and Peter — came into the house, I felt my heart drop. There was the Pharisee from earlier with a second man wearing the tefillin and the slight ennui of the learned.

So the one had gone and gotten another to take the teacher to task. I had seen meetings like this many times in my years at the Temple and in my association with scholarly friends — and had often been the second man brought in for such verbal wars.

But I sensed no nervousness in Jesus. As the servant came to pour water over each of our hands, he greeted the host and each of the Pharisees, too, with a kiss.

"I hear, Jesus son of Mary, that you told some stories today near the water," the second Pharisee said.

I cringed at the way he said "son of Mary." It was the address of a bastard, to be called the son of his mother rather than father.

"Did I?"

"A charming tale, about some weeds." He chuckled and gestured vaguely. "What is this story about? A farmer? A husband whose neighbor 'sows seeds in his field' when he isn't looking?"

Chuckles, all around.

Before Jesus could answer, a chunk of straw and earthen ceiling fell abruptly onto the table. And then we were up and leaping back over the cushions, the Pharisees tripping over their robes, Simon falling against the wall with a look of such utter shock that I would have laughed at him were the ceiling not now falling down in great clumps and dusty nuggets.

"Who's up there? Stop! Make them stop!" Nahum was saying, clapping his hands to his head. He was a proud man, but not a wealthy one. He had not counted on ruin to his house in hosting this prestigious dinner.

A group of faces appeared above us, brown and dirty-faced, and there was John yelling up at them that they were killing us. They pulled more of the dirt and straw away and the branch support beams with it leaving a clear expanse of starry sky.

"What is the meaning of this?" James shouted.

And then the sky was blocked out by what looked like a pallet.

"Steady!" someone yelled. I had never seen anything like this Galilean chaos, this commotion of the country folk.

"Teacher! Please!" Someone shouted from above. One of the wall stones came loose and tumbled into the room. The ropes creaked. A groan issued from the pallet.

A young man was lowered right onto the table. His face was drawn tight and a line of drool escaped the corner of his mouth. I had thought him a man but he was barely thirteen, if that. I had seen paralytics before near the Temple steps, and been afraid of them. He was not the kind of beggar that a man could even pity well, because he seemed half out of his mind, eyes looking out from the prison of his own bone-thin limbs. A smell filled the room — urine, perhaps, overpowered only by the stench of one who is wasting away inside his own body. Across the table, one of the Pharisees covered his nose with the edge of his sleeve.

The boy lifted his arms, just a little. They didn't work right. His legs were askew, no better than sticks. I shuddered and looked away in time to see Simon avert his eyes. But Andrew was looking at the pallet with strange interest.

As was Jesus.

He leaned over the pallet and sighed, smoothed back the young man's hair. The paralytic made a sound that was not a word.

155

Bubbles came out of the spittle at the edge of his mouth.

I would never forget the look on Jesus' face. I had seen it before on the face of my mother once when Joshua and I, roughhousing, had knocked a bowl of rare painted pottery to the floor, shattering it. It was the most precious thing she owned and her eyes had filled with tears even as she had gathered up the pieces on her knees.

How was it possible that I should see that look in this man now? What man was this, who could look at a paralytic that way?

He held the young man's wrist gently. I saw Simon glance toward the door.

It was an impossible situation. How could we gracefully leave this place, this house — the presence of this broken man — with so many nearby?

"Son," Jesus said, loud enough for all of those to hear, and yet in a way that seemed as intimate as though he had whispered it. The young man's gaze was fixed on his, rapt. "Your sins are forgiven."

I must have heard him wrong.

Across the table, Simon had gone white.

What was he doing? Every man of Israel knew that only God could forgive sins!

Over in the corner, where the Pharisees had drawn back against the wall, the one stared, eyes bulging, no longer indulgent.

Jesus' gaze snapped up as though the man had screamed at him.

"Why do you entertain evil thoughts?" he said.

The Pharisee started to open his mouth.

"What is easier?" Jesus said, his voice rising in the direction of the teachers in the corner. "To say to this man 'Your sins are forgiven'?" He returned his attention to the young man on the table. "Or 'Get up. Take up your mat . . . and walk'?"

The young man closed his mouth, still slick with the line of saliva running down past his jaw to his throat. Slowly, he turned his head straight, as though he were gazing not up at the faces of his family, but past them, to the heavens themselves. And then he lowered his chin toward his chest . . . and began to roll upward.

Gasps from overhead. From the windows. From my own mouth.

The man came up as one emerging from the surface of the mikva or the waters of the Jordan, into the air. He sat straight up as Jesus took him by the wrist. One of the thin legs twitched on the pallet. Overhead, a woman cried out.

The leg slid over the edge of the pallet and table both, dangled toward the floor.

The other slid toward it until his feet had come to the ground. He bowed his head, his free hand grasping the edge of the table . . .

. . . and pushed up from the edge.

His breath came out in a slow, unsteady exhale, ragged like a pant.

No — like an incredulous laugh, where his jaw and his tongue had not seemed to work before.

Shouts from the roof. But those within the room stared in utter silence as he stood before the teacher, hand now clasped in his. And then he slowly let go, reached up and brushed the line of saliva away from his cheek, moved forward a step, and then another, and clasped the teacher in shaking arms.

At that, an explosion of pent breath, of cries and laughter came in through the windows and down through the ceiling. Across from me, John was hollering as though with the might of the heavens, and his brother had rushed to the window, crying, "Did you see that? Did you see it?"

The house erupted. It shook like Jericho itself at the clamor outside and on top of it, as though it would all come down upon us.

But the Pharisees in the corner were as

pale as the dead.

That was how the trouble started.

13

It was three weeks until the Feast of Tabernacles and I had never experienced a more astonishing two months of my life.

Now everywhere we went, people said, "Are you not one of the ones with him? Are you not his disciple?"

I was gratified at first by the look in their eyes. It surpassed what I had imagined as a child when I wanted to be a teacher of the law, going beyond respect to strange awe.

Then again, it was an easy thing to awe peasants and fishermen. It was an altogether different matter to move the learned. And though there were more peasants than teachers, it was the Pharisees and teachers whose opinions mattered . . . and who found themselves the most offended by my new master.

And then there was Simon.

When people asked him these same questions, he did not answer, but kept his eyes straight ahead. They grabbed his sleeve and his tunic anyway, as though having been in the company of the healer he might have some vicarious power. But of course none of that was true.

He was often in prayer, his shawl over his head, and I knew that he wrestled with something that he would not share with me. In those days and hours, he reminded me of Joshua as he had been in Sepphoris. The way my brother had struggled so valiantly and beautifully. Perhaps because of that, I was gentle with him in the only way I knew how to be: I left him alone.

A few days later Simon and I accompanied Jesus down near the lake. James and John had gone ahead of us.

I welcomed the breeze, the smell of the water — if not the fish themselves in the shallow pools where the fishermen brought in their catches. The father of John and James — the "Sons of Thunder," as Jesus called them — had invited us to his house for dinner that evening. I was curious to meet the father who had spawned the brash brothers, but when I asked the teacher about it he said, "We will go, but not tonight. Tonight we eat at a wealthy man's house."

I was secretly relieved for that news, hopeful that a rich man might serve something other than fish.

Near the catch pools of the southernmost dock stood a stone hut. It was attended by soldiers and a line of peasants, their pack animals laden with baskets of barley, jars of pickled fish, oil, wine. Behind the hut a large wagon stood half-filled with similar goods under guard by two more soldiers.

The tax booth.

Had the teacher come to pay taxes? I followed him to the hut where James and John were already arguing loudly with the collector behind the table.

The man was a Jew — nearly all of them were, having bid and bribed for the privilege of extorting their countrymen. My father had never failed to spit in the direction of a tax booth when he could for the simple fact that such men used their learning for love of money over the law. It was the reason Shammai had permitted lying to a tax collector as long as it didn't involve an oath . . . and the teacher Hillel permitted it even if it did.

"I tell you, that was a freak catch," John was saying. "You can't base our lease on one catch alone! So here it is, the usual payment and we're done with it!"

The tax collector, who could afford to be

far fewer volatile with soldiers at his side, spoke so quietly that I couldn't hear him. John's brother, James, however, was another matter.

"Fool! We've only got the two boats and there's fewer of us fishing now than before! We've paid you enough to fill your table for days with only a pittance left over for our own children. Don't think we don't know who you are, son of Alphaeus. You're a Levite. Your calling is the Temple! But here you sit stealing our food and livelihoods and giving them to Herod and Rome." He spat on the table, right onto the man's books.

The soldiers watched the exchange with a lazy eye, apparently accustomed to these conversations.

Simon stepped in front of me and tried to draw Jesus away.

"Please, Teacher, you dirty yourself here," he said.

The tax collector, who had lowered his gaze at the onslaught of the brothers' anger, suddenly looked up. His cheeks were full and anyone looking at him could see that he was well fed, that his skin was not dark from the sun, and that his clothing was made of the highest quality linen. But now I also saw the lines around his eyes, the ring of his mouth drawn tight over his teeth as though he sat there by an act of will — no, as though he sat there chained by the very wealth of the fine linen on his back, fixed to his position by the hatred and scorn of others.

"Are you the teacher they're all talking about?"

"I am," my master said. "Come with me."

I stumbled back. I told myself it was not possible that I had just heard the same words my master had spoken to me offered to a *tax collector*. That I did not hear the scrape of a chair, or the audacity of the man rasping as he fell to his knees: "Have mercy on me, a sinner!"

That night, my heart pounded as I entered the Roman-style villa in the upper hills of the city where the wealthy had their houses. We had come to eat at a rich man's house indeed — the house of Matthew, the Levite tax collector.

Simon had refused to come.

We sat down stiffly on the sofas, as though scorpions might come out of its cushions. Peter and his brother reclined rigidly, holding themselves high on their elbows rather than sinking into their shoulders.

Another wealthy man arrived not long after us, gold rings heavy on his fingers, his

164

fat cheeks flushed in the early evening heat. Matthew greeted him with a kiss. And then to my shock, the teacher himself rose from among our company and kissed him as well, as one kisses a friend.

I saw the surprise on the faces of the others, the ire smoldering up from the fishermen. But none of this surpassed the sheer stupefaction of the man himself, whose bravado slipped the moment Jesus released him and brought him to the table to sit among us.

Two more rich men arrived soon after and they, too, came to the table with darting glances, as apparently uncomfortable as we were.

There was not a Pharisee or man of the law to be seen. But of course not. We were dining in the company of tax collectors.

Outside the Roman-style house, a small crowd had gathered to peer at the guests through the courtyard and windows, to gawk at the sheer wealth of the table and the delicacies upon it. But they let out a collective gasp when servants went out to them with platters of the same food served at the table within: Jerusalem dates and rare melons off the coastal plain, almond cakes and lentil stew, salt fish, jugs of wine, and loaves and loaves of bread. Within minutes the courtyard had swelled to bursting, and Matthew had gone himself to invite in as many of those outside as the room could accommodate.

Sometime during all of this, the Magdalene woman who indeed followed my master came in with her friend, Joanna, who I had been alarmed to learn was the wife of Herod's own steward. They sat down not even three arms' reaches from the teacher himself.

It was chaotic, anarchic. As vividly aberrant as Jesus' healings, with the fishermen looking as though they could barely swallow and the tax collectors glancing from the women to the plates of food going out to the courtyard as though they were goats flying across the sky.

One of the tax collectors, whom I had heard the others refer to as Kaniel, suddenly put down his almond cake and hissed, "What is *that* woman doing here?"

At first I thought he meant the Magdalene or her friend. And then I followed the line of his gaze to a woman in the corner of the room. Her face was painted, her veil not properly tucked around her hair. I wondered if Matthew had any idea that a prostitute had entered his house. She was eating hungrily and when she got up to make room

166

for another woman who came in to sit beside her, I saw that she was pregnant.

They would ask her to leave, surely.

The tax collector looked around and summoned a servant, whispering to him. But when he had finished, Jesus reached out a hand to the servant's sleeve and said something I could not hear. A moment later, the servant went to the woman, but rather than ask her to leave, he brought her a basket full of bread and figs.

I watched all of this, the way she clasped the basket as though it were not a basket at all, but an amphora of something far more precious.

Clearly offended, the one known as Kaniel got up and left.

I told myself that I should not be here, that I insulted myself. The sages said that a man was not to associate with an evildoer, even if it brought him closer to the law. That to take something into oneself from a contaminated environment would draw the impurity of that company into oneself.

And here I sat with tax collectors and sinful women.

But for the moment, the vigilance of purity seemed like a distant thing. As I ate, a strange sense of liberty came over me, as if a coarse cloak had been removed from my back.

I drank deeply of the wine. It was very strong and I wondered if it had something to do with my musings, my observation of myself as I realized that in the company of Pharisees, where I ought to have felt more pure, I felt less so. I was the child of a woman who had lost her purity. I had dwelt in a cave with corpses, and had seen the nakedness of my father on a cross. If there was anyone impure here, it was I.

My master had dirtied his hands on the leper and the paralytic both. Now he dirtied them publicly with the tax collector. I began to wonder if that was the way it was, that one must dirty his hands to heal.

It was as though the world was backward with him, and that purity was the truest contagion.

I was thinking all of this the minute I saw them: three forms moving through the courtyard. As the crowd parted for them I could see the tassels hanging long on their garments, tefillin on their foreheads and arms, the way they did not stop to help themselves to food, but rather shied away from it.

Pharisees.

A few minutes later, one of the peasants from the courtyard came into the house where we were eating and stood before Jesus.

"Please, Teacher," he said. He was one of the better attired of the lot outside in that his clothes were less ragged and he had a pair of sandals on his feet. The stilted and awkward conversation around the table fell away. "There is a Pharisee outside who asks, 'Why do you eat with tax collectors and sinners? Why this display of impropriety?' "

Jesus set down his cup. "You might ask why I heal the sick rather than the healthy," he said, loudly enough for those in the courtyard to hear.

His face was no longer that of the man who had grinned at the others upon their arrival. He looked off to the side and shook his head slightly. "Tell the one who sent you in here to learn the meaning of 'I desire mercy, not sacrifice.' I haven't come to call the righteous, but sinners!"

The Pharisee outside visibly stiffened as the other two glanced between themselves, apparently at a loss as Jesus picked up a date and went on eating and talking to the guest beside him as if nothing had occurred. After a time, the rest of us followed in uneasy suit.

That was the first night that I realized the tenor between Jesus and the Pharisees had changed Before, they had come questioning, wanting to know which faction or school he followed and where his loyalties lay. In every synagogue and even in the Temple this same ritual played out like dogs sniffing one another's tails.

But as the Pharisees left, gathering their robes close around them, I saw the way the first one glanced back, a terrible look on his face.

14

New Year came in with the harvest. It was now two weeks until Tabernacles and we turned our eyes south, toward the Holy City.

I had both anticipated and dreaded this journey up to Jerusalem. Anticipated it, because I wanted to enter the Holy City with this new headiness of purpose and because I missed my family.

Dreaded it, because I knew Simon would leave me and the company of my new master.

The teacher's family joined us in Bethmaus for the journey. I was surprised by the prick of impatient envy I felt in seeing them surround him and steal his attention away, even at the way Jesus attended to his mother. She was petite, her small stature lending her a girl-like appearance until one saw her eyes, lined with years, filled with secrets.

I told myself that in Jerusalem I would

take Jesus to the porticoes. I would be there to usher him about, to show him off to those in the Temple. Jerusalem was, after all, my city.

All this while I had been chewing on the cud of what to say to the Sons. That he healed lepers? That the lame walked? Or that he ate with sinners and had taken a tax collector into his company?

I knew that I had to make a decision — to proclaim him to them as a healer and perhaps a messiah, or as a lawless man of questioned birth and potentially a blasphemer.

I wrote at last, swiftly figuring the cipher in my head:

Tell the Teacher that the sick are healed and masses come to hear. Our friend is coming for the feast.

I felt like a prophet, writing it. Had felt the thrill of it coursing up my arm even after I folded and sealed the note and sent it ahead with a merchant.

The kingdom of heaven is like leaven, Jesus had taught only days ago.

I wanted it to be. And now I understood that it was: spreading quietly, until it has taken over the entire dough. The teaching itself was a message, I believed, a code of its own. Perhaps by the time any more Pharisees took offense to his ways, we would stand on the steps of the Temple itself, and the kingdom would be at hand.

I shivered in the heat.

At night I allowed myself to consider that I might go to my deathbed free of Roman rule, able to say that I had walked with and even been the disciple of the Messiah. Perhaps, even his adviser.

I began to inwardly rage at Simon for his shortsightedness. I told myself that when the kingdom arrived, he would miss his place at the high table and only have the comfort of knowing he had not eaten beside a tax collector — one who walked with his chin lifted and more peace on his face now than any of us.

More had come to follow us up to Jerusalem so that whenever we moved, the dust of so many feet seemed to be everywhere — in hair and eyes and nostrils.

We made camp along the Jordan and went down to the river to wash. We shook the dust from our tunics before donning them again. Later, I sat on the bank next to my master, savoring the rarity of this moment alone with him. Simon was nowhere to be seen, having gone farther downstream.

"Tell me how I can serve your cause," I said to Jesus. "I have friends I would have you meet. Friends in the Temple and who frequent the schools and others who teach in the porticoes."

He gave a small smile. "I am longing for the Temple. It was the first place I heard the voice of my father. I couldn't bear to leave it." He laughed softly, the corners of his eyes creasing, damp hair curling over his ear. "My mother was so angry at me. It took her three days to find me . . . but I didn't want to leave."

There was a sadness in his voice as he said it.

I realized then that I wanted to know him more than I had ever wanted to know anyone in my life. My friends. My father.

My brother Joshua.

I had so many questions to ask of Jesus still. How he healed. How he could presume to forgive. How he felt any peace at all about schooling the Pharisees and teachers of the law. How does one do these things?

"Teacher," I said, turning toward him. I would have gotten to my knees, so weighty was that word when I spoke it. "Please tell me. When will the kingdom come?" I felt like a boy, a child, asking it.

"How do you know it is not here, in this

evening, with you now?" he said quietly.

I felt my brows draw together. "But the Romans. The Sadducees and corrupt High Priest. When will the priesthood be restored and the Temple cleansed?"

"One day Rome itself will look toward Israel. But Judas . . . remember these hours and savor them. In days to come, the kingdom will cost us both much. It will cost me everything. And it will cost you all that you hold most dear."

What I held most dear? What had I not already lost, other than my own life and good name?

"But that is not your greatest question, Judas, is it?" he said, quietly. Suddenly, I realized that he had stayed to talk to me. That he had remained here on the bank not to laugh at Peter and the others dunking one another like boys in the deepest part of the water, but merely because I had wished it.

My heart began to pound in my temples. I couldn't bear the direct brunt of that gaze, fearing how I might see myself reflected in those limpid eyes.

You do not know me. If you knew me, you would not want to be near me.

Sweat rolled down my sides inside my tunic. I opened my mouth to say it, knowing that with the effort of only several words

I could alienate him forever. And gone would be the only peace I had felt since the days we left Sepphoris.

I spat at my brother. I dwelt in a tomb. My father died, and my mother sold herself to keep me alive. I may keep the law, but what does it matter, knowing this?

I am not worthy of anyone.

But when I looked at him, I saw a great tenderness in his eyes as though everything within me were already laid bare. And yet I knew it was not.

If he looked at me like this, when I had voiced nothing so ugly as the truth, what would he do the moment I did? I couldn't bear his turning away. And I would crumble beneath his pity.

"My greatest question is simply . . . when will these things come to pass?"

His gaze lingered on me a moment before dropping away and I felt an inexplicable disappointment within myself.

"Stay with me, Judas," he said, finally, quietly. "One day you will understand all these things."

I could not sleep that night.

Two days later we entered Jerusalem amidst the press of pilgrims flooding her streets, singing their hymns and waving myrtle and

176

palm. To the hawking of street vendors, the smell of refuse, the baking of a thousand ovens within the city.

It was a time for spectacle, and people were ready to be moved and awed. The throng had come ahead of us and everyone seemed to stare at my master. Even those who had not traveled with us seemed to recognize that here was a man of importance that he came into the city with such a following, and they fell in alongside us, singing and slapping the Galileans on their backs as though they were long-time friends.

The boys of Galilee glanced around, apparently amazed at the marvel of my home city. By the Temple rising up white in the morning sun, the gold facade of the sanctuary on fire with light. But even its brilliance could not match the shining of my pride in it, the most beautiful building on earth.

I had seen many soldiers in Galilee, especially in the garrison town of Capernaum, but now it seemed that I saw them everywhere: standing at the gates of the city, at the cascading stairs of the Temple's entrances, outside the Antonia Fortress. Even though the Temple guard was comprised of Levites, when I looked up and saw them striding atop the royal stoa, with their short tunics and swords, they looked as Roman as the rest.

We paid our coin to immerse in one of the mikvot near the southern steps, handing our things to one another as we donned clean tunics. It was the first time I had immersed in days, though we had all bathed in preparation to come to the Holy City. Stepping into the water, I felt renewed. That I shared new kinship with the men with whom I had traveled and eaten with for weeks. I was also anxious to go home, to see my mother and Nathan and tell them about my journey and new teacher. But first, I would go to the Temple.

When we came out of the mikva, freshly dressed, Peter glanced around. "Where's Jesus?"

"I thought he was with you?"

"Some followers we are," James muttered.

We found him in the porticoes, already surrounded by a growing group of pilgrims and some of the regular students, those who came to the porticoes on holidays hoping to hear a visiting rabbi from Alexandria or Antioch or even Rome. They had not come looking for a teacher from Galilee, and yet a group had already gathered at his feet, including several children.

"You've heard people talk about loving their neighbors and hating their enemies," he said, his voice carrying easily through the arched basilica. "But I'm telling you, you should love your enemies. If you love those who love you, what reward is there? If you greet only your own people, what are you doing more than others?"

Mere months ago, I had known nothing of this man except that he was the emaciated cousin of John. Would have disdained the teachings of a laborer from Nazareth.

How much had changed in the space of a few months.

Soon I would learn how much could change in a day.

My brother greeted me in the front room of our house with the cold decorum of a stranger as his children came rushing at me. I could not remember them ever doing this before, and I scooped them up in surprise.

"Brother," Nathan said, standing back.

"Don't jump on your uncle," Mother said, coming into the front room. I let them go reluctantly.

I clasped my mother and she clung to me, girl-like joy sheathed in the wrinkles of her face. And then she drew back and cried, "Judas, how thin you are!"

That evening, as the horn sounded from the corner of the Temple announcing the coming in of Sabbath, we sat down to the meal.

"You should have seen it," I said, gathering lentils on my bread. "His face was whole again. I tell you, it had been covered with rotting flesh and it was whole — and his fingers were on his hands!"

My niece and nephew watched with rapt gazes.

"So you've seen them, then, the wonders they talk about," Nathan said. "People compare him to the healer Hanina bar Dosa. Have you met him?"

"No, though I've heard his name. He's a Pharisee." I hesitated, then said, "The teacher does not always have the highest respect for Pharisees."

"Brother, you've been too long in the countryside," Nathan said. "Any would-be messiah who does not earn the approval of the Pharisees is not a wise man. Perhaps, if you are truly intent on this cause, you should go sit at the feet of Hanina for a while."

"No," I said with a vehemence that surprised me. "Don't you see? That's exactly it! He doesn't look for approval from any Pharisee. Or priest. When he healed the paralytic —"

"He healed a paralytic?" Mother said.

I had almost said too much. Already, I saw the way she raised her brows, the slight frown.

"Yes," I said. I did not add that he had also pronounced the man forgiven.

"Are you certain he was a true paralytic before?" Nathan said, squinting.

"Yes. Quite."

"Hmm," Nathan said. "Well. I would have liked to have seen that."

Mother glanced up at his wife. "Rebecca, is there more good wine?"

I stared at her as she went back to her plate, to chasing lentils with a bit of bread. How could they continue to eat? A paralytic restored! A leper, healed! Didn't they understand? How would I ever be able to tell them about the dawn I had met Jesus on the trail, or the way he had summoned the tax collector I now knew as Matthew to come with him? Or the strange dinner that we had eaten at his house that night?

And then I realized: I couldn't.

There was a new hardness in Nathan's eyes. I had missed him while in Galilee. I had longed to say so, but now I felt a great gulf between us. What could he understand of my need for the strange thing Jesus carried within him, for the purity I had felt in the company of those sinners, so unlike that

181

of the Pharisees? Even if he did understand it, he could never, as a good man of Israel, condone it.

Sitting in my house with my mother and brother, I felt alone. I longed for my teacher, gone back to the house of his relatives, Mary and Martha, where we had spent our last night before entering the city.

"This teacher is a man free of the burden of convention," I said, trying again. "I've never seen anyone without fear, as he is. He speaks his mind, without worry of consequence from the rich or the learned."

"Well that's not wise, to not fear the consequences. He's in Herod's territory. Didn't you say his cousin the Baptizer was arrested? Is he so foolish?"

I fought back the sudden wave of my anger.

"You could see for yourself. He's in the city now. Perhaps —"

"Judas, you look as though you haven't eaten in days," Mother said. "Eat. There is plenty of time to talk about these things. You've just come home."

Her meaning was clear: *No talk of messiahs. We are here. It is enough.*

Nathan glanced from Mother to me. It was a thing I had seen him do uncountable times throughout the years since his birth.

And then he gave a hard laugh and looked away as though not knowing how to deal with me.

"Tomorrow we'll go to the Temple," I said. "He'll be teaching there."

"As you wish, brother," Nathan said, a sardonic turn on his mouth that made me want to strike him. I had done that once, when he was very young, around the time he had first lifted his chin in defiance of me.

That night I sat in the courtyard by the light of a lone lamp, pretending to be in prayer but only wanting to remove myself from the house.

My mother came out to bring me a cup of wine.

"He won't say it but he missed you. You are his greatest hero, Judas," she said, handing it to me.

I glanced down at the cup.

"I abandoned him."

"But you're here now."

"I mean I abandoned him years ago. And you." I glanced up at her. The lamplight was playing along the wrinkles on her face. When had she acquired so many? And yet I could see within her the woman I remembered coming down from Jerusalem with my father and Joshua that day. The same one who had survived the days after Sepphoris if only for my sake. I wanted to smile at her. To say that I thought she was beautiful. Instead, I looked away.

"You did not abandon us. You never left."

"That's not what I meant."

"Do you think I don't know why you struggled to love him? To look me in the eye? I don't blame you and neither does Nathan in his heart. He craves your approval even if he doesn't say it."

She sat down beside me. "But now, listen to me. Whatever it is you seek in this teacher you can find here. Your brother needs you and I want you near. Go to Nicodemus. You can see about a place in the school of Gamliel or Zadok. A teacher respected by other teachers. Not a laborer from Galilee keeping the company of bandits."

"He doesn't keep the company of bandits," I said, instantly defensive despite the fact that the company of tax collectors was considered far worse. Bandits, at least, were often heroes of the people.

"I hear the tales as well as anyone!"

"Then you know the signs he performs. And remember what I say, because I tell you one day this nation will throw off the shackles of Rome —"

"No!" she hissed. "Do not say such things.

You know how dangerous a game it is you play. I forbid you to speak such a word again!"

She was shaking in the flickering light of the lamp. "I will not count my son among those men. Do you know what it is to answer the other women and say that yes, my son has gone to follow this strange preacher? The way they look at me?"

"There was a time when you were not afraid of how others looked at you."

"That was a different time. I did what I had to do. But I did not do it so you could fall into the same fate as your father!" The line of her jaw, illuminated by the glow of the lamp, hardened, but her lips began to quiver like a girl's. "I wouldn't take back anything I've done. I would do it again! Because in so doing, I kept at least one of my sons and I gained another. I would do what I did for a lifetime to keep you alive and safe."

I touched her hand.

"All I have ever wanted is my sons near me."

"Forgive me, Mother." I said, because I knew I would soon leave.

We sat in silence broken only by the sound of her quiet weeping.

The song of the Levites was still in my ear when Nathan and I emerged from the Temple's middle court into the porticoes the next day.

"I don't see anyone resembling your description of this Jesus," Nathan said.

"I'm sure he's here."

As we passed near the double gate, I noticed a clot of priests walking toward it. It was unseemly to walk too fast, let alone run on the Sabbath, but the priests came striding with great purpose, their robes billowing about their feet, furrows in their brows.

With a gnawing pit in my stomach, I hurried out after them.

Outside, the priests had stopped atop the steps. Below them stood several Pharisees I recognized as those who oversaw the nearby mikvot. All of them were staring at something farther down the wide stair. A voice soared out in the clear autumn light.

"My father is always working, and so am I!"

I hurried down the steps, skirting the long robes of the priests. There, a little lower down, surrounded by a crowd of gawking onlookers, as well as Peter, Andrew, Matthew, and several others of our company, was Jesus, his arms outspread.

"What happened?" I asked one of the others standing nearby. And then I saw James and John standing a little farther down, uncharacteristically silent, their eyes darting this way and that.

"They said he went to the Siloam Pool," the man said in a hushed voice, gesturing toward my master. "And that he healed a man, and that he told him to pick up his mat and carry it. And that one of these Pharisees saw him carrying it and told him that the law forbade him to carry his mat on the Sabbath, but the man said that the one who'd healed him commanded it."

"So you admit that you told a man to do what is unlawful on the Sabbath?" one of the priests was saying. "You admit that you told a man to break the Sabbath?"

My hands were cold. This was far more serious than dining with a tax collector or not washing before a meal.

"He's mad," the man said. "Who would say such a thing, and to such men as these? He claims to heal by the authority of God!"

Would he go so far? I thought of the paralytic, whose sins he had called forgiven.

I caught Peter's eye. His expression was stark.

"What's more," Jesus said, turning to look up the steps at the priests. "The father has entrusted all judgment to the son that all may honor the son just as they honor the father."

Outcry from the priests, hisses and exclamations from the Pharisees and some of the onlookers. Dumb stares from those on the steps — including Andrew and James.

"Who's his father?" someone else whispered. "Is he a priest?"

Nathan caught up to my side, having circumnavigated the growing crowd of those coming out the double gate and others stopping to stare from below, astonished by the spectacle.

"Don't be amazed at this!" Jesus was saying, his voice carrying out over the steps. "A time is coming when all who are in their graves will hear his voice and come out — those who have done what is good will rise to life, and those who have done what is evil will rise and be condemned. I judge as I hear, and my judgment is just!"

Uproar from the priests.

"My judgment is just!" Jesus shouted over them. "As I seek not to please myself but him who sent me!"

"Blasphemy," someone said from the group of priests. And then louder, "Blasphemy! Do you hear him?"

I pushed through the Pharisees toward Jesus.

"Please, Teacher," I said. He glanced at me.

One of the Pharisees stepped forward. I recognized Narada bar Hakkesset, an elder Pharisee and a rich man, who also served on the high court of the Great Sanhedrin. And there, now that I could look back at them, were several of the Sanhedrin among the priests, their richly hemmed robes standing out among a sea of simple linen. They had gathered like vultures.

I no longer cared about Nathan, about the others emerging from the gate behind us. All that mattered was silencing him before these hostile witnesses.

"Teacher, please!"

By now even more had gathered, and I could see far below the form of a man pushing through the pilgrims gathered to watch the spectacle: Simon. He came up the stairs and stopped, his face blanched nearly white.

"You are accused of telling a man to violate the Sabbath," one of the Sadducees said. "How do you testify on this?"

"By law, I can't testify about myself.

Because anything I say about myself will be deemed untrue. But the father who sent me testified himself concerning me!"

And then the priests were shouting, and the Pharisees, too, and some of the Sadducees began to shout at the priests because of something one of them said about the oral law, which the Sadducees did not acknowledge.

Quickly. Quickly. I hurried to Jesus' side as Simon came up the stair, the brothers John and James closing behind us. The Pharisees were waving their fingers and shouting, the old rivalries ever beneath the surface.

Ahead of us, those beggars and sick and others who had come over from the Siloam Pool began to hurry toward him, some hobbling, some being led by others, clamoring for him. Enclosing him.

As we hurried our master away, I glanced back, looking for Nathan. He was gone and what I saw stole the heat from my veins: Helcias bar Phiabi, the chief treasurer of the Temple, standing at the top of the stair, watching us go.

That day I understood, if I had not fully before, that Jesus was more than a mystery. More than unconventional, more than a faction able to unite some and divide others.

He was dangerous — to himself and all of us who followed him.

15

I came home badly shaken.

I had seen the eyes of the chief treasurer upon me. I knew him by name and face and reputation, all. Phiabi. It was one of the great ruling houses, among Hanan, Boethus, Cantharus. They ruled the Temple, the high priesthood, the captains of the Temple guard.

I had wanted to be seen with my teacher. And a Sadducee had seen me indeed — ushering him away.

I was terrified.

I had no doubt Jesus had healed the man. I had never seen him turn away anyone who came to him, had never seen him fail to walk up to any man or woman or child who caught his attention, as though they had cried out in a voice that only he could hear.

Even on the Sabbath.

I reminded myself that the Maccabee had attacked the Seleucids on the Sabbath and that God had blessed him for it.

But for the moment, I knew too many people associated with the Temple who would want an accounting of me. And then there were the Sons — what would I say to them?

He was the gatherer of multitudes, this Jesus. A man of questioned birth, who claimed the Lord himself was his father . . . and then healed on the Sabbath in violation of God's law. Man of contradictions! Didn't he know that there were those who might seek his ruin for this?

I briefly considered leaving the city, relocating my family to Kerioth, taking them away from here. For the first time in years I remembered the night we had fled Jerusalem, so long ago.

But Nathan would never go back to Kerioth and I wasn't certain Mother would, either.

And I would not leave my new master.

I was in a state of fear when a man arrived at our door. He handed me a coded note:

It is time we met in person.

Nathan stared at me as I read it, must have noted the color that fled my face.

"Who is that from? What does it say? This is because of what happened today, isn't it?"

I barely heard him. And I don't know how I answered him, my mind on the summons in my hand. From all that I knew, this was highly unconventional. It was not done.

I thought: *It is a trap.*

But even then I knew I would go. The mystery of the faceless Sons had hounded me for months, and I was ready to excise that boil — along with the fear of today — before it burst.

My mother caught me by the shoulders. "You're going to him, aren't you? Don't. I beg you. Don't."

"No. I'm not. Stay inside and do not answer for anyone until I return."

And then I went out, leaving Nathan's anger and my mother's fears behind me as I followed the servant, who did not speak, not knowing where he would lead me.

I walked quickly, noting the fine quality of his sandals, the mantle over his shoulder. Within minutes we had come to the upper city and a home I recognized as that of Rabbi Zadok.

The great Shammai's most obvious successor.

It was well known that Zadok was wealthy

— he was married to a woman of some standing whose family supplied the wood for the Temple.

Shammai had always liked well-to-do students.

I expected to be taken around back, up a narrow flight of stairs to meet with my faceless source. A servant of the militant teacher, perhaps, or his steward. Such goings-on were not unheard of by those who were quietly almost as powerful as their masters, if only for the people they had access to. But we came in through the courtyard, where we were greeted by another servant.

"The teacher asks that you join him for the meal," the servant said. And with amazement I realized that the rabbi *himself* must be my contact. The servant led me to a side room where he brought water and a clean garment for the meal. I hardly noticed any of the fine hangings on the walls or the mosaic tiles beneath my feet as I washed. Only after I had removed my own tunic did I look down at the bleached linen one with distant consternation. Only months before, I would have eagerly accepted this welcome, even as I felt that I dirtied the garment by donning it. Now I stared at it, a clean tunic of good linen, no doubt washed in ceremonially pure water. I flicked the sleeve of it.

Would this protect all within this home from the horrors of my past?

I put on the tunic and went out to the servant, who was waiting for me. He led me to an expansive room boasting several lamps, many of which were hanging upon the walls, and a large table set with food and attended by a stack of cushions.

There, sitting at the table, was Zadok, already sipping his wine.

I knew him to be several years younger than me though the hair of his beard was already grayer than his head. One side of his face pulled downward slightly, one brow lower than the other in a way that made him appear perpetually skeptical, even when he smiled.

"Judas," he said, rising to greet me.

"Hail, Teacher," I said, kissing his hand, still in shock.

"Judas of Kerioth." He seemed to try out my name as he gestured me to recline. I was careful to do so with my heels away from him as the servant poured me a cup of wine. Zadok, I noticed, didn't bother to pray the blessing for wine but waited until the servant was done and then gestured for him to leave.

"After what happened today, what choice did I have but to invite you here?" he said when the servant had gone. "Despite the risk I take in doing so."

"You can trust me," I said.

"It's not you that I worry about. Informants flourish among us. There are those who pander to our oppressors, who would take any opportunity to expose us. That is why we do not meet or gather. Why if one of us is captured we do our best to free him but not at the expense of informing upon one another or revealing ourselves. That is the oath we take, and that you have taken, let me remind you — that even upon pain of torture we would rather kill ourselves than inform."

"Yes," I said, remembering the night I went to Levi's house. He had refused to name any other members of the Sons, saying he would not even give up their number to me if he knew it. And I had made the same vow before God and Levi both.

"I, myself, do not know our full number — nor do I even want to. But I will tell you that we extend to the palaces and the hills. That there are Pharisees among us — and slaves and merchants and bandits, too. Even Judas bar Hezekiah's own sons. Thus, the truest Sons of the Teacher."

The name never failed to incite a visceral response in me. Even now I could feel the sweat beading against my nape.

"I can speak of them because they are wanted already. They seem to have made zealotry something of a family business. But I suppose it runs in other families as well," he said with a meaningful look.

"So I hear," I heard myself say.

"Meanwhile, this country teacher you now follow inspires the imagination of the peasantry with his stories and purported miracles. You see, Judas, we are on the cusp of several opportunities converging at a very important time."

My heart was by now beating very fast. I had forgotten the wine before me, the food on the table. The sons of Judas bar Hezekiah! What might be accomplished if they joined with my master? We would rouse the entire countryside. Our movement would be unstoppable! In my mind I saw all of Galilee rising up, rushing south to Jerusalem like a mighty flood.

"Perhaps now you understand why I am mystified about this Jesus," Zadok said. "About the things you have said about him and his sway over the people. And why I am confused about the things I've heard even today from others who were there at the southern steps. So now I need to know: Does he call himself a messiah?"

I swallowed, aware that I must now choose my words carefully. Because suddenly I didn't know what my greater mission was: to win the Sons to Jesus' cause, or Jesus to the Sons'?

And then I told myself: It was all one and the same.

"No. He has not."

"I hear he is one of questioned birth, and a Nazarene."

"He is a man of the people. He speaks the language of the Galilean poor. The taxed and the landless — of which there are far more than the rich."

"Is he raising an army?"

I hesitated.

"You may speak safely and freely here. I know you are a follower of the teachings of Shammai —" I noted how carefully he distinguished this, as we both knew I had not been his student truly — "and among brothers." Was it my imagination or did he purposefully point my loyalty toward the school that he now had effectively assumed?

"Perhaps," I said. And then, "I don't know. He hasn't said. He speaks in riddles and stories, even to us."

"And these peculiar stories. Are they a message? A code to others? Who are his affiliates?"

"His cousin, John —"

He waved his hand. "John is imprisoned and as good as dead. Herod will not forgive him."

No one had stated it as starkly as this until now in my hearing. I reached for my wine, hoping he wouldn't see how that jarred me.

"I understand that Jesus has acquired many of John's disciples."

"Some. Yes. Teacher, I've meant to ask — have you seen or heard from Levi?"

He studied me for a moment, his fingers on the edge of his cup, before he said, "No."

Why was I not certain I believed him?

"Who are his sponsors?"

I pictured in my mind Mary the Magdalene and Joanna, the wife of Herod's steward. But I dare not say so, knowing it would only discredit my master. "The people themselves," I said.

"These lepers. Does he heal them truly? What is his method? How does he do it?"

I saw again the way the leper had dropped his head and how, when he reached up, his hand was whole. How does one tell that?

"He told the leper to be healed, and the paralytic to get up, and they . . . they obeyed," I said.

He narrowed his eyes.

"Did you witness this healing at the Siloam Pool?"

"No," I said. "But is it such an ordinary event that we see a crippled man healed? It is a work of God, is it not?"

He looked at me sidelong. It was a grotesque angle, given the incongruity of his face. "If it is done on the authority of the Lord, then the Lord who commanded the keeping of the Sabbath will not also then command the breaking of it."

"Respectfully, Teacher, . . . but was it not Abraham whom God told to sacrifice his son on Mount Moriah, beneath the very Temple Mount, and then told not to?"

Or was it possible I even now rationalized the actions of a blasphemer?

He considered me for a long moment before giving a slight smile. "As you say."

He had acquiesced, but somehow I felt I shouldn't have spoken. That I had thrown a stone into a river and created a ripple that might come back to me as a wave.

"So he has no affiliation with the Pharisees or the Sadducees, or even, as some have said about John, with the Essenes. That is a dangerous kind of man. Because it means that he has no loyalty or accountability."

"His loyalty, Teacher, is to the people."

"It is a careful balance we must strike, Judas," he said, sitting back. "It is an easy thing to say 'no king but God' or to talk about Messiah, but until the day that we are ready to mean it, and to back it, such a cry gains us nothing and loses us everything. Rome will not hesitate to crucify us by the thousands. But here is something: We hear that Pilate's sponsor, Sejanus, has fallen from favor in Rome. Pilate must walk carefully here or he will find himself recalled and sent back in disgrace. There will not be another situation as happened with the treasury — he dare not risk it. Another reason why if there is to be a time, it may be soon."

He leaned forward, eyes locked on mine.

"So now listen to what I say. Your master must leave the city. It is not safe for him here. Not after today. At this rate he will not live to see Passover and he won't be the only one to suffer."

My heart thudded in my ears.

"Do you understand what I am saying, Judas? When the time is right, he must return with an army or not at all."

16

"You keep it," Matthew said, tossing the moneybag to me. "I'm not blind — I see the way they look at me. None of them trust me. But you, you're a man of standing and know your way around a counting table."

I had not trusted him either — up until that moment.

I tucked the bag into my belt. It was far too light.

With Zadok's warning still in my ears, I was anxious to be as far from the Holy City as possible, as quickly as possible. As we entered Galilee again and the smell of fish thickened in my nostrils, I felt I could breathe for the first time in days.

But that wasn't the only reason. Simon had returned to us.

I wanted, with boyish exuberance, to laugh and tussle his hair. But the Simon who had come to us outside the city gate was not the same man. He was thinner in the space of days, as though he had fasted through the Feast. His face was drawn and gaunt, and he kept to himself. I left him alone, missing him even as I followed ten paces behind him. I had not thought that anything would compel him to follow my master again, that in fact the events at the Temple had turned him irrevocably away. But as we traveled he walked with the resolution of a man who shed with each step a part of himself as though he carved it from his own body.

Time enough to learn about this change of heart later. For now, I was content.

By the time we reached Heptapegon, the small coins left in the moneybag would not buy food enough for those in Jesus' innermost circle, let alone supply us for the days to come.

On the Sabbath, we followed Jesus out of the city to pray. It had become my favorite moment of the day, the sight of my own feet following after him as he went out in the morning. Of his laborer's fingers as they drew the mantle over his head and gathered its tassels together, the reverberation of the Shema rumbling up from his throat.

I never felt so close to him as I did in those moments. Salvation seemed to swell up even now beneath us, brought not by the Maccabee or the priests or the Pharisees, but by this man.

Hear, O Israel . . .

Here was something more base and transcendent and holy so that the very air seemed not so much to blow as to breathe, as though taking its cues not from cloud or sun . . . but from the one praying beside me.

The Lord our God is One.

I had wanted nothing in my life but to believe in a man such as this.

When the sun was over the mountains on the eastern side of the lake, we went down from the hills, passing by several fields on the way to town. The stalks of wheat on the fringe of the field had been left unharvested — food for orphans or widows to come and eat without penalty.

Or hungry disciples.

I was not such a city-dweller that I had not plucked at heads of wheat before, chewing the kernels into a gum as a boy. Matthew, however, had to watch how Peter crushed them between his hands before reaching tentatively toward a stem himself. I wondered if, having been a rich man, he had ever eaten this way in his life.

I glanced farther down the way, and there was Simon, pulling kernels from the stalk, rubbing them in his palms and putting them one after another into his mouth, chewing them doggedly. There was something primal and desperate in his eyes so that the working of his jaw seemed to have a focus all its own. I did not know what drove him, but I began to eat now in earnest as well. The sun was climbing, warming the dark curls of my head. All my life, Sabbath had been a thing of duty, but today it was beautiful, sitting among the other days like a queen.

Several of the town folk had come out to meet us, children bounding ahead of their parents, some of the young men, poor and landless and out of the habit of rising early, still bleary-eyed from sleep.

And I thought: *It is well. All is well.* One day soon the mass of these followers would overflow these hills, and I would look back on this day with the wistfulness of remembrance. I must cherish this, I knew it even then.

But then, as we made our way down the hill and more people came out to meet us, I saw that two men among them were wearing the tefillin of the Pharisees. They stood at the edge of the field, their robes billowing in the crisp morning breeze, and I knew that they would not go farther than that, having restricted themselves to the thousand cubits prescribed by many teachers as the limit one should walk on Sabbath.

I resented the sight of them immediately, even though I knew I must make it my mission to mend ways with them. For the sake of Zadok. For the sake of my master's mission. And yet I had wanted this moment — this hour, this day — to pass as one never-ending day, without interruption.

As we came toward them, the first threw out his arm as though to indicate a mess around him.

"Your disciples are doing what is unlawful!" He was an older man and his jowls shook when he said it.

My master looked at him as one reluctantly returned from reverie.

"Why do you accuse us?" he said.

"Are you not reaping, grinding, and sifting on the Sabbath?" the Pharisee said, gesturing to our hands.

I glanced at Simon as he picked a last kernel from the palm of his hand and pushed it through his lips into his mouth. It wasn't defiance, the look on his face, though he was looking directly at the Pharisee. It was something else.

Hunger.

"David entered the Temple and ate the consecrated bread, which wasn't lawful but for the priests," Jesus said.

"You are neither David nor a priest," the Pharisee said. "You break the Sabbath, and you teach your disciples to profane it with you!"

My peace, so great only a moment ago, cracked. Why did Jesus provoke in this way? The entire nation was hungry for a messiah. Did he not know that they would follow him for his signs and healings alone?

The accusers left us that day, outrage in their gazes . . . foreboding in their eyes.

The synagogue in Heptapegon was not as fine as that in Capernaum, but it was filled with people that day — rich men and peasants alike, squeezing onto the stone benches and standing along the walls and near the door until the sheer warmth of so many bodies heated the room like the embers of a fire.

Jesus taught in his characteristic way, without citing the sages, reading from the scroll of Isaiah and saying that the scriptures had been fulfilled this day. How I wished he might at least quote Hillel! But no matter. The people had come to see him and they had come in numbers.

It was then, toward the end of the teaching, that I began to notice something strange. There was a man near the front, where we were, looking uncomfortable all the while. I hadn't thought much about it; I had seen men tremble in the presence of my master, and women inexplicably weep at the mere sight of him.

But this man, who looked to be poor by all accounts, looked often from Jesus to the Pharisees sitting off to the side, including the man who had come out to the field earlier, now sitting in the Seat of Moses. As soon as Jesus had closed and returned the scroll, the man pulled out his arm from beneath the edge of his mantle, and I could see that it was twisted like something withered on the vine, his fingers curled inward like a dying flower about to drop from the stem. He held it out, as though he had not five withered fingers but five sound ones, and as though he would point toward Jesus himself.

Jesus looked at him for a long moment as a hush fell over the synagogue. But the look on his face was not the same I had come to know so well in him — that of one bent down over something shamefully broken, in sorrow. This time, his brows drew together and he looked from the man, holding his withered hand out like a trembling weapon, to the Pharisee sitting too comfortably in the seat of honor.

Fatigue hovered around Jesus' eyes like shadows.

"Stand up," he said to the man.

The man got shakily to his feet with a frantic glance toward the Pharisees, who leaned just perceptibly forward where they sat. And then I understood the situation: The man had been approached and given a small coin — a dinar, perhaps, enough for bread — and told to come to synagogue and sit here, near the front. Told that if he were very fortunate, perhaps the visiting teacher might take pity on him, that he might be healed, even, by the end of the day.

Jesus faced the Pharisees. He shook his head and dropped it. When he lifted it again a moment later, he said through tightened jaw, "Which is lawful on the Sabbath — to do good or to do evil? To save a life . . . or to kill?"

I knew, and the Pharisees surely knew, that it was lawful to save a life on the Sabbath if that life was in danger. To not do so would be to kill. But surely this man was not going to die from his withered hand.

The Pharisees refused to answer his question.

"Teacher," I hissed. "It is a trap!"

Jesus sighed and then with another shake

of his head said to the man in a loud voice, "Stretch out your hand!"

The man looked struck, blanched, as though he might fall over dead. But then he slowly lifted his arm again. And uncurled those furled fingers. Long and straight. They flexed back, arcing like small bows, the bones within them taut beneath the skin.

Gasps. Cries from the first rows, as others in the back leapt to their feet, some of them pushing against those ahead of them to see.

They came down from the rows of benches like stones falling down a hill, to seize the man's hand and examine it, the man himself stark-faced, his eyes bulging, his lips stretched over his gums in amazement. They came grabbing for Jesus' sleeve, to say that their aunt or uncle or small cousin was ill, or that he must come eat at their house this evening, or only to touch him, to whisper the word that had become an offense to me, but that now sounded like "Hosanna" from any lips: *Messiah.*

Peter and I pressed close to our master as they swarmed around us. As I pushed against the most aggressive of them, I managed one glance toward the Seat of Moses.

Empty.

I did not need imagination or intelligence, or an inkling of anything other than basic law, to know that their case had been satisfied.

They had gone to determine how to seize him.

We must move quickly.

We left that evening by boat for Capernaum. I knew that the teachers of the law had gone to conspire against my master. But why did he provoke them so — and why rise to the bait? Would it be so hard to say to the man with the withered hand, "Come join us. Rest. Eat. Tomorrow you may be whole?" But he lived for the moment.

The last time I had asked him about the kingdom, he had said it was here, now. I had wanted to shout: "Then where is it? The corrupt High Priest is still in the Temple, and the Romans in the fortress, and the Herods on their thrones. When is that kingdom to be gone and the new one come at last?"

But my master would not say. He spoke in riddles. He was a riddle himself.

17

"Judas."

I opened my eyes to find myself staring into the face of Jesus.

"Come with me."

I got to my feet, put on my sandals and drew up my mantle. Peter was already in the front room with Andrew. James and John waited outside with Matthew and Simon. A moment later, Jude and Nathanel and Philip of Bethsaida came with Thomas, the smaller James, and another man also named Judas. These last had come from the house of Zebedee, to which James' and John's houses were attached.

We followed him out of town beneath the first tinge of dawn, a couple of stray dogs at our heels. They followed us as they did most mornings, stopping just beyond the city wall to stare as though waiting already for our return. The crowds were still sleeping, put up in guesthouses or with whoever would take them in, or curled up in their mantles in market stalls and stables, nestled in the straw against the chill. In the waning darkness I could make out fresh snow on Mount Hermon. I drew my mantle closer around my neck and longed for the warmth of lamb and lentil stew.

"He's been out here all night, as far as I can tell," Peter murmured to me.

Out in this cold? And come back to get us and come out again?

We gathered on a hillside where there was an olive press set back in a cave, and went in out of the wind.

When the last echo of the Shema had faded from the walls of the cave, Jesus said, "I have gathered the twelve of you to myself. You will face great opposition because of me. Because of me people will hate you. Families will be divided and they will not understand what you do. You will give up everything to be with me."

His voice broke. We looked at one another. Waited. Jesus covered his face with his hands.

"Teacher," I said, tentatively, feeling that I spoke for all of us. "When is the coming kingdom? How will it occur? How can we serve you to that end if we do not know this? Meanwhile, there are others who are going out to see about your ruin for the things you say!"

"Don't you understand?" he said, turning on me with such a look as though I had cut him. "It is here! Now!"

I glanced around. Was I the only one who saw both the opposition and opportunity before us? What was wrong with him that he seemed more interested in healing the sick and telling stories?

He clasped me by the shoulder and said, "Listen . . ." and began to tell the story of a rich man who gave a great banquet, and about how all the guests had excuses not to attend so that he sent his servant out into the streets and alleys of the town to bring in the poor, the crippled, and the blind instead.

We all looked at one another. We had all thrown livelihoods and reputations aside for this man. What was there for any of us, but to see this through?

Did he not see the danger of the Pharisees, conspiring against him? The Sons would expect a report soon. The Sons, whom I realized I must win to our cause rather than the other way around. I already knew Jesus would not abide by their rules, could not be tamed. But how could I win their support for this Messiah when so many of them were surely Pharisees like Zadok himself?

These were deadly games!

That night, the demons returned, exhuming the memories of my father and brother, my wife and son, smearing my conscience like a stain.

At last I shoved up from my mat, took up my mantle, and, wrapping it around me, went out of the house. Down near the breakwaters, the boats were gone from their moorings — the fishermen out for the night. I stared out at the lake, trying to spot the light of their lamps in an effort to distract myself, having learned that they would be there if I only looked, standing out in the moonlit air above the water.

There! There was one. I drew a slow breath. Now that my eyes were adjusted, I imagined I could even see, faintly, the cast of a heavy net, could hear the slap of it on the water before the stone sinkers pulled it down.

"Judas."

I started at the sound of my name, but not at the familiarity of the voice. Now I saw him, his mantle drawn close, sitting atop a low wall near the dock.

He had been there, right before me, all this time.

"Teacher," I said, my voice inexplicably thick. "Forgive me —"

"Judas."

"I couldn't sleep," I said, feeling emotion rise up like strange panic within me. "I came out to clear my head. I couldn't stop —"

I felt, more than heard, him step away from the wall. His hands on my shoulders, his arms wrapping hard around me. Felt the keen rise up in my chest, tight and stifled.

"I just —"

I was a boy, missing his brother. I was a child, looking on the broken body of his father. I was a young man, knowing that my new brother existed out of my mother's shame, and only because she had wanted to feed me.

I was held in those Galilean laborer's arms, covered in shame. My knees buckled and I slipped down like a sack of grain in those arms.

I was unclean. How could he embrace me? How could he kiss me and greet me as he did, or bear my greeting in return?

I wanted to tell him that I was afraid. That I was so afraid. That I was desperate for something that even in my learning I did not know to name. That I was fearful for him, that he could not do or be all that he said. That I had not received the hunger in Simon's eyes or the love in the Magdalene's

217

and, what's more, wasn't certain that I could. That I envied Peter his simplicity, and even Thomas his frowns, because he seemed to struggle only with disbelief, which was the least of the demons that rode me like the sins of the atonement goat, running for Azazel.

Beyond all that, I was worried that my bowels, so very familiar to me in behavior, would begin to lurch, and I would shame myself even further.

But most of all, I wanted to tell him that I would stay, because I had nowhere else to be, no other thing or person in this world to cling to, and no other answers but what he might give me. That I prayed he could give me the answers I sought, because if he could not, then I did not know that they could be found in this world.

All that I had carried within me like a diseased cistern cracked and spilled out. I had thought myself spent, empty, and that there was nothing else he could say, in mercy or in belittlement, to me to cause me to excise any of it more. I was wrong.

"Judas," he said. "I will not leave you."

I covered my face and wept.

Finally, when I thought I must have been there for hours, and realized that somehow I had come down on the hard pebbled ground, and was bent over against his shoulder, when I imagined that I saw the faintest light again on the lake, and beyond it, the barest trace of light in the sky, he spoke again.

"Come with me where I am going."

"I — I will remain with you." *If you can have me. If you can stand my shame.* The words, too thick, mangled in my throat.

"There is so much upon you. Come. I will show you even greater things than you have seen."

We got up together, me staggering on leaden feet, stiff from the cold. But the turmoil, the panic, the roiling questions, at least, were gone. Unanswered, but gone. All, except one.

"What were you doing here, when I disturbed you?" I sniffled like a child, wiped at my nose.

His smile was simple. "I was waiting for you."

18

They came from Tyre and the Decapolis. They came as pilgrims on their way to Jerusalem. Always, there were pilgrims. All with one word on their lips:

Messiah.

Our numbers grew. I was nervous because I knew Herod's spies were everywhere. The Pharisees already conspired against us; soon Herod would come for my master as surely as he had for John. We were running out of time.

But I was also elated, because that meant soon the day would come. Jesus would have to proclaim himself — by Passover, I was certain. The holiday I had learned to fear and then even to loathe, I would have cause to love once more.

And so these days were precious because I knew they were numbered. For now, my master was mine in rare and quiet moments. But soon I must share him with the world.

Rain came with the winter, turning the Galilean countryside green after the scorched gold of summer and autumn. The first anemones speckled the hills like droplets of blood and yellow flowers carpeted the valleys.

All this time, John remained a prisoner of Herod and I had heard nothing of Levi. I asked after him when I could, but heard nothing so that I began to think he had been killed in the arrest.

We went west, to Cana. I feared Jesus would take us to Sepphoris, but he never showed any desire for the city an hour's walk from his hometown. I had long since given up trying to discern the logic of each city that we visited — or passed by. It only mattered to me that with each stop news of him increased . . . along with the growing multitude.

Meanwhile, the whispers became a roar across the country as more and more came to look on my master in dread amazement.

Messiah.

A week after the Feast of Dedication, we returned to Capernaum. And a day after that, I laid eyes on Levi.

He came to us at Peter's house just before dusk and ate for nearly an hour straight, scooping lentils and bread and olives up all at once with dirty fingers and blackened nails.

I hardly recognized him, shrunken nearly to the skeleton that my master had been the first time I had seen him. His eyes were wild in his head. His hair was long and tangled with bits of grass and twigs. Every so often he paused to scratch at it, or at one of his ears, flinching, as though from invisible insects, or from the very air itself.

"We hide near Macherus. Sometimes one of us is allowed to go in and speak to John, and when we find or are given food, sometimes we're allowed to take it to him," his companion, a man named Gidon, said. I saw the way their eyes darted this way and that, wondered how they had placated the guards.

I didn't ask.

Levi, for his part, hardly looked at me and only greeted Simon with the barest of nods, but glanced often at Jesus with an emotion I could not discern. I wanted to take him aside, to speak privately with him, but it was as if the history between us never existed.

"What does John say?" Jesus said. "How is he?"

"He is alive, though I fear he will never leave that place," Gidon said before he looked at his plate as though it were suddenly an alien thing.

"Are you the one?" Levi said abruptly to Jesus, strange hardness in his gaze. "He sent us to ask you. You, his cousin. Are you the one? Are you? Or should we expect someone else?"

"John baptized our master himself!" I said, trying to see in Levi the man I had known. "He called him the lamb of God! How can he now ask if this is the one?" How dare they question it?

All this time there had been people at the door, peering in through the windows. As we were speaking, a woman came with a piece of woolen cloth and laid it in the hands of Peter's wife as we were sitting there.

"Please, it is for the master. You see? My child is well — see how he walks now without even a limp!" she said, bidding the little boy walk inside a few steps before he ran back to his mother on two sturdy legs.

When they had gone out, Jesus said quietly, "Tell John what you hear and see. The blind see, the lame walk, those with leprosy are cleansed, and good news is proclaimed to the poor."

Levi slammed his plate down. "Why do you not come to his defense? Why do you not come to rescue him? If you can perform miracles, why do you not cause his cell door to fall open and release him from that place, or do your powers not work in that way? Our own men die in the wilderness for him!"

"The kingdom of heaven has been subjected to violence since the days of John, and violent people have been raiding it," Jesus said. "I do as my father wills. There will be far greater trials than this."

He was not looking at Levi, but me, as he said it. Levi abruptly got up and walked out into the courtyard.

That night, Levi took me aside.

"Leave him," he said, his eyes blazing behind a beard so grizzled that I would not have known him in a crowd.

"Haven't you heard all that we've told you?" I dropped my voice to a low hiss. "Besides, I cannot. I am sent here by Zadok himself. Don't you know this?"

He gave a wild laugh. "Zadok no longer responds to my letters. He has abandoned John for the cause of your master. But I'm telling you, be cautious. Be warned. Nothing good will come of this."

"Zadok said he hadn't heard from you."

"Oh, I'm certain he did. He's hungry, you know, for any power he can seize. He only wants to know if he can subjugate your master as he wanted to subjugate mine. But John will not be any man's slave but God's. And your master . . . what is he but a shadow of John grasping for popular opinion?"

"You haven't seen what he has done. But I have seen with my own eyes."

"Then ask yourself, Judas, by whose power he performs his signs. Ask yourself if these are the acts of a man who loves the law. Are you deceived, Judas? You, of all people?"

I blinked at him. "Why do you say this? What's happened to you?"

"Ask yourself that," he said, sucking spittle from the corner of his mouth, as though it were too precious to evaporate even in the winter night.

"Why would Zadok show any interest in my master if there were any question about the source of his power?" I said, picturing him the day I had gone to his house, reclining at his table.

"Why do you think? To aid their cause! But mark me: They would have only their own men in the place of power. In the coming kingdom, do you think they care for Galilean peasants who preach against the Pharisees? They want to oust the Sadducees, but do you think they'll suffer dissenters against themselves? They have one vision for the coming kingdom, Judas, and it is not John's, and it is certainly not your master's. Beware of him, Judas. Ask yourself what source his teachings come from. I hear he doesn't even cite the sages. Do his disciples — do you — now follow the law better than before?"

I almost said: *It is not the same. I follow the spirit of it.* But a part of what he said niggled, like something caught between the teeth, as I thought of the broken Sabbaths, the meals taken with tax collectors and prostitutes.

"Do not be deceived."

He left me then, without a clasp or a kiss, striding away on his bare heels into the darkness.

I was deeply unsettled after that. If Levi, whose learning and mind I once trusted, could say this about my teacher — no matter how deeply changed or calloused Levi might now be — what did that mean?

No. I had seen what I had seen — not only in the sign of the lepers, but in my heart the night by the lake.

That night I penned a message to Zadok:

The blind see and the lame walk. The

multitude grows.

I did not mention Levi.

19

It was good that I sent that message then and not delayed a day. Two days later, I am not certain what I would have said.

The first thing that happened was that the Magdalene returned. She came, waiting until the end of the day after Jesus had healed enough people for them to seem like one long sea of faces to me.

There were by now a thousand gathered in the foothills of Capernaum to hear him speak. A thousand —

But still not enough.

When I saw her climbing up the hill through the crowd, I was struck by the look on her face. I had always thought her comely, but now, wearing her anticipation like a bridal veil, her hem in her hand like a girl as she hurried toward us, I wondered what it was that made me unable to look away.

And then I realized it was the very purpose

in her gaze, the joy shining on her face. She was beatific.

When she had made her way through the crowd to Jesus, who was always answering a question or holding a child or taking into his arms for blessing whatever baby some peasant woman handed him, he laughed and kissed her as though she were his mother or sister.

I would never understand him! Why? Why must he flout propriety? Did he not see the turning heads? Did he not hear the gasps of those nearby or note the scandalized looks?

I remembered the words of Levi: *Beware of him.*

And yet, even as I thought it, a pang of jealousy shot through me as she took his hands and kissed them, and I wasn't sure who I envied more — her, or him.

Later that day, she came to me, having brought more coin with her for the communal purse. It was a strange thing, taking money from a woman like a fishwife taking an allowance for market from her husband, and I was conscious of her hands, so slender, as she passed the bag to me.

"Why do you return?" I said to her. "Why do you return, knowing they'll call you harlot or worse for the mere fact that you follow him, knowing others watch and judge

229

you both — and not kindly?"

"I've enslaved myself to him," she said. "I wanted freedom once, but no longer. I want no freedom without him and his teachings. Ah, I see. You worry I come to him as a woman to a man. Do you really think it's like that? You, Judas, who misses nothing?"

I felt the heat rise to my face. I had never heard a woman speak so bluntly, having been all my life more accustomed to the silent and passive languages of women that were a code all their own.

"No. I don't." I knew my master too well. "But the appearance —"

"You love him. Will you begrudge me the same?" She gave a bitter little laugh. "Ah, but I am not allowed the same as you, am I? Not by the teachers or the schools or the priests."

"They could brand you a whore for the rest of your life. You would never live it down." Already, she might not.

"I don't care what they say. I care what he says. I care to be near him. I leave him only when I must because one of these days I fear I'll be separated from him for a long time. But I know I must somehow want that, too, when the time comes, if only because he does."

I felt shamed by the beauty, the sheer

purity — not of what she said, because it was scandalous that she followed a teacher and spoke alone even to me at all — but by the emotion and love pouring off of her like perfume. Would I have the same courage as her, I wondered?

That night I thanked God I had not been born a woman.

The next evening we were to dine at the house of Simon the Pharisee. I thought it a good sign, an opportunity to win back some of the vitriol that we had incurred from the others. It was an invitation and statement of equality, a truce of sorts from the Pharisaic party. Mary and Joanna and another woman named Susanna, who had come with her, had decided to stay back, as this was a Pharisee's home. I had made this request of the Magdalene myself, drawing her aside quietly on the hillock earlier that day, as improper as it was to speak to her again.

"As I think of it, I believe a cousin of mine has invited us to visit this evening, and that we won't be able to come," she said. I nearly fell down at her feet in gratitude.

Simon the Pharisee was a wealthy man, a grain merchant with a gentle demeanor, who carried himself with a sophistication I had not thought to find in Galilee. As with

Zadok, we were given clean robes to wear. Thirteen of us!

His house was a quiet house of quality. The mosaics on the floor bore no improper images of man or animal but only the curved pinwheel crosses and geometric patterns that are appropriate for a home or a synagogue. Simon himself was a lean man, and I assumed he fasted more than the prescribed amount — perhaps even three times a week. As we reclined at the table, I happened to glance at our own Simon, called the Zealot. He had dined so often with Pharisees I had thought he might look as at home as the Pharisee Simon himself. But today he seemed strangely out of place.

In Jerusalem we pretended not to hear or watch what others did on their rooftops. Because of that, I used to find it disconcerting, this Galilean way of dining before the audience of those who came to watch the spectacle, to listen to the gossip and conversation, to see what graced the table of those who could afford to eat well.

But unlike the dinner at Matthew's, with the Pharisees standing outside, this time it would be the Pharisee who welcomed us, with the unwashed congregating outside. For once we would be the very vision of a visiting teacher dining at a Pharisee's table.

I only prayed the rumors of this night would circulate with as much swiftness as every other rumor about my master.

How it all went wrong.

We had barely prayed the prayer for wine when a woman slipped in from the court-yard. Not only did she come into the house, but made directly for my master.

"You!" one of the servants said.

I blinked. Hadn't I seen this woman somewhere else before? I recognized those painted eyes. Yes! At the dinner party at Matthew's house!

Where she had been known as a sinner.

I remembered all of this belatedly, as she fell down at Jesus' feet.

The air left the room with a hissing breath. Mine. Peter's. Simon the Pharisee's. But it was too late.

She touched him — laying her hands across the tops of his toes, her pale fingers caressing the arches of his foot in such a way that would haunt my dreams for weeks and months to come.

Her expression strained, as though she had fallen into concentrated prayer, but her eyes were open. She hitched a breath, and then her mouth twisted as she began to weep, her hands curling around his heels, and when she looked up at him —

I caught my breath.

Such exquisite devotion! Such pained love!

In the way the air had left, it now exploded back as she produced a glass jar from her sleeve and broke it open. The smell of expensive perfume filled the room — strong and sweet, washing down the length of the table.

Spikenard. I had smelled it before among a rare cache of my brother's imports. It was the incense of the Temple, the scent placed before God himself.

It came out in a rivulet the color of roses. Of wine. Of blood.

It was undiluted, infusing the nostrils, as exquisite nearly as the expression on her face.

I couldn't tear my gaze away — from those fingers, coated with the expensive oil, from the image of them sliding from his ankle to his toes. I hauled in an abbreviated breath, closed my eyes, but the scent was in my head and the upturn of her face was before my mind, and there was the perfume, as prevalent as joy, as heady as sex, devotion, as beauty.

She slid the veil from her hair.

Skin. Hair. Tears. Such unabashed tears. Such trembling in her hands and shaking in her shoulders, the hair like fine black wool with which she wiped his feet. It was unseemly. Lascivious.

And yet I had never seen anything more sublime in my life.

Simon the Pharisee had gotten to his feet in outrage — her presence defiled the entire assembly.

"Teacher!" he said.

A good man, a decent man, would have shaken the woman off. Would have sent her out with a curse. But Jesus did not.

I knew that he must condemn her — here, openly — one woman, one soul, for the sake of the kingdom.

And I also knew that he would not do it.

Simon the Pharisee had a terrible look on his face — the look of a man who has gravely misjudged.

"Simon," Jesus said, his fingers lightly touching the woman's head. "Let me tell you something."

"Yes, please do explain." His voice was stony, his eyes averted.

"Two men owed money to a moneylender. One owed ten times as much."

Perhaps Simon the Pharisee had never owed money to a moneylender, but the faces of those beyond the gate had surely paid with coin and pride both. And I knew it was to them that Jesus truly spoke.

"Neither had the money to pay him back, so he released both debts. Who will love him more?"

The Pharisee's face reddened. When the servant came into the room with a tray of food, she was given a sharp gesture to retreat with it.

"I came into your house," Jesus said. "You did not give me any water for my feet, but she wet my feet with her tears and wiped them with her hair."

No. I covered my face with my hands. *No.*

The woman left, heads swiveling to follow after her as though she were not a common prostitute at all. She had come in with tears. She went out with peace, the smell of perfume and God wafting behind her, her chin held level as though she were the one, rather than us, wearing the fine ritual tunics.

She might be saved, but now we courted ruin.

20

It was the Sabbath and I could only hope for the hours to speed by, and that they would take with them the Pharisees and priests and teachers who had descended on us, some of them come from as far as Jerusalem.

It was the crowd and the renown I had hoped for — only not the way I had hoped for. They came, loudly, some of them wagging fingers at the women in our group. I tried to put myself between the Magdalene and the mob, to even find a way to get her out, but the growing crowd had followed us into the synagogue early in the morning and kept us there, like prisoners, late into the day.

"Are you the Messiah?"

"They say you are Elijah!"

"Please! My brother is blind —"

At one point someone pulled a man through the press at the door. He was like an animal in their hands — a blind mute, making his animal sounds and grabbing at the air.

It was the Sabbath.

But I knew it would not matter.

My master went to the man — in that moment I saw the lines around Jesus' eyes, how very weary he was — and covered the man's face with his hands and whispered to him. And I watched, as I had watched and seen before, the look of seeing return to milky irises, and the sound of words — rudimentary at first, and then well formed as though he had not just learned them but had spoken them all his life. It was one thing for a mute to hear and begin to mimic sounds, and a wholly other thing for him to shout his Hosannas to the roof.

I thought the synagogue ceiling would collapse that day.

"He uses no herbs! What about Solomon's incantations?"

"Was this man really deaf or blind to begin with?"

"It is by Beelzebul, the prince of demons, that he casts them out!"

My fist lashed out.

And was caught by Simon.

"No, Judas."

Jesus shouted over the ruckus of the

synagogue. "Every kingdom divided against itself will be ruined, and every household divided against itself will not stand!"

"Do you hear that?" I said to the one who accused Jesus of casting out demons by Beelzebul, spittle flying from my lips. "He is speaking to you!" But the Pharisees — there were some twenty of them now surrounded by a horde of curious, desperate, and gossiping spectators — were shaking their fingers and shouting to be heard.

A man was pushing through the mob, past James and John, and finally let through — pulled through as though he were being born anew — by the arm by John.

It was James, the elder brother of Jesus.

"Brother!" he shouted. The head of Jesus snapped up at the sound. "Come, we are outside. We've come for you. Mother is here, too."

They had come for him as a family comes to collect their mad son. Their wayward one, before he can disgrace the family or himself anymore.

"Make it rain," one of the priests was saying. He turned to me. "Honi the circle-drawer made it rain."

"He just healed a man!" I snapped.

"None of us was close enough to examine him, to be certain he was not seeing before.

239

Tell your master to make it rain. To give us a sign. Tell him we have come from Jerusalem." We both swayed, jostled by several more who had burst into the overcrowded synagogue. He grabbed me firmly by the shoulder, dragging me toward Jesus. "Tell him —"

I stopped short. Jesus stood alone, his gaze downcast, his head shaking. Alone, jostled every so often by someone pushing against him, a growing despair on his face. As I looked on, his chest lifted and fell as though he breathed not so much air, as the tar of sadness.

The man was pulling at my sleeve, commanding me. This was not the way I had expected other teachers and learned men to look at me. This was not the way I had envisioned that my time in any synagogue would be.

"Leave off!" I shouted, compulsively, shoving the man back. His eyes went wide.

Next to me, I saw Peter reach toward his waist where I knew his sword to be, but Simon stilled him with a hand.

"Brother!" Again, James.

"THIS IS MY HOUSE!" The voice of Jesus rang out, jarring us all, ringing off the very lintel over the door. Beside me, the arguments fell silent.

"If I drive out demons by Beelzebul, by whom do your people drive them out?" He leveled his finger at one of the most venomous Pharisees, spittle on his lips, his face red. "So then, they will be your judges!"

In the stifling press of the synagogue even on that cold day, my skin prickled.

The man next to me started forward, but Jesus thundered, "Whoever is not with me is against me! And whoever does not gather with me scatters!"

"A sign!" the man next to me called out. "We want to see a sign! We have come from Jerusalem and will take back the word of you. But prove all you say. For all we know, this man's ears were awakened by this noise. Command the rain to come and to cease again! If you can do these other things, what is one sign to you?"

Jesus turned away, his hands going to his head, the heels of his palms over his eyes.

"Bring the rain! Or are you a fraud?" the man demanded, angrily.

"A wicked generation asks for a sign!" Jesus shouted. "But I'm telling you, none will be given."

I covered my eyes.

Why. Why? It would cost him nothing to still this controversy. To silence them all!

But of course he wouldn't. Of course not.

The synagogue rang out with fresh chaos. The blind-mute was staring, his hands over his ears, the ruckus no doubt cacophonic and too loud, so that I pitied him and gestured him toward me.

The room was about to erupt in earnest. I looked around at us, at everyone red-faced, there with their agendas, their demands, angrily compelling him to do this or that, and even angrier that he would not make a sign or side with one party or another, or even come home with the family as placidly as a good son, a good man of Israel, should do.

A woman's voice was shouting over the outside din. "My son!" The diminutive form of a woman was ducking beneath outstretched arms, grabbing at the upper arm and shoulder of James, the brother of John, at the door.

"It is his mother. It is his mother. Let her through!" I shouted, shoving past the Pharisees and teachers in their fine linen, who could not be bothered to help a peasant through the crush.

"Teacher!" I called out, drawing her through, my arm winding around her from behind as James and John held the doorway. It was improper, but I couldn't help it. I took her by the hand and as I did, her veil came askew.

I caught at her veil, tried to help her cover her head.

She looked not so much like a mother as a woman on the brink of losing her heart, her tiny fingers clasping at my sleeve, and then the hem of her veil, her eyes — those uncanny eyes — fiercely searching the crowd.

"Master! Your mother is here with your brother!" I shouted.

He glanced up with a strange look. "Who?"

"Your mother! Your brother!" Let them take him out from here at least.

"Who is my mother and who are my brothers?" Jesus said.

I blinked.

Surely he had misunderstood. But then he pointed at me. And then Simon. And then Peter. "There is my brother. There —" he pointed to Andrew, and then Nathanel and then James and John at the door. "And there," he pointed to the Magdalene, "is my sister."

James stared, his arm wrapping around his mother, who had covered her face with her hands. I thought I had reached the end of shock with this teacher. But I had been wrong.

He shuns his family. He shuns them and claims me — I, who spat at my brother and neglected my half-brother.

What was a man without his family? Here, in Galilee, where so many died before they were even weaned, to be cut off from family was to die.

"How can you follow this man?" a man next to me said. He was gray-haired, an elder of the city. And though I saw the words come from his mouth, I heard them with the voice of Levi.

Beware.

21

The throng grew like a dust storm out of control. It swelled into the thousands. Our meals, our getting up and lying down, our praying and going to immerse, were now open to every eye that cared to see. We could hardly find a patch to lift up our tunics and relieve ourselves without someone looking on to see that we were indeed Jews.

Jesus healed. He taught. He also spoke more and more openly now about the kingdom of God, the kingdom of heaven. Seditious words, to any king or Roman ear. It was one thing to tell a story of leaven to a small group of hungry fishermen in Capernaum. It was another to tell it to thousands going up to Jerusalem for the feast of dedication of the Temple.

We were all aware that we were in increasing danger; Herod would not — could not afford to — overlook such a mass of people gathering together around one man beneath his Roman masters.

It must be soon.

One evening Jesus was leaning heavily against James' shoulder as we came down from the hills. A young man, thin as a reed, came pushing through the crowd. His exuberance told me he had only just arrived in time to see the teacher departing.

"Please, Teacher, let me follow you wherever you go!"

Jesus' head was hanging forward, his arm around James' shoulder. Exhaustion overcame him more and more often these days. "Foxes have dens and birds have nests," he said. "But the son of man has no place to lay his head."

"What — but what do you mean?" the man said, looking from him to us.

"He says go home," James said.

Just then we saw a new group rushing up from the city, coming across the fields toward us. Simon groaned.

"No more. He's delirious," Peter murmured, fatigue etched like furrows around his own eyes.

"Quickly," James said. "The boat."

The thought of water did not sit well with me. I was weary to the bone, wanting nothing but to collapse on the floor of Peter's house.

"He can sleep in peace on the boat," Peter said. "And the night air on the lake will revive the rest of us."

I did not want to be revived. I wanted only to lie down and hear nothing of the clamor I had heard for the last three days. But I said none of this as Peter and John went ahead to arrange for boats and to fetch food from the house.

Galilean fishermen, I had learned, were superstitious about the lake and its weather. I had seen them look to the sky and utter a prayer as though it were an incantation on numerous occasions. Now as the two of them went on ahead, I noted that James was murmuring under his breath and looking to the east.

"What. What is it?"

But then the crowd was coming up toward us, some of them shouting, a few of them singing.

"Hurry," I said.

Jesus was staggering by the time we came to the promenade along the shore and got him into the boat.

I saw, just once, Peter's worried glance back toward Capernaum, as though he feared it might not be there when we returned. And then we were setting out onto the lake.

Without the constant harassment of the people jostling for a chance to see Jesus, to ask for a blessing or healing or the answer to a question, the night seemed filled with strange and sudden relief and eerie stillness both. As James, John, Matthew, and Thomas took the oars leaving Peter and Andrew to work the sails, I realized it was indeed a beautiful dusk.

Jesus all but collapsed beneath the stern deck, a ballast bag under his head. As the boat sailed out past the breakwater onto the lake proper, he barely moved. Had I not known better, I would have been alarmed to see him so still, his sandaled feet swaying just slightly with each undulation of the water. He lay as one dead.

I turned away from the sight.

I leaned back against the side of the boat, lulled by the slip of the oars into the water, and eventually found my eyelids pulled down as though with the stone weights of the fishermen's nets.

A brief sense that I was floating . . .

The mismatched boards of the boat hit me hard, knocking the breath out of me.

Shouts. I pushed up against the floor of the boat, my hands nearly elbow-deep in

248

water. Rain pelted my face like icy daggers. Someone was bellowing orders. Above me, Peter and Andrew hauled in the sail against a churning sky.

"James!" John said. He was diving across the boat to fall on the rudder, adding his weight to Andrew's or I wouldn't have heard him at all, the storm swallowing the shouts of the others like a maw. The sail whipped loose, one of the ties lashing Matthew across the face so that he reeled back against the side of the boat and almost went over. Across from me, Nathanel clung to the side of the boat with both arms as it lurched and spun sideways like a twig. Lightning lit Peter's stricken face, and the look of his expression turned my veins to ice.

"Teacher!" Peter was shouting, trying to get hold of the sail. A black wall of water loomed before us and the stern went up against it, climbing until the boat nearly stood on end. James threw himself against Jesus, still sleeping, one arm thrown over the ballast bag. "Teacher!"

I leaned low, clutching the edge of the boat as a second giant wave rose up from the lake like a watery Goliath. For a moment I felt the panic of one drowning. I lowered my head and gulped for breath.

Tonight I die.

All I could think was that I had not been to the mikva. I had not cleansed myself all these last several days. I had not said the Shema tonight. I had done none of these things. I had flouted the authority of the priests and my face was known as renegade to the Pharisees.

I would die alongside my teacher and master, my hoped-for Messiah. The crowds along the lake would eventually disperse, and John would rot in Herod's fortress as Roman soldiers looked on during the Feast of Dedication. Perhaps the true sons of Judas bar Hezekiah would come rushing from the hills, only to be cut down by the legions.

I clawed rain from my face, tried to pray. Felt Nathanel grab on to me, clasped him with shaking hands. Together we would go to a watery Sheol. And all I could think was: *This wasn't supposed to happen. It wasn't supposed to end like this.* The masses, the signs, the inexplicable moments of sight. It would all amount to nothing.

The boat pitched, the stern of it jerking up out of the water. In a flash of lightning I saw the sandaled feet of Jesus, flagging against the floor of the boat, loosely in the water like the body of a dead man. Had he drowned, then, there beneath the stern?

Had he departed from us silently, without even a word of farewell? Soon we would all be fortunate to float like that on any water here.

I told myself to let go, to lunge forward and seize him by the legs. Then the boat jinked sideways, throwing us all backward. For a horrifying instant, I thought we would capsize.

I opened my mouth to cry out to him, only to be smashed in the face with a crashing wave that slapped my ears and sent my head ringing.

It was John who fell down over us, grabbing me by the arm when I nearly went over the side. "Master! Save us!"

It was a horrid sound, that scream. I would remember it the rest of my life.

I covered my face, trying to shield my eyes. Against the dark, I saw him, the pale of his tunic in the sluicing blackness, rising up. In my deafness, I heard him when I should not have against the screeching gale:

Be still.

The words had not been shouted to the furious wind or issued to the sky, but spoken as though directly to my heart.

The boat fell to wild rocking as the waves subsided into hillocks. My hair and beard were plastered to my head and face as the roiling sky turned away like the long and tangled tresses of a woman spinning on her heel, departing to the east, the way she had come. Below, against the shore, the lights of Capernaum and Heptapegon glimmered in the twilight.

In the silence, twelve men stared at one another, dread-sick and drenched, faces and hair and beards dripping with soft music into the pool of water within the boat.

What would have happened had John not cried out at last? Had he not been able to wake him?

Beyond the distant hulk of Mount Tabor, the last of a ruddy sunset stained the western sky.

Next to me, Thomas murmured through lips still faintly blue, "How can it be that the winds and waves obey him? Who can do that? What kind of man does that? No man, no man." He fell into the whispered words of the Shema after that, saying them again and again. I wiped my face with an arm that ached when it moved, so tightly had I clutched the side of the boat. I bowed my head, still trying to steady my breath, to will the shaking from my limbs.

The Pharisees had asked for a sign. But he had given it, instead, to us.

■ ■ ■ ■

When we came to the other side of the lake, we bailed out the boat, wet and shivering as James started the boat's small cook fire. The flames danced without bending even once, untouched by wind.

I closed my eyes, thinking myself too exhausted to stay awake, but unable to surrender to sleep. I went back again and again to the sight of Jesus standing up in the boat, speaking words that I should not have been able to hear to a wind that should not have obeyed.

I must have slept eventually because before long I became aware of birdsong and the rocking of the boat — of Andrew leaning over the fire to feed it twigs and grass and dung. It was morning and my clothes were not dry, but stuck to me with the same consistency as that mostly dry dung, moldered and rank against my skin.

I vaguely remembered that we had pulled the boat up onto a sandy stretch of shore. We had crossed over and tied up here to the pier — where? And then I realized: We had come to the eastern side of the lake, to the territory of the Gerasenes, a part of the Decapolis.

Several of the others were ashore with Jesus. But next to me, Simon refused to get out of the boat, sending his morning stream directly into the lake.

"The people here are worse than Samaritans. That isn't sheep dung burning on the fire there, but pig."

Why had they gotten out? The only advantage of this place was that it put us outside Herod's territory, but I wasn't sure what was better — the impurity of a pagan land, or moving about beneath the eyes of Herod's spies.

And yet there was my master, walking toward the hills. Would he pray the Shema here, in this pagan place?

West of us, where the hills jutted up sharply, the ground seemed to move. But then I saw that it was not the ground at all, but animals grazing, not so very far off, the color of stones or earth or —

Pigs. Perhaps a hundred of them, or more.

As a boy, I had seen them for sale in the marketplace of Scythopolis. They had fascinated me then, but they disgusted me now if only for the memory of that place and the shame that had come to us there.

I went after the others, hungry and short-tempered, anxious about my master's purpose. Surely he did not mean to preach here? The town was far inland and we had little coin to spend. And what would the pagans do — take us in? Feed us? Welcome us to their tables to eat their pork and drink out of their impure earthen vessels?

Ahead I could see a short basalt scarp on the next hill, and the pockmarks on the rugged face of it — some of them too obviously closed. Too carefully closed, with stones.

Graves.

"Master!" I shouted. "Master!" I called again. But this time a strange gust sounded from higher up as though in reply.

Peter faltered, looked back at me. The sound came again, but this time I saw that it was not the wind.

It was a man, running down the hill, hurling himself down from it, dirty and screaming.

My first thought was that he was a bandit. But then I saw that he was completely naked.

The scream came again, his mouth a gaping hole in his face.

He was not only running, but running as I had seen a horse charge once. His ragged hair flew out behind him, and his arms were wide at his side like wings, keeping him aloft so that it seemed impossible for him to stumble. Something dangled like a manacle from his wrist. His gaze was locked on the small group in front of me, and the look on his face was that of no man I had ever seen.

Malice. Hard and rabid beneath his eyelids, as his tongue flicked out over the lower lip of his open mouth.

It was the stare of the deranged. A murderer's gaze.

He was flying toward them, the lean muscles of his thighs corded beneath the skin as he went straight at one man in particular: Jesus.

I thought, *He will kill him.*

I had my knife out, was running toward them, but I was still twenty paces behind them, too far away.

"Peter!" I shouted. "Your sword!"

His fist was already closed round the hilt, but Jesus held his hand out toward him and the sword never came free of its scabbard. I yelled again as the madman closed the distance between them, a boat's length away, mere paces —

He fell hard to the ground, as though flung down by an unseen hand.

Peter and John both leapt back as one, nearly knocking into me as James threw his arm out before our master. But Jesus had pushed him aside in a way I did not know a man James' size could be pushed away.

"What do you want with me, son of the Most High God?" the man said.

His voice was the sound of stones grinding together. There was a gummy froth at the corner of his mouth. Naked and bloodied, he clawed his way forward and pitched back onto the ground, his back arching off of it as he said again: "Son of the Most High!"

Son of the Most High?

The man was mad.

"Master," I said, but it only came out as a whisper. There was a dark light in his eyes that I had not seen in the eyes of any other before.

Jesus said, as though he were any other man who had come to him from the multitudes camping even now outside Capernaum, "What is your name?"

"Our name is Legion," he said with an awful smile. He rose up and landed on the ground again, not so much as one falls down, but as one is flung down. There was fresh blood on his face, coming from his lip, out of his mouth.

"Stop! Do not throw us into the abyss!"

Us?

A chill crept up my spine.

This man was not mad.

Several bees had begun to buzz in a nearby broom brush. At this, the man went wild, batting at invisible insects around him. It was a moment before I realized that there were, in fact, no bees at all this early in the season, and that the buzzing had come, somehow, from him.

He cocked his head to the side at what seemed an unnatural angle as though straining to hear some one, some *thing* we could not see. Jesus took a step toward him and he flung out his arm toward the high hill and cried, "Do not torture us. Send us into pigs. Let us go there!"

Above us, the pigs were a sea of swine, churning on the hill as the waters had on the lake just last evening. In the distance, the figure of a man standing off to the side of the herd stopped, seemed to stare, and then point at us. Now I saw there was a second man with him.

Jesus crouched before the possessed man.

"Master!" I found my voice. The demoniac would lunge for him, would throttle him or jab out my master's eyes.

Jesus pushed James' hands away as the larger man tried to pull him back. He leaned forward, looked into the man's eyes as one peers through a window.

"Go."

So softly.

I didn't hear at first the gust that started behind us. And then it blew, raising my hair against the wind, causing my mantle to flap, and James' to come flying off completely. The man fell back as one trampled beneath a wagon, pinned to the ground. The air was far too chill for so sunny a morning, the air too filled with unnatural shadow. The man twisted back along the grass and screamed.

Above us, the hills continued to churn. Screaming — from the wind, the man . . . the pigs. High above, the herd roiled like the sea. Shouts from the swineherds, the one barely leaping out of the way of an onslaught of animals, coming straight for him. No, not for him, but for the edge of the hill. And then they were barreling past him, a flood of grotesque and swollen animals, running down the hill, the earth shaking even here.

Down, down they came as a deluge of flesh rushing from a cliff. The ground did not slope gently into the water as it did where we had put in with the boat, but dropped in a raw scarp toward the water. The pigs dropped with it, disappearing from view. Faster and faster they came, like the face of a mountain sliding into the sea. Below, the water had become a swarm.

Within minutes they had all rushed over the edge and into the water. One moment more and the water was still.

The hill above was eerily silent, the smell of freshly turned earth carrying to us on the breeze, a wide swath of it churned in their wake. Below, the lake lapped against the shore, and the rocking of the boat began to subside.

There was not a single pig in sight.

The swineherds, silhouetted against a beautiful morning sky, stood hands to heads. And I understood that the entire wealth of the city — an entire city's livelihood — had just disappeared completely.

I fell to my knees.

After Jesus had lifted the naked man from the ground, taken off his own mantle and covered him . . . after he had told the man to return to his people — the swineherds had begun to shout, and to run toward town, no doubt to bring others to kill us — I picked something up off the ground: the manacle, fallen from the man's wrist during the ordeal.

It was split open, twisted at an angle that no man but a blacksmith with a hot forge could have bent it. But there it was, broken open, as though it could not, dare not, stay shut.

The voice of Levi was silenced within me. I looked at this man, this teacher to whom I had pledged myself, unconventional as he was, with renewed awe. I understood the meaning of this sign very well.

What were Romans but pagans and pigs and demons in the land of Israel? Didn't the famed Tenth Legion bear as its standard — a thing in itself against God's law — a wild pig?

He could not have spoken more clearly had he said it. Had he screamed it.

By this one act alone I knew that this man would drive the demon pigs of Rome from the hills of this land, and that Israel would at last be free.

By spring, we would advance on Jerusalem. Within a few years we might advance on Rome. Anything was possible to me then.

I determined then to enjoy these last days and weeks as one enjoys the last hours before Passover, having prepared and brought in relatives and made the arrangements for the lamb and the feasting space and food, when he can finally sit down and remember the feast itself at last.

My heart soared. *Messiah.* The one sent of God. I had not waited, or suffered, or hoped, or lost in vain.

22

They came to us on the Sabbath, having broken it to bring us the news. But they need not have spoken; by their haggard faces alone, we knew.

John was dead.

One of his disciples, a man named Dael, fell down at Jesus' feet and wept. "Herod has cut off his head. We've just come from burying him."

For once, Jesus did not have ready comfort to give another. He reeled away. His hands covered his face. Andrew, across the room, cried out. He had been John's disciple once.

I could not imagine it, the charismatic wild man of the Jordan, silenced even in this way. But of course he had to be. Herod would not — could not — afford to let him live. He had spat in Herod's face, and so Herod had relieved John of his head.

I remembered the night I had met with Zadok, and how he had waved away John's name as though he were already dead.

Now fear seized me by the throat.

Jesus was the cousin of John, so alike at first that they even preached the same words in the beginning and had often been mistaken for one another until Jesus had grown more rampant than his wild cousin, and his cousin had been caged.

If John was a dead man, it was only a matter of time until my master was, too.

But Jesus didn't seem to be thinking of any of this. He lurched outside, tearing his hair. A terrible, grief-stricken cry came from the courtyard a moment later.

Dael looked up from the ground, his face streaked with tears, dirt. "There are men with me — nearly twenty. Others, who would not break the Sabbath, will soon come."

"Twenty? But there were so many!"

He shook his head. "The rest have fled. In these last days there were less and less of us as they realized they followed a condemned man." He wiped at his nose and then fell forward on his hands again.

"Where is Levi?" I demanded.

"He's gone. I don't know where. He left us in the middle of the night."

"Come. You will follow our master now," I said. "It is the Sabbath. Come, eat and rest."

I did not feel any of the reassurance in my voice.

That night I thought back over every word I had uttered about the coming kingdom, everything I had ever said or repeated of John's or Jesus' that might be considered seditious against either Herod or Rome.

I wondered what Zadok and the Sons might say about the things I had spoken. They themselves would never have spoken such things, preferring to wait until the moment that another put his neck out there to do it for them, so that they might only rise up at the last minute.

Cowards. Cowards, all of them.

And I was a coward, too. Because the more that I told myself that I had said nothing seditious, I knew it for a lie meant to cleanse me of guilt. I had gone from town to town spreading word of a kingdom not of Rome. I had rejoiced at the swelling hundreds and thousands that had come to accompany our travels, envisioning an army. No matter how I tried to reason with myself, I knew the truth: Following my master had put me soundly outside the safety of the law. One of any number of hundreds might identify me as having preached his message, acting in his name.

My lot was inexorably tied to his.

I did not want to die as a bandit in the hills, or as my father upon a cross. I had already given — and lost — too much for the cause of freedom.

But my master was not another Judas bar Hezekiah or even John the Baptizer.

He was the Messiah. And if not him, then no one. So now we must move, and quickly.

But we did not move quickly.

Jesus' charisma began to flag. He became thin and drawn. He went to the hills at the going out of day and did not return sometimes until dawn. The pall of death seemed to hang over him as though it were he who wore the shroud, and not John in the grave.

In the middle of the night, many from the throng began to sneak away. The next night, and the next, more disappeared.

I began to reconcile myself to the fact that we would not march on the Holy City at Passover.

I consoled myself by saying that Jesus was like David. And like David, he must hide out before moving to claim his place as king. He was of the line of David. This story had been enacted before. I told myself this, again and again.

Until the whispers began in the back of my mind.

You could leave. I could leave now, and return home. I could collect my mother and family and go south. To Kerioth, perhaps. Or to Alexandria. I could study under disciples of Philo or another great teacher. The Sons of the Teacher knew all they needed to know by now. Surely they no longer needed me.

You wanted to be a scholar once.

But no scholar could do the things Jesus did. I had seen my teacher perform deeds only the greatest prophets might.

None of them was Jesus.

And so there it was: I could no more go back than I could put back the many months that I had spent following my master.

I went out with him in the morning and evening when he would allow me. I held him at night when I heard him weeping. I feared. I prayed.

"Do you love me, Judas?" Jesus asked one early morning. We had been out all night, praying in the hills.

"With all my heart," I said, tired and worn, desperate for him to return to us. To life once more.

To me.

23

A merchant brought me the coded letter:

I was recently summoned to an inquiry about this Jesus. I called him a man of questioned birth and no consequence. But he is quickly becoming known as seditious by those in power, and a blasphemer. One cannot be a Messiah and commit blasphemy. Already there are those who call for his death.

Tell me: is our brother, Simon the Zealot, among you still?

That night when I knew Simon to be alone, I went and flung him to the ground.

He looked up at me with surprise in his eyes — which only ignited the fire in mine.

"What's the meaning of this?" he shouted.

I threw the letter at him, picked it up again and, leaning down, held it before him. "Do you read what this says? You, who I counted a brother! Why did you never tell me you were one of the Sons?"

He glanced at it, not touching it, his eyes scanning the coded message, putting it together, reading it, getting to the last line.

"I stopped responding to them after Tabernacles," he said dully.

Tabernacles. When he had joined us in leaving the city, to my surprise.

I clasped my head, the message still in my fingers. "All this time we could have been in this together! All this time, I might have had a confidant and not been alone in it!"

"No. They wanted your reports to check against mine. They would have played us off one another — don't you see? They're doing it now. I should never have brought you into this!"

I grew very still. "What do you mean 'brought me into this'?"

"Who do you think told Levi to come fetch you? Who do you think recommended you to Zadok?"

I stared.

"I saw the passion in you for the coming kingdom," he said. "You covered it well but I saw it, dormant all these years — before it flared to life after Susanna's death."

I took a step back.

"And so I brought you in, not meaning to

stay with you or to leave after Tabernacles
with you. With him. But once we had
returned to Jerusalem . . . I was ruined by
then for the man I now call Master. I can't
go back to Jerusalem or that life. I never
will. I'm ruined for all but him. He's set
something free in me. That is what has mattered most, even above the freedom of
Israel. Hate me if you like, but that is the
truth. That is how I knew I could no longer
be a part of the Sons of the Teacher. That
teacher. And now, whatever fate you work
with them for our master, I will share in its
outcome, but not its shaping."

"I have no hand in his fate!" I said.

"Don't you? What do you think they are
doing with all that you tell them, if not pulling the strings of their sources in the Temple
or in the courts of Pilate or Herod even as
they rile up the young students, those
zealots ready to die or kill for the law,
unaware that they will never be free as you
and I are free?"

"What do you mean never be free? What
are we here for if not for that? And we are
not free yet!"

"Are you listening to nothing? Do your
ears hear nothing? Do you think your
anxious heart will be silent if the Romans
are gone?"

"Yes!" I roared.

He was shaking his head. "I will not go back to them." He got up. "Tell them whatever you like. My family may suffer. They have all but threatened my brother in this —"

"Zadok called me to his house."

"Of course he did. These are men of consequence, and they wanted you to know that. Rich and powerful men and Pharisees."

"Pharisees!" Our master had done nothing but offend Pharisees as long as I could remember!

"Who do you think wants to see a Messiah come to Jerusalem more than anyone? I'll tell you. The Shammaites. The militant Shammaites. Students of my teacher, as I once was — many of whom in Jerusalem are Pharisees."

I stared.

"Ah, but what if our master doesn't do it the way they want him to? If Jesus is too peaceful, what do you think they will do? Do you not see this deadly game you are involved in, Judas of Kerioth? The Shammaites will grow to hate him. I've already seen it. He will not move the way they want. It is not his way. Didn't you hear him the other day, preaching the turning of his cheek after one strike to receive another?

The giving away of one's mantle should another need it?"

"I thought — I gave him my mantle after he gave his to the demonized man . . ."

"Judas! Judas," he chuckled, but the sound had no mirth in it. "Is it a demoniac who demands our mantles of us . . . or is it the Romans who may demand anything they wish?"

I felt sick.

"You're saying . . ."

"I'm saying that you must be wise. Look around. Do you look for a reign of peace? There will be no peace. Do you think to usher him in to his seat in the Temple? The Pharisees will not have it. The Shammaites tire of him because they are confused by him. He is not one of them and so they will condemn him. And the Sadducees — they would have him put to death now, before the talk about him grows any further. Before Rome comes in and deals with him themselves and they lose any more privilege than they have."

I was stuck on something he had said earlier.

"You said they threatened your brother . . ."

"Who knows," he said, reaching up to clutch at his head. "I asked my brother to move. I spent the entire Feast of Tabernacles begging him to go away, trying to convince him to return with his family to Galilee, to Gamala. But how can he go away? No, of course it's ridiculous. There is the business. My family is too wealthy to move. They are weighted down with it like a millstone. I fear for him. For his wife, his children. He has said it, you know. Our master. That brother will turn against brother."

"*Why?* If you fear for them — why?"

"Because this is where I belong. I belong . . . with him." His voice cracked. "And because despite all I have told him, he will have me. I have told him everything, including things I have not told you, Judas, that I dare not, because you are so very good and so very tortured in your goodness already — how can I tell you? You, who are perfect — you love the law better, even, than I."

"That's not true. If only you knew. And you, Simon, have been called zealous all your life."

"Yes. I am zealous," he said, sounding very tired. "And everyone loves me for it. But they do not know me. He —" He pointed in the general direction of the hills, where I knew Jesus to have gone, as he did nearly all the time now since John's death. "He knows me, and he loves me in spite of who

I am. No — because of who I am. I am not worthy, and yet he loves me."

"Simon! What are these secrets? What terrible thing can you have done that a man would hate you? You have lived for this kingdom as much as I!"

"You do not know the things I have done — in Gamala, when I first joined the Sons before coming to Jerusalem. I have spilled blood for them, Judas, and no amount of zeal has atoned for it. He alone has."

Simon — a murderer? But Gamala was a hotbed of nationalism. Surely he killed a Roman?

"When — what . . . ?"

"Don't ask these questions," he said, looking up at me, a dangerous expression on his face. "Unless you truly want to know."

"The Sons know?"

"They've known for years and have kept my secret. But now I've abandoned them and they could use it against me at any time."

"Write to them. Tell them you'll return to them. We'll work together to protect your family and one day soon it won't matter —"

Though even as I said it, I thought: *Here is a man who by his own admission deserves to die.*

He shook his head with a faint laugh.

"Still the idealist, Judas. No. No more. My future is here. I have come here with all I am, and our master has accepted me. I cannot go back."

"But your family —"

"This is my family. He is my family. You, Judas, are my family now. And I beg your forgiveness for every deception or for disappointing you. For the blood of that man, whose name I never knew, did not want to know. For that as well. So now you know my secrets. I know none of yours, though I have surmised many about your past. Yet it doesn't matter. You are my brother."

I didn't want a brother who was a killer. I felt, inexplicably, as though by knowing it, I had blood on my own hands.

"You'll immerse tonight, having heard this, I know."

I looked away.

"The law says —"

"I don't care what the law says," he said quietly, and I could not believe my ears.

"There is a greater law at work here, and a greater redemption. I made the sacrifices. I have done everything I could short of spilling my own blood to atone for the blood-guilt. But in the end, it never did anything to assuage me. Nothing did, until I came here. And for that, I thank you, Judas. I am so deeply grateful to you. But now, perhaps, you understand why I have distanced myself from you, knowing that it was I who brought you here with me, not the other way around. I am sorry for deceiving you. But there are now no more secrets between us."

I turned away. In coming here he had found — what. Atonement? But how could he? For all my belief in him, Jesus was not a priest. He preached the release of sins, he pronounced it. But what did that mean for a murderer?

I held on to the letter for a day more, eventually writing only:

They call him seditious because they fear him and his coming kingdom. Be ready. The Sadducees and the others will lose their place in it, but those who support him will be made great. He has said himself that the first will be last, and the last first.

I said nothing of Simon.

24

They came from Bethsaida, from the Decapolis, where they had heard the tales of the swine — some of them angry, come to harass him. They came from Tyre and Sidon and even Syria.

They came out of curiosity, or because they were desperate. But what they did not know — could not know — was that we were the desperate ones.

We were now north of Bethsaida in the territory of Philip, Herod's brother, where it was safer for us. I had not spoken any more to Simon. I did not look at him when he was near, nor did he seek me out.

I had thought in coming north we might lose more of our number. But after three days the crowd swelled to the largest I had ever seen it. By early afternoon of the third day I counted nearly five thousand people carpeting the hills and foothills. We moved among them constantly, repeating the familiar stories and blessings, even recruiting a few of our staunchest among the throng to help us.

By mid-afternoon, the sun was hot overhead. Hunger churned all of our stomachs.

"Teacher," Andrew said. "We need to let them go to find food and lodging. Some of them will have to go as far as Capernaum or Heptapegon. There's not enough in Bethsaida alone to feed them all."

Jesus, seemingly lost to his own thoughts — it was the way he had been ever since John's death — glanced up at him. "Why don't you give them something to eat?"

Andrew blinked at him. "Teacher, there are so many."

He looked around. "Do we have any food?"

I stared at him and then looked at Andrew as though to say, *Is he even with us?*

"There's some here," Thomas said. Thomas, always the literalist. He had been carrying the basket of what food we had, which had dwindled.

"There's hardly enough in there for James alone, Master!" Andrew said.

"Make the people sit down."

"To what end?" Andrew said, visibly exasperated.

Jesus looked up at him, the expression on

his face weary. "Make them sit down in groups of fifty. And then give them something to eat."

"I'm telling you we hardly have enough to feed —" Andrew started.

Jesus gestured impatiently for the food as though we were the ones who did not see. Andrew turned away, shaking his head.

Lifting the fish and then the loaves, my master said the prayer for the breaking of bread. His face was haggard. I thought, with a tinge of fear: *He is not in his right mind.*

He laid the food in the basket and then handed it to James as though it were settled.

I closed my eyes in wordless frustration, trying to tamp down the desperation I felt growing within me. We had plans. For the spring. For the mob, for our advance on Jerusalem. Plans and hopes! How long would he wallow like this?

I had loved his question to me just before dawn: *Do you love me, Judas?* He asked it near-incessantly now, and it had been with pleasure that I had said, "Yes! Yes. I love you." Again and again. And I had meant it. Had found pleasure and purpose in knowing that this man, this teacher . . . this friend . . . who healed lepers and calmed the very wind asked me with such urgency: *Do you love me?*

I had relished that I could hold sway over such a heart. That for as many as looked to him . . . he should look to me. As though none of it mattered without my love.

And as he had wept through the night, my heart had soared with the knowledge that I was known and not rejected. That I was somehow necessary to this enigmatic man, this powerful man . . .

This broken man . . .

In ways I did not understand.

I glanced at James, still holding the basket. The look on his face was strange.

"What is it?" I said, wondering if there were an insect or a scorpion in it.

"Bring another basket," he said, oddly.

Andrew, still standing a little ways away, shook his head and chuffed.

Matthew brought him another and James began to pour bread and fish into the empty one in Matthew's arms.

Bread.

Fish.

So much bread. So much fish.

"Another!"

Matthew's laughter rang out and someone brought them another. He hastily put down the one and hoisted the empty as James poured.

Bread. Fish. Another basket.

It went like this until there were ten in all. By the time we had poured the last of them and taken them out to the throng and sat down ourselves to eat, we were laughing, the heat of the day forgotten, the tension over us breaking like a spring thaw, like ice cracking beneath the sun.

Elijah had given bread once, to only a hundred men. If Elijah fed a hundred, how much greater was the man who fed five thousand?

Hope. It was the one thing that the countryside cried out for. Food. It was the main requirement of an army. It was for that reason that Rome had coveted the wheat fields of Egypt. But we would be invincible beyond even Rome. Because what man here would not follow a man who could give him food without end? Who might heal him if he fell ill?

That night my master went off alone. I wanted to talk to him. I felt humbled, broken by my doubt. But he slipped away before any of us could follow him.

I told myself it didn't matter — that he could have every malaise he wanted and I would be gentle with him. My spirits were high, and I was renewed, and from that reserve I would give him every patience.

But he did not ask me to pray with him

the next night either. Or the night after. And as the mob grew, my master grew increasingly distant.

A week later Jesus came down to the piers of Capernaum to see us off. Crowds of hundreds waited for him here, some having traveled for nearly a hundred miles to see him. We had returned for a few days but dare not stay longer — but the crowds had not yet had their fill of him.

"Go. I'll join you there," he said, untying the rope himself.

"Please. Come away, Teacher," I said. It was by now nearly evening and I was none too eager to go out on the lake without him after what had happened the last time, but he gave me a smile and pushed us off. Earlier, I had offered and then asked to stay with him, but he had sent me with the others.

I had not admitted, even to myself, how that injured me.

I watched him look back at us before turning away. His back was bent, and as he turned toward the low hills, he faded into the dusk so unremarkably that I wondered if he had disappeared. For a moment I even wondered if I would ever see him again, or if, in that odd and quiet departure, he would exit my life forever.

The thought unnerved me so that my pulse began to pound.

I closed my eyes, willed my heart to quiet. I had been in a state of gnawing anxiety since my talk with Simon. In a state of fear, too, for my mother and my brother so that I sent them a message via the Roman post saying only that I missed them and wanted to know if they were well. I could not say more.

We passed the trip wagering when we would march into Judea, and when Jesus would enter the Temple to claim his throne at last.

"Tabernacles," Peter said.

"Spring," Andrew said.

"Sooner," Thomas said.

"Yes. Let it be sooner."

Matthew and some of the others were silent.

"What if we don't live that long?" Matthew said eventually.

"Of course we'll live that long," James said. "He's promised us a place in the kingdom. The only question is who will be greatest."

"The one who has been with him the longest," Andrew said.

The one he loves the most, I thought to myself.

Evening descended across the lake, thick and buggy. There was fear in the darkness of the lake for me, and I kept a sharp eye on James and Peter. But I never saw them glance to the sky even once. The wind did pick up, but only enough to slow our progress, so that Peter cursed and Andrew briefly took down the sail, the wind seeming intent on blowing us all the way back to Heptapegon.

As the night wore on without a storm but without a wind to see us to Bethsaida, a few of us slept when we were not taking turns at the oars.

It was sometime before dawn when a swift prayer and the hissing intake of a breath woke me. I had been sleeping lightly and came awake all at once.

But there was no gale, no gusting wind or even rain. It didn't seem we had moved at all since Andrew had taken down the sail.

"There," Nathanel whispered.

What was he pointing at? The clouds were thin, the moon full so that it illuminated the surface and waves of the water.

"I see it!" Matthew said, sinking lower in the boat. The gazes of the others were as intent as wolves — but not nearly as brave.

But it was the fishermen who had begun to pray, the fear on them palpable.

I had heard them murmur about strange things on the lake at night. I considered it the product of uneducated minds and Galilean suspicion and was about to close my eyes again.

But then I saw it.

It rose up like a pillar of moonlight, growing taller by the moment as though it had risen up out of the lake itself.

"A ghost!" That, from James.

I had heard more talk of ghosts in the Galilean countryside than I ever had growing up, where we had learned of the spirits brought back by the witch of Endor. But I had never fully understood and therefore never fully believed in these things.

Until now.

James, beside me, shrieked with a voice that I might have thought to come from a woman. I would have laughed at him, except that I could see it walking, striding out over the water. I could see from here the movement of the figure's tunic around its legs, the way the mantle was drawn up over its head as my master was often wont to do . . .

"Don't be afraid!" the figure shouted.

His voice.

My heart leapt within me. Before I could say it, though, Peter had gotten to his feet.

What man but Peter would leave a perfectly good boat in the middle of the lake, climbing over the side of it so that we all cursed ourselves for our fear? What man but Peter, who, flagging in the moment, began to sink, so that we were grateful we hadn't spoken out?

And what one of us did not envy him that saving grasp in the end?

By the time they came into the boat together, the wind had picked up so that we took in the oars and let out the sail. It was then, in the first tinge of dawn, that I saw the tears on Peter's cheeks, just before he lowered his head beneath his mantle and wept.

The crowds in Bethsaida were ravenous for him by the time we came ashore that morning.

"We're ready to do the work the Lord requires," a representative for many other men said when we had gone into the synagogue. It was not safe to speak of these things out in the open.

I was excited for every man who came to Jesus like this, like a warlord pledging both men and fealty.

"But give us a sign first so we know what we've heard is true. Seeing it with our own eyes, we'll follow you."

Inwardly, I groaned. The last time anyone had asked for a sign we had nearly drowned on the lake.

"We heard about the bread!" someone called out. "Show us that you can multiply bread!"

My master's face tightened into a look of absolute frustration.

"Yes! Show us!"

"Don't do it for the food that spoils!" Jesus suddenly shouted. "But the food I give you! *I* am the bread of life. Whoever comes to me will never go hungry!"

Silence in the synagogue. Was this to be the moment? I barely breathed. Those on the benches leaned forward. Waited. But when he did nothing, they began to look around, confused.

"So where's the bread?" someone said.

Today was not the day. Because just then my master's expression twisted. He spun away, looking as though he might inexplicably weep.

No. No.

He was far too worn. When was the last time he had slept? Ate?

They must not see him like this. We

needed these men. These numbers. But this was not the charismatic leader and revolutionary that they had come to see.

"Master, come away," I whispered, reaching toward him.

He pushed my arms away.

"The bread is my flesh!" he said, stalking back. "Whoever eats it will live forever. I'm telling you the truth, that unless you eat my flesh and drink my blood, you have no life in you."

I went cold and then instantly hot, heat searing my cheeks, enveloping my head. Next to me, Simon blanched.

No. No. No!

He was raving. He was mad. It was the only reason he could have possibly said something so perverse.

Shock on the faces of those standing closest. Outrage from the stone seats. Men had gotten to their feet. Even the uneducated peasants were staring. Across from me, Peter covered his face with his hands.

"Stop," I cried, reaching for my master but he ignored me and began to cry out: "Whoever eats my flesh and drinks my blood has eternal life! And I will raise them on the last day!"

I closed my eyes. When I opened them, men were already angrily going for the door.

A man did not talk about eating the flesh of another man. He did not speak of drinking blood.

The blood of birth and the blood of circumcision tied a man to the Lord. But blood belonged to God alone. For that reason a woman segregated herself at the time of her bleeding. For that reason, the blood of sacrifices ran from the Temple into the ground. It was not to be shed without purpose or lightly, lest it cry out to God in the direct connection that it had to the divine. These were not our laws, but God's.

Jesus would not just ruin our mission — the vision for an army, for Israel, marching against Rome — he would ruin us. And with such words, he would kill us.

Quickly, Simon said: "Even the prophet Isaiah has said, 'Come all you who are thirsty, and you who have no money — come, buy and eat!' " But it was too late; the people were in uproar. I turned away.

I watched them filter out of the synagogue, my peace, my heightened hopes, going with them.

"Does this offend you?" Jesus said, his voice rising. He followed a group of them as they made for the door. "Then what if you saw the son of man ascend to where he was before? The words I speak are full of life and of the spirit!"

He stood there and watched them go and did nothing to stop them. And we stood there, powerless to stop them, watching them go.

"You. You don't want to leave, too, do you?" he said to us as we stood there, his head lowered as though he had vomited or emptied his bowels onto the floor. The synagogue was nearly empty.

"Where would we go?" Peter said, looking utterly lost.

Indeed, where?

Jesus dropped his head. I thought for a moment he might weep. He looked for all the world like a man utterly alone. But I had nothing with which to comfort him.

"I would not be bought by bread, or by power, or swayed by riches. How can I let them be, either?"

Was he even speaking to us?

He covered his face with his hand, the strain of these days and weeks and long nights showing in the droop of his shoulders, in the lines of his forehead even as he slid his fingers against them. A moment later his knees buckled. James was there to catch him, his arms going around him, this man who had been a hand-laborer, whose strength seemed to have been bleeding out from him these last days.

"Master!" he held him up. My arm went behind his neck in James' arms.

"I chose you twelve," he said, so quietly that I could barely hear him even in the empty space of the synagogue. And then he said something else that I could barely hear.

"What do you say, Teacher?" I said, wearily.

"One of you . . ."

"Yes?"

"Is a devil."

"Why do you say these things?" I demanded.

"Because," he said. "It's true."

"He's lost himself," Peter said that night. "He hasn't been right since John's death."

Across our small fire, Simon sat, stony and pale in the dark. I did not need to ask his thoughts to know he wondered what he'd done in coming here, in leaving everything to follow this man. I knew these were his thoughts, because they were also my own.

That night I dreamed I was returning from Galilee. But as I went up to Jerusalem, there was no gleaming Temple facade, no gold or marble. It was all burned to the ground. As I got closer to the city, I could see what I thought were fence posts along the road. But then as I got closer I saw that they were not fence posts at all, but crosses, their patibulums wide enough only to accommodate the span of a man's arms.

There were hundreds of men and women upon them. And the city itself, as I passed beneath that grisly parade of crosses, was empty.

"Mother!" I shouted. "Nathan!" I shouted the names of my sister-in-law and my niece and nephew. But there was no one left within the city. Only then, when I ran back to my house, did I discover the coded message written on the wall: *You have done this.*

Many left in the middle of the night, and more, openly, in the morning. I stood outside the house in which we had stayed — some relative of Zebedee — and watched them head northwest to Sidon, or west, toward the countryside of Galilee. Some of their faces I recognized as having followed us for months. I wondered if they would go to the hills, to be welcomed into the ranks of bandits. Maybe even by the true sons of Judas bar Hezekiah, themselves.

Countless times through the night I had thought of going. Of asking Simon if he would return with me. What else could I do here? I could only slant my reports to the

Sons for so long. They had their own spies among us — I knew that now. They could easily check the veracity of any account I gave and know I tried to sway them. To hide that my master was slowly collapsing beneath this weight.

Of madness.

But when I would have rolled up my meager pack and slung it over my back, I didn't. I didn't, not because I had more courage than the others, or because I had so much to return to . . . or even because I wanted to know what he would do next or if there was in his madness some true plan, some genius that I had not seen or anticipated.

I did not leave because I had never felt so fearfully alive than I had with him. Because I believed him.

So I would wait. I would nurture him and coddle him back to health if I must.

In the end, I did not leave because I loved him.

25

By the time we came to Caesarea Philippi,
it was not as conquerors, but as fugitives.
The throng was gone and the dream of the
coming Passover faded with every mile.

Jerusalem might as well have been a world
away.

As we made our way toward the foot of
Mount Hermon, I began to wonder why he
would bring us here, to the source of the
Jordan in the cliff face. It was a pagan place
where the locals worshipped the Greek god
Pan and our prostitute king had built a
temple to Augustus.

As we made our way up the face of the
rock toward the grotto, I could see even the
niches in the walls carved out for offerings
to the god. No good man of Israel should
be here. Had my master come so far, then,
that he not only blasphemed, but sought
those places rife with the worship of other
gods?

I wanted to laugh my own mad laugh. Why not. Why not? Should we eat the offerings left to the idols as well?

And yet the closer we got, the more crisp the air became. It smelled of water. Not in the way that air might smell of rain, which was a blessed smell, as rain was always a blessing in the land, but of living water.

Of purity, and cleanliness.

It should have smelled of death.

Above us, the snow was on Mount Hermon, pristine and clean, the source of the water. How could the cliff face be so polluted by these niches and this grotto dedicated to Pan, by the temple here, built by the traitor Herod of my youth, who built a temple to every Caesar who shined his crown . . . and it smell so beautiful?

How could I possibly feel renewed by the water coming out the mouth of the cave — the same one the pagans believed to be the gate to the underworld so that the nearby city literally sat upon the gate to Hades? I had even heard once that they enticed their gods out from this very grotto by perverse acts performed between women and goats!

The air picked up, riffled through my hair. The breeze was filled with the scent of cypress and almond trees, of the orchard that the townspeople kept near here, of mossy rock and snowmelt.

"Who do people say that I am?" Jesus said, when we had come to stand just before the cliff face. We had bread and olives with us, but none of us dared suggest we eat or drink here, despite the fact that these were the very waters that became the river Jordan.

Peter and I glanced at one another.

"John," Matthew said. "Many people think you are John. Even Herod, Chuza's steward says, thinks this."

At that, Jesus gave a sad smile.

"Elijah," Thomas said. "Or Jeremiah."

"Yes, any of the prophets," Simon said.

"What about you?" he said, looking around at us. "Who do you say I am?"

In that moment, I had the distinct impression that if I said he was my friend, that is what he would forever be. If I said he was a hand-laborer . . . that is who he would be. I don't know why I thought that, only that his face struck me as a blank slate, devoid of the anguish or madness of before, ready for inscription.

My friend.

My heart whispered it.

Messiah.

My past, my pain, cried out for it.

Silence stretched around me and I knew

that each of them voiced the thing they wished only in their hearts.

We hadn't known how to talk to Jesus of late, each of us watching our words, none of us speaking with the same impetuousness we had known. A year ago we had been children. Now we guarded what we said, measuring it, knowing when our words would be futile or even go unheard. He had grown so contrarian of late, so unpredictable, that most of the time none of us knew what to say at all.

The moment stretched over the running of the water like the thin web of a spider, taut with expectation. I all but heard the glances of the others, darting around us.

And then I realized I was afraid. That my heart was a cudgel in my ears. I was afraid because I feared that whatever I said, he might say it was not true.

That he was not the Messiah.

That he did not love me.

Worse yet, I feared I would believe him.

They were the twin badges on all our hearts for so long now: hope and fear.

The strained silence stretched on, unbearably. I glanced at Simon, who was searching the ground in front of him, his eyes moving back and forth as though reading something there. I looked to Peter, impetuous Peter, who had leapt from the boat.

Speak. I thought to myself. *Say it. Let it be said, spoken into existence.*

Or let it be said, because I cannot bear it anymore. Let it be put out like a shard to be crushed, and then let us no longer pretend. As though in voicing it, it would be bound in heaven and earth, both.

Speak.

"You are the Messiah."

My pulse hammered into my skull.

"The son of the living God."

There it was.

But it had not come from me.

Across the circle of us, no one moved. Only Peter, who rose to his feet. Hope shone from him like a fever. He was radiant.

Jesus lowered his head. For an instant, my heart sank.

"Blessed are you, Simon bar Jonah. But I call you, Peter. And this is the rock I will build my church on," he said, glancing up.

The temple of Augustus seemed to fall away behind me. The niches in the stone face ceased to exist. There was only this: Peter's simple proclamation, and this ground, separately holy, where we stood.

"And the gates of Hades will not overcome it," he said, over the water gushing from the underworld behind him.

At last, I thought, and fell down to my knees.

At last.

I left there in a state of alternate hope and euphoria. Hope, because I had never heard him say it or consent to the label of Messiah before until now. I understood that as in Galilee there would be strife surrounding us as we did our work — as the trappings of the pagans and Herod had surrounded us in this moment.

Euphoria, because as we left, he said he would indeed go up to Jerusalem. It was the thing we had hoped for.

But then on the way down from Caesarea Phillipi, he began to say things that at first confused me, and then filled me with desperate frustration.

He began to talk about suffering at the hands of the priests and the teachers of the law.

This had already happened. And, if I was honest, he had brought much of it on himself.

Why must he harp on it now?

And then a few days later, as he was saying this again, he said something that turned my blood cold.

"I will be killed, and on the third day be

raised to life."

Even as I was thinking that I would speak with him in private, Peter forgot his former restraint.

"Never! We will never let that happen to you!"

Jesus pulled up short and cried, "Get behind me, Accuser!"

Peter froze.

"You, stumbling Rock. Behind me now."

We were stunned. Any one of us might have said the same thing; it was the sentiment in all of our hearts. For what had we given these months and, some of us, years?

Or, others of us, a lifetime?

That night Jesus went apart from us as usual. This time, none of us tried to pursue him.

Peter came to me an hour later.

"I'm leaving."

I got to my feet.

"No. You can't."

"Can't I?" He threw up his arms. "What else can I do? In trying to do what seems right, I do wrong. When I am with him, it is as though all the world is turned upside down. So that if I say, 'You must live,' he calls me Accuser, a satan."

His eyes were filled with the deep cuts of confusion. "How does one please a master like that?"

I didn't know. None of us did.

It was a paradox. He was a paradox.

"Meanwhile, my family is in danger as I follow this teacher I cannot please! At least in Capernaum I know what I am doing. I am an expert at what I do. I never feel off-balance, not knowing my right from left as it changes each day!" He covered his face with a hand. "You, Judas, have been closer to his heart than any of us. You, who understand the ways of teachers. Tell me!"

There was a moment, a bare moment, when I thought, *Yes. Go.* Perhaps the fewer there were of them, the more influence I might exert over him. Even to the point of saving his life. Because that's what it was rapidly coming to. My master was right; he would die if he followed this course. Herod wanted him dead. The Pharisees wanted him dead. The Sadducees. Who else would there be but the poor and the sick and what would happen on the day that he refused them bread and signs? Even the Romans had to buy favor where they went with bread and circuses and offers to lower taxes or build roads or of privileges. I had thought the coming kingdom different, but perhaps it was the same for any kingdom — God's, or man's.

But Peter loved him, and our master loved him in return. I knew this. For Peter to leave would crush him. And so it was for the sake of our master, and for our movement more than Peter himself, that I said, "No. You must not," and begged him to stay.

At the right time, and in the right moment, I would speak to Jesus if he continued with this. I would speak plainly. I would rebuke him if I must. His grief was choking him and making him irrational. We could not afford to be irrational. We were now gambling with our lives.

Spring became summer. The jackals were out on the hillsides. Somehow they sounded closer than ever.

I forgot the sounds of Jerusalem, of Capernaum. I knew only the rhythm of the coming and going, the prayers of my master. He preached to whoever came to hear and whatever towns we came to during the day, but then left us alone at night seeking solace not with us but with God.

I had in my things some parchment. Now, I began to write. To chase the account of all that had befallen us and record as many words of Jesus as I could remember. To have them for posterity. To distract myself from the new and gnawing hole in my gut. Every time I thought he had abandoned his morbid distraction with death, that we might at last talk of the future, he would announce to us again that he would die. Recently he had begun to say that any of us who wanted to follow him must even take up his own cross.

He had not said it to the crowds — there were no longer multitudes that followed him at any rate — but only to us. Didn't he realize that he must not think this way?

And each night I went to my bed in a sweat and dreamed of my father.

One day late that summer, Jesus went away to pray on the slopes of Mount Hermon. He was almost always in prayer now, taking Peter and the brothers James and John with him. Though I missed him and our nights of prayer until dawn, I resolved not to begrudge Peter, who had been so wounded by him.

And so I tried to savor the time to myself, resting during the day when I knew I would not dream, and writing at night by the fire, glad that Jesus was not alone in his solitude, even though it seemed more and more that he preferred the company of only these three.

They came back with strange tales of Moses and Elijah, come to talk with him. I didn't believe them at first, but then I was intrigued with what it could mean, and made them tell the story again, and then again. I was excited by this, anxious to ask my master about it — until Peter sheepishly told me that they were not to tell the story to anyone. Not even the rest of us.

Not me.

I, who made constant excuses for him, who rationalized what he meant, who did everything I could to blunt his rough edges and to sharpen his soft ones . . . was not to know.

I hated the weakness in myself that made me feel like a child or a sulking fishwife. But somehow, I had fallen away from him, and he seemed to shun my company so that I had to learn, now, what he had said from one of them.

The three of them were strange after that, often quiet. Too quiet.

"What is it?" I said at last to Peter. "What is it that puts the fear on your face?"

It was fall and the rains had begun to come, and I looked forward to the green on the hills, hoping that we would all, somehow, be restored to new life with them.

His eyes were hollow when he looked at me. "He says again and again now, that he will die — die and be raised from the dead.

Why does he say that, Judas? What does he mean?"

I just shook my head.

We were in exile for months, until the day that Zebedee sent word that the fervor had died down and most of the crowds had given up waiting for him and gone their way.

Finally, that fall, we returned to Capernaum.

We returned as men who hide in open sight. I saw the way that they looked at us, the people and the Pharisees. I saw the wide berth some of them gave us, thinking it might hurt their own image to be seen talking to us.

For the first time, I missed moving about as one even who offended the Pharisees — at least then we had not scuttled around like those who fear being caught in some act. I missed, even, the throng.

And now who was there following us in earnest but a few stray dogs? They had come with us so far that when I opened the door in the morning to go out and relieve myself against the garbage heap, there was always one of them there, manged and haggard, choking by the side of the road on whatever it had found to gnaw on. And I could not ascertain who was in worse condition — them, or us.

But for as much as I missed our life before, I relished this time with my master. Between his many admonitions that he would die — he was obsessed now with the idea of death — he began to spend time with us alone again as he hadn't been able to before, in the presence of so many. And now he told us stories of prodigals, of forgiveness and debt, of missing sheep and coins.

Pray in this way. Forgive us inasmuch as we forgive others.

Seventy-seven times.

His teachings were not new to me — these were the things spoken of in the teachings of the sages, and debated in the schools of the Temple and in the synagogues. But his stories were.

We sat by lamplight at night. As men who share stories holed up in a cave without food while a storm blows outside, knowing they may starve.

We pretended there were no soldiers waiting to seize him, that there were not, even now, ready witnesses willing to testify that he was a blasphemer. That he was not caught in the grip of a malaise and fixated on death, and that he would not take us all to that grave with him.

I could believe, in those days and weeks,

that we were alone, we twelve, in fighting an invisible Accuser, that we twelve were somehow army enough.

Until I woke up in the middle of the night, bathed in sweat, having dreamed again of the burned city, the coded message on the wall.

This last time, it had read only one word: *Unclean.*

26

Standing on the road and looking up toward the Holy City, my heart hammered within my chest. But not for joy.

It was Tabernacles, the time of harvest. I could not escape the dream that had haunted me now for many nights. The crosses, the burning buildings.

The Temple, destroyed.

I did not confide in Jesus; I didn't want to tax him in any way with my macabre dreams — he, who thought only these days of death.

We had left Thomas, Jude, Philip, Nathanel, and James the smaller behind and joined a group of pilgrims as we came closer to the city. But first we had begged Jesus not to go.

"There are things I must do. But don't worry." He smiled slightly. "It isn't time yet."

Time for what?

But I knew I would get no good answer

from him. At least there was no throng following us. In this way, we might be any other pilgrims on this road.

Last year I had anticipated that by this time we might be in our new base in Jerusalem. Perhaps in the palace itself. But here we were, skulking about, going so far as to stay in Samaria, where we were issued the gravest insult of all: the refusal of hospitality.

I never thought to enter Samaria, let alone to pass an evening there out in the wild. I did not sleep well that night even though Peter stayed awake most of it with his sword unsheathed.

The night before the feast began we arrived at the home of Mary and Martha in the darkness of early evening. Their brother, Lazarus, clasped all of us in greeting.

Even this close to her gates and my family so near, Jerusalem did not beckon to me. A sense of dread had settled like a pit in my stomach, so that I had to slip out constantly to empty my bowels, which would not hold food properly.

When, on the fourth day of the feast, Jesus started out for the city, I slipped away.

The day of our arrival I had sent a message ahead. Now when I came to the house of Zadok, I was let in without preamble.

I was not given a garment as before, but only some water to wash my hands as I was taken to a smaller room to wait. A short time later, Zadok came in.

"Hail, Teacher," I said, kissing him, feeling strangely false, as though I betrayed my own master in greeting Zadok this way.

He seemed to have aged in the time since I had seen him last. And then I thought, *He will outlast us all.* The thought sent a strange wash of cold up my shoulders.

"So your master returns to the city. Despite my warning to you."

"Please. Help me protect him." I was ready to beg, to promise him anything. He was so close, my master, to recovering from the thing that had seized him all these months. Soon, I thought, very soon, he would be nearly his old self again.

"I think you overestimate my power," he said, reaching for a stone cup and pouring some wine. He offered it to me, and I took it, but I could not bring myself to drink. "I told you he shouldn't return at all unless he was ready to march on the city."

"We lost the throng after John was killed. And now today he'll go to the Temple and soon everyone will know that he's here." Simply saying it, I was close to panic. "But the Pharisees have influence to exert in this.

You can protect him."

Zadok sighed. "Judas, your master has made his own choice of friends. I hear he has routinely flouted the ways of the Pharisees — and for what? The man is no idiot. On the contrary, he is a brilliant teacher, by all accounts, if contrarian and manipulative."

I wondered about who had reported those other accounts. "No," I said quickly. "He is not manipulative. Contrarian, yes. He is a paradox. If only you would meet him yourself. Please, will you go to the Temple? Look behind the provocative words he speaks. There is more there —"

I caught myself. I had almost said, "than the law," but said instead, "than what you have heard and the heresy spoken about him. He is himself a sage, whose way would have caused Hillel to smile and Shammai to nod."

Zadok set down his cup. "Judas. The messenger of Annas has already asked what I know of your master's appearance so that the guard may arrest him. He's prepared even now to take him the moment he enters the Temple."

I fell down at his feet.

"Please, Teacher!"

"Why did he cause such offense the last

time he was here?" he said, shaking his head. It was genuine frustration on his face. Frustration and anger, too. But rather than alarm me, I felt an anger of my own, rising up in me toward this man that he should presume frustration from so far without knowing what paradoxes and hardship and fear we had lived with . . . and then toward Jesus himself, that he had caused this rancor in us all.

"Is he a man of such compulsion that he can't stay away, that he can't choose his time, that he must go to the porticoes as a dog goes back to his vomit?"

I felt my face turn red. "You insult my master." Were it not for my dire need for his help, I would have stormed out of his house. Were it not for circumstance, I might now sit in his place, as an even greater teacher of the law, and he in mine. But need compelled me to stay, even on my knees.

He raised his hand. "Forgive me. I mean only, why can't he temper passion with prudence? If what you say is true and he would be Messiah, why doesn't he act more strategically? You say he lost the throng that surrounded him — how does a man lose a whole army?" He shook his head.

"It was a choice," I said, in a bald lie. "And if you were there, you would have seen the prudence in it. But don't think he can't recall them all with a word. All across Galilee, his name is known. Even to Phoenicia and Syria, into the territory of Herod Antipas' brother, Philip. The people love him, or how else would he have evaded the soldiers of Antipas? But now he has come here —"

"Yes, and why?" he demanded. "Didn't I say he shouldn't return until such a time that all was ready and we might support him? Besides." He sighed heavily. "He's from Galilee. There's no overlooking this. What prophet comes from Galilee?"

"Nahum," I said swiftly.

"Nahum," he repeated and gave a slight but mirthless laugh as he sank back into his seat. "Let's not argue, Judas. This changes nothing between you and me. Your master won't be the first messiah to fail. There's no shame in it. But it's time to leave his side."

Leave Jesus? No. Impossible. Panic rose up inside me at the thought of my brother, my mother. What might happen to them because I disobeyed an order from this man? Even now, Simon lived in fear for his family.

But I knew without question I would never leave Jesus.

"He won't fail. The signs, the healings!"

"Yes, the signs, the healings. What messiah hasn't made the same claim?"

And then I knew.

Zadok was supposed to be the new Shammai. He was supposed to want the freedom of Israel, and the perfect keeping of Torah that would bring about that day. But in that moment I understood that he would want it only as he had envisioned it or not at all.

"Please," I said. "Go to the Temple. You have every pretense to be there even now. Please, hear him. Test him yourself."

"Perhaps, Judas," he said, sighing. "But perhaps it's time for you to consider that this man is not the Messiah."

27

There was a crowd gathering around a teacher at the far end of the royal stoa. Some of them were shouting.

It could only be him.

I slowed my stride, sure that anyone near me would hear the dread thud of my heart.

A man standing a little ways off said, "Isn't this the one that they were talking about, the one they're trying to kill?" He looked up and around. "But no one's stopped him. Maybe they really do think he's the Messiah."

"That can't be," another man said. "They know this man is from Nazareth. He's a Galilean. A Nazarene. What messiah comes from Nazareth?"

I saw Simon through the gathered crowd, caught his eye, but did not move toward him.

Through the afternoon, we stayed like that, our vigilance never relaxing. At one point, I looked across the court and saw the form of Zadok. He had paused to glance in my direction, but if he saw me through the horde of pilgrims, he did not acknowledge it.

That day we walked out of the Temple, free men. I didn't know if I had Zadok or God to thank for that.

The next day he stirred up the pilgrims and Pharisees in the Temple like a hornets' nest. But when some came to seize him, others moved to keep them from doing so.

The Pharisees came to challenge him every day now — many of them men I recognized. I had seen them like this before: intent as vultures, about to cast a teacher out, to argue him into a corner from which he could not escape, to pass judgment on him by the evidence of his own words. They had ammunition enough to call for his death, and yet they came day after day, bringing others with them.

Again, I begged our master to leave the Temple.

The last day of the Feast, I glanced up from the gathered crowd — larger each day — in time to see several Temple guards coming toward us.

I had prayed so many months now for the day that we would stand in the Temple like this and Jesus would make himself known as the son of David — as the coming One. But now I prayed for the very opposite thing. Unless he would enact a miracle — throw himself down from the height of the Temple itself and be miraculously unhurt, or cause the sun to go out as had the prophets of old — they would not believe him. And I knew he would do neither.

So when I saw the soldiers, I braced myself.

But when they came, they stopped to listen, and as the sweat trickled down my spine, they stood there just like the rest of those who had come, pausing once or twice to murmur between themselves. At last, I could stand it no more and made to move toward them, but Simon put out his hand and stopped me. When Jesus was done, they went away.

Now I had seen every sign there was to see.

Each day that passed like this contained the longest moments and hours of my life. I stayed with him constantly. Only on the going out of the third day, after I had seen Jesus safely to a cave in Gethsemane where he liked to pray before returning to the house of Mary and Martha, did I finally go home.

My mother did not get up from her mat when I arrived. But I knew with a glance that she was not ill. No, something more grave had passed.

My brother appeared in the front room, sunken-eyed and thin as I had ever seen him.

"What's happened?" I said, at which my mother covered her face with her veil. My brother came at me, railing.

"I heard you were in the city! Did you think once to come directly to us? No. You stayed with your precious teacher, the blasphemer, didn't you? All the while you have been out defending your Messiah, did you think to ask once what has happened here? No! Of course you haven't!"

I looked from one to the other. My first thought was for the children. But then I saw the face of little Hannah peering around the way from the next room.

"Where's Joses?" I said suddenly.

On her pallet, my mother began to weep.

"He is here," Nathan said, the blunt anger draining out of him with each word. "He is out in the courtyard. He spends all day there, and won't come in unless I force him. He will not speak . . ." He laid his forearm over his forehead and I thought for a moment that he might weep, too.

And then I realized the one person still missing: Rebecca.

"Nathan, where's your wife?"

"We have needed you and where have you been?"

"Brother!"

He covered his eyes and even when I shook him it was several moments before he opened his mouth, twisted and ugly, and said, "She went out for water, later than usual. Hannah had been ill and Mother was ill, and she had not been able to go sooner. It was late in the day that she went to the spring. And the streets were crowded with the huts of the coming Feast . . ."

He drew in a breath.

"And?" But I already knew I didn't want to hear what he would say.

"The soldiers of Pilate were in the city for the Feast, and the men of one of the watches saw her —"

On the pallet, my mother's weeping had become a soft keen.

"She came home so late. Her face —"

I stared.

"Tell me they didn't kill her."

"Oh, they didn't. Not directly." He bared his teeth like an animal.

Rage. Indignation as I had never felt it. It boiled up inside me.

"She clung to me when I would have gone out to death after them. I was crazed. But she begged me. And she was so broken, bleeding . . . I was prepared to go to the elders, to the Temple, the synagogue. I was prepared to go to Nicodemus. She begged me not to. She begged me. Do you understand? For the sake of her honor."

I was shaking.

"Where were you?" His expression had shattered to a thousand pieces — and my heart with it.

Tears streamed down his cheeks, sputtered on his lips. In that instant, he was not a full-grown man and a father, but the boy I had left to the bullies of Kerioth before going back to defend him in guilt.

Where were you?

Then, as now, I had been chasing messiahs.

I wanted to say I would never leave again — no, that I would take him with me. That I would never see him defenseless again, that somehow this was my fault.

"We found her in the mikva," he said, all the anger, all the emotion stripped from his voice like flesh from a corpse's skull.

I covered my face. Staggered back against the wall.

I was overcome with horror — for Re-

319

becca, whom I, too, had loved. But most of all, for Nathan. Because I heard it in his voice: the cry, the pain that even he had not been enough to keep her in this life.

That night I did not return to my master, to the hospitality of Mary and Martha in Bethany, intent instead on keeping a watchful eye on my family.

I thought often of the mikva, wanted nothing more than to use it. But I could not bring myself to do it for the image of Rebecca floating in it, her dark hair an inky fan in the living water.

28

The slave of Ananias bar Nebedeus, one of the Sadducees, was murdered in the market. He was stabbed in the middle of a crowd, and no one knew who had done it.

Except for Simon and me. His single glance said: *It is the Sons.* It could only be them.

We feared for our master every hour that he was within the city gates, and feared, too, that murder of Ananias' slave would be somehow put upon him. I had no more currency left in the way of leverage or influence by which to protect him. Every day, I had prepared for his arrest. Every day, we begged him to leave, but he would hear none of it.

Meanwhile, his teachings became increasingly contentious and explosive.

"I am going away and you will look for me and you will die in your sin," he said one day in the porticoes.

Simon and I turned away. How much more could he push? How much more could they take?

Could we take?

I had thought that the Temple authorities had not wanted to cause a stir during the Feast when so many others would be there to see it — including Pilate and Herod themselves. But the Feast was now over and Jesus had begun to gather such a following that they dared not cause an uproar right in the Temple.

The multitude was forming again.

But this was not the adoring multitude of before. Each day it grew in size and vitriol. Each day the words of my teacher were met with greater and greater reaction as Jesus became his most incendiary yet.

They called him a Samaritan, demon-possessed.

And then the last day he went too far.

Jesus cried out, the vein in his forehead bulging: "Before Abraham was, I Am!"

I Am. The very name of God.

A chill ran down my spine and up over my arms. Several of those men who had been listening crossed the courtyard to a pile of stones where the stoa was still — endlessly — under repair.

The law dictated I should stone him myself.

Love dictated something else.

"Master," I said, pleading.

"Please!" Peter said.

Impossibly, we escaped with our lives.

That night, when he said we would return
in the morning to Galilee, I should have
fallen down in relief. Except by then I didn't
know if it would matter.

Nowhere was safe anymore.

When I went home my mother cried out at
the look on my face.

"You're leaving?"

I was silent.

"You are the elder son!"

I wasn't always. I wasn't supposed to be.

Nathan came into the room, a piece of
parchment crumpled tight in his hand.
Scriptures, I assumed, to comfort himself in
his grief.

"So you will follow him into the hills," he
said. "You disappear with this would-be
Messiah, this blasphemer who no one wants
to follow? You follow him into obscurity!"

"You don't know —"

"Oh, I've heard about everything your
great teacher is doing — he called himself
the One, the equal of God! He deserves to

be killed! He will get you killed with him. Do you think he will care whether you follow him to Sheol? No. Because he is no messiah but a madman and a devil."

"You will not speak of my teacher that way!" I roared, my fists clenched, shaking.

Across the room my mother cried, "Judas! Nathan!"

"Oh, but it isn't a messiah you care so much about — it never was that for you. You only care that he's made you believe he loves you."

I was across the room in a flash, slamming him against the wall.

He laughed in my face.

"Of course you defend him to me. What else should I expect? Be done with your charades, brother —" He shoved me away, and I felt the younger strength of him and my own age in a way I never had before.

I staggered back, distantly aware of the cries of my mother to stop, her shouts and stern words, which had long ceased to have any effect on either of us.

There was something on the floor. The parchment he had been holding. I blinked.

He bent but I got to it first, spinning away with it in my hands. I was a boy again, taking away his things, but this was no boy's game.

This was no scripture.

It was a coded message. I stared at it until Nathan tore it from my fingers, the first real hint of fear in his eyes.

He had joined the Sons?

A thousand questions spun in my mind. Had they recruited him to spite me? Because of my absence?

"Brother . . . tell me you haven't joined these men."

"You will not dictate to me!"

"You don't know what you are meddling with," I said. "You have no idea the extent of the thing you have touched."

"Who are you to me? I am not even your brother." There were tears in his eyes, prisms of rage. "I know the reason you were ashamed of me. I have known it always. I have always known why you despise me. Well, I release you! Leave and let me be."

"No. You are my brother. The fault is mine. It has always been mine."

"No, it isn't. And I don't even think I can blame you for hating me." He pushed angry tears away from his cheek. Across the room my mother was weeping, and my heart went out to her most of all.

"I don't hate you," I said. "And I only blame myself."

He looked up then, his teeth gritted

together. "Do you know who you should blame? You should blame the Romans that did this to us. To your father. If not for them, you would have Joshua, rather than some bastard replacement. Rather than some would-be Messiah. You would have your father. It is he you have loved and missed all these years, and I have always known it."

"Nathan! Judas!" Mother cried again, as much in upset as in fear, I knew. These were not things to be voiced aloud.

"Leave your so-called Messiah." Tears were streaming down his face. "He will not strike the eagle down for you. Leave him, Judas! You've been deceived. He will only get you killed."

"If you knew him, you wouldn't say this," I said, but I had no anger left, and my words sounded hollow.

"I don't need to know him to know his deeds."

"For your sake, for Mother's sake — for your children, take care, Nathan. For their sake. Do not leave them without a father."

"How soon are you leaving?" he said coldly, collected again.

I glanced at the message in his hand, desperate to know what it said. "Soon. Now."

He went out without saying goodbye. Mother cried after him, her hand to her heart as though the earth had rent open before her.

"Please, Judas. Does this teacher need you as we do?"

I wanted to comfort her, but there was nothing left to say. I had chosen my master over them already. Whatever his fate, whatever he was — madman or Messiah — I would live or die with him.

It was this thought that propelled me out of the house that night. Through the streets, my sandals slapping against the worn stone that had survived war and the shedding of a multitude of lives. He was of questioned birth. By the law, he was a blasphemer. A breaker of the Sabbath. I did not understand his cryptic sayings. Why, even as he talked of freedom, he talked of death.

But none of that mattered.

Even as the voice within me screamed that I dare not ignore the fact that the priests and Pharisees wanted to kill him, I knew I would not trade him even for the law.

Or for Israel herself.

I loved him. I loved him.

I lurched through the city, out the gate — there to the cave, where I knew they would be.

I threw my arms around Jesus as he rose upon seeing me — this master who had been so broken with his own grief, for whom I had tried to be so strong.

"Hail, Master," I said, choking. My knees buckled and I sagged in his arms, weeping.

No, he did not need me. But I desperately needed him.

29

The Jerusalem we left was no longer the place I had known, the shining city of Zion. It had always been filled with capricious mobs and Romans, with radical students and the insurmountable wealth of the Temple, with Pharisees pursuing the law of God with the exacting edge of a knife. I had always known this, but until now never understood what it meant to be the object of such righteous hate. Her streets ran now with murder, and when I dreamt of the Temple, it was not of the golden facade, but of the sacrificial blood that poured from her gutters.

Our last night in Bethany, I sat in the house of the sisters Mary and Martha, and listened to my master teach. I sat beside Mary as though we were both men in the synagogue or students in the porticoes. It did not seem amazing to me anymore to do this. I pretended that we were no longer a group of disciples following their uncertain master, but all that existed in this world. Like Lot and his daughters, thinking they were the only survivors in the world at the burning of Gomorrah, leaving the city for a place where the former order held no more sway.

And like Lot at the burning of Gomorrah, none of this was how I had hoped it would be. Jerusalem was as good as a mass of burning embers to me and what had I taken away?

We hadn't gone far north before a group of Pharisees caught up to us in their fine linen robes. I braced myself with what little reserve I had left, but these Pharisees had not come from Jerusalem, but Perea, east of the Jordan.

"We've come to tell you that you have to leave here. Leave and go someplace else. Herod wants to kill you."

They would kill him in Jerusalem. They would kill him in Perea or Galilee. Now where were we to go?

That evening, we camped near Bethany by the waters of the Jordan River where this had all begun.

"Please, Master," I said a few nights later. "Come away from here, where you will be safe."

"Judas," he said, his eyes filled with the injury I could not understand. "Don't you believe that there is work here I must do?"

Months ago, I might have cried out: *But you are not doing it!*

But tonight I only said: "Can you not do it in Philip's territory? Why must it be here, always in the place of danger, with men who would kill you? Don't you know that I love you, that I can't bear the thought of you in danger? Please, come away."

"Judas —"

"Please." I felt my vision swimming with tears. "I don't care what you do. Please, will you come away from this danger and live."

He lowered his head and I knew I had disappointed and hurt him. Desperation rose up in me and I swiped at my eyes, no longer caring how womanish it looked.

"Judas, no one lights a lamp to put it under a bowl. It is put on a stand so that those who come can see the light."

"Yes, but there are those who are coming to extinguish it!"

He blinked at me. "Do you still think I've come to bring peace?"

I covered my face. What was the use of reasoning with a madman?

"Judas, we are almost to the end of this journey. We are almost there. Trust what I do and say."

"I have trusted. I have, I do," I said, with bone weariness.

"He is not in his right mind," I said to Simon that night when we could talk alone. Our master's brother had intimated the same thing long before and we had defended him. But now I wondered if we should have listened.

Simon was quiet.

"Are you well?" I said.

"We could leave," he said. "We could go to Gamala. If you truly want to serve this cause, there are men there who knew Judas bar Hezekiah and follow the sons of his loins."

"Maybe we could go meet with them in secret," I suggested. "Join our forces together —"

Simon was already shaking his head. "Open your eyes, Judas! Do you think the Sons of the Teacher will wait on a man like our master? They see only a man who won't raise the muster he's capable of. Who shuns the violent ways they crave. Who won't tell them to kill Romans or to not pay their taxes."

"We can't leave him," I said.

He glanced down. "I have left all to follow

him. But he's bent on his own death. He will bring about ours. That's what he meant when he said to take up our crosses." His brow wrinkled when he looked up at me again. "Are we ready for that?"

Several people came down from Galilee. More a few days later and more the next, including several bandits. They might be any landless men or day-laborers except that I saw the feral look in their eyes and, on occasion, the flash of one of their swords.

Jesus healed everyone they brought to him. His teaching took on a tone of greater urgency, as one who is rushing to say all that he must in too short a time. And his parables turned strange.

"I'm telling you, don't be afraid of those who kill the body. Be afraid of the one who, after you're dead, can throw you to the fires of Hinnom. Fear him."

Peter, who had been sitting near me, turned his head and whispered, "What is he talking about?"

I shook my head, because I didn't know. But it didn't matter; the crowd increased. Within a week, it had doubled.

The throng was returning.

30

We took up our camp and went into Jericho. It was two months until Passover.
There, in the city, was a woman with a bent
back. It was the Sabbath but Jesus healed
her anyway.

But this time was different. When the
synagogue leaders began to rail at him, Jesus
shouted, "You hypocrites! Doesn't each of
you untie your donkey or ox on the Sabbath
and lead it out to water? Shouldn't this
woman, a daughter of Abraham, bound so
many years by the Accuser, be set free on
the Sabbath day?"

The people were cheering. I couldn't
believe my ears.

"I've come to bring fire on the earth," he
said, "And how I wish it were already
kindled!"

I saw how the bandits with us received
this with gleaming eyes and knew their
thoughts immediately: Surely what he spoke

of was nothing less than war.

It was too early after our flight from Jerusalem. I dare not lay claim to my hope. But that day I felt the return of something I had not felt in a very long time. Love, I had felt for Jesus now for a long while. Fear and confusion, I had felt for him. Need, I had felt for him, too.

But that day, I felt pride.

In Cypros, my master told stories of banquets thrown not for the rich but for the poor. Those men I knew to be bandits among our group approved. They approved, too, when a few days later my master said, "Suppose a king is about to go to war against another king. Won't he first sit down and consider whether he is able with ten thousand men to oppose the one coming against him with twenty thousand?"

When he was not teaching, he seemed to gather silence around him as one gathers stores before a storm, or strength, as though shoring himself up. He prayed often through the entire night until dawn, so that he looked gaunt by day. Andrew and Peter and James and I often went with him to protect him, often falling asleep to the sound of his murmured words, often waking to find he had gone on farther without us.

The day that Talmon, servant of Martha

and Mary, arrived at our camp, Jesus was talking again about the kingdom of heaven — not that it was leaven or a pearl, but that people would be eating and drinking as in the days before the flood destroyed them all.

"Teacher!" Talmon all but collapsed in the arms of my master as though he had run all this way. "Please! Lazarus, whom you love, is sick. Come quickly — they fear he will die."

Jesus, holding the man by the arms, cried out. I knew the look in his eyes and was afraid he might leave with him that very moment. But it was Peter who issued the caution.

"Please, Teacher," he urged. "You dare not travel so near Jerusalem. You barely left with your life last time!"

"Please!" Talmon said. "He is dying. He won't live long!"

I looked from the desperate slave to my master. We all knew and loved Lazarus. But we loved our master more.

"It is for God's glory," Jesus said, slowly letting go of the servant. "So that the son of God may be glorified." I thought then that he said it to comfort himself, that he said it because he knew he could not return and live, and therefore could not — dare not —

go. He took a step back, saying again, "It is for God's glory." And though his words spoke reassurance, his expression was deeply troubled.

"Please, Teacher, hurry!" Talmon cried.

But Jesus let Talmon go, telling Andrew to get him something to eat. And then my master went off for a little while, pulling his shawl up over his head. He was gone through the day and into the evening — so long that Talmon began to pull at his hair and beg Peter and Andrew to please go after him and make him come.

"Don't fear," Peter said. "Our master has healed from afar many times. It might be even now that Lazarus is well again."

But I had seen the look on Jesus' face. He was tortured as one who all but stands by the bedside of one dying.

Would he truly not heal Lazarus and leave his slave to kill himself with worry? It was nothing for him to say only "He is healed right now — go home." He healed any person who came to him even on the Sabbath. Would he not heal his friend? I did not understand him!

Late that evening I went out to the hills where I knew he would be praying. When I came to him, he lifted his head. His face was streaked, and I knew he had been weeping.

"Peace, Master," I said, coming to join him, wrapping my mantle over us both. I did not ask about Lazarus or Talmon but simply sat with him through the night.

The next morning Talmon returned to Bethany, weeping and alone.

A day later, Jesus said, "Today we go."

I saw my alarm mirrored in the faces of the others.

"Teacher, we can't go back to that place — they'll kill you."

A bandit standing nearby whose name was also Jesus said, "We will come with you."

But how could we keep him safe, even with their protection? What if the Temple guards were already waiting near Bethany for him? What spy wouldn't know or hear about Jesus' friends there — he had gone down from Jerusalem to their house often enough. What if they were lying in wait for him?

"Lazarus is sleeping," Jesus said. "I am going to wake him up."

"Then he is well!" James said. Fear and frustration were plain on his face. He had been there with us the day the men had picked up the stones in the Temple to kill him.

338

Our master turned away from the group of bandits and said, very quietly, so that only we few could hear him: "Lazarus is dead."

"But you said —"

"Now we go to him."

Peter threw up his arms and walked away from us. I went after my master, and James fell into step beside me. On the other side of him, the look on John's face was grave.

"Let's go," James said. "He is our teacher. We will die with him." And I remembered what Simon had said.

But I did not want to die. I watched the form of my teacher as he prepared to leave and could not reconcile these words from him. Now that the multitude had begun to grow again would he walk blithely to his death?

But I went. I went, because I had learned by now that he was the author of the unlikely. And I went because I could not stay back and live if he were to die.

Martha came out to meet us. Her eyes were swollen and I hardly recognized her at first.

"If you had come he never would have died!" she cried, beating my master on his chest. But after the first few blows, her fists seemed weighted down with iron so that she no longer had the strength to pull her arms back. He didn't stop her, but only turned his head as I had seen my sister-in-law do when one of her children flailed at her face.

"Your brother will rise again," Jesus said, his voice thick and guttural as tears ran down his cheek to his lips.

"Yes, I know . . . I know!" Her face twisted in grief. She shook her head with it, as though she had wrestled through the night with this very thing. "He will rise on the last day in the resurrection. I know!" But it was no comfort to her now.

Just as it had been no comfort to me when Susanna had died.

And then I heard him whisper in her ear, "*I* am the resurrection . . . the life. Do you believe this?"

Martha turned her face up toward him and though swollen, red, and splotchy, it was beatific — beatific as though filled with the raw need for something even greater than her dead brother. Her expression crumpled and she cried, "I believe you are the Messiah, the son of God."

I blinked to hear such words from a woman. *Son of God.* By all accounts, she might be guilty of sedition for even saying the words we had danced around for so long. I flinched, that she had spoken them so loud.

He whispered something else to her that I could not hear. She nodded, lowered her head as he helped her to straighten her veil, which had come askew. And then she smoothed her tunic and turned and went back toward the house.

Mary came out and broke into a run. She threw herself down at Jesus' feet, weeping over them, her tears making dark splotches in the dust that coated them.

Jesus lifted her like a rag doll in his arms.

"Come and see, Lord —" It was all she could manage, her lips pulled back in the grimace of grief. "Come, I will show you."

She took us to a place nearby where tombs had been cut into the side of the hill and stopped before one of them, unable to even level her chin at it. They stood there together, Lazarus' sister weeping, her forearm held before her face as though shielding her eyes from the sight . . . and my master, his shoulders shaking with the cries of a man whose heart has broken, and who has had no strength in him now for days. Here was the man who had prayed through the night, who had grown gaunt with some great burden that only he could see or know. He bent over, his hand on his knees, great sobs wracking through him.

Behind me, the bandits were silent. I sensed in them a profuse respect for the dead that only comes from those too familiar with it. At last a few of them turned away, to fasten their gazes on the hills in the direction we had come.

Finally my master straightened and said, "Take away the stone." When no one moved, he cried, "Take it away!"

Mary grabbed his arm. "What are you saying? He's been in there four days. There will be a terrible stench!"

"Take it away," he said again.

And then the bandit Jesus and the brothers James and John were there, straining against the rock, their faces turned toward their shoulders against the smell of rot from within. I thought I heard the tomb open with a gasp as though sucking at the fresh air and I instinctively covered my nose. Next to Jesus, Mary's hands shook over her mouth.

Jesus was speaking quietly to someone — at first I thought it was to her. But then I realized that he was praying. When he had finished, he lifted his head toward the grave.

"Lazarus!" His voice broke.

Silence. I imagined that I heard my master's voice ringing off the back of the tomb itself, the echo of Sheol.

I covered my face. Finally, he had gone too far.

"Lazarus. Come out!"

I turned toward him to take him by the shoulder, to tell him to stop and let them grieve without this cruel trick.

But then someone gasped. James, beside me, screamed.

I lifted my eyes, my heart drumming in my chest, fearful to see what I knew I would see, even before I had seen it.

I staggered back as cries erupted around me.

Ahead of me, Peter sank to his knees in the dirt.

31

They came in droves to see and hear the teacher who had raised the dead, to touch him and gape, and to be healed.

I was rapt, drunk with anticipation I had not felt since the day I first saw Susanna and knew she would be mine. Since the night of our wedding, when I knew I would have her in my arms. My hopes had died at the hand of tragedy before but it had all given way to something greater. Nothing could ruin my happiness.

Two days later, I received a coded message.

Leave. Go away, far from the lands of Herod or Judea. Your master has performed one sign too many. Caiaphas is jealous to keep the high priesthood and knows one single sneeze in the wrong direction and Pilate will relieve him of it. Do you think he has forgotten that his predecessors held their office only a year apiece? And so he has increased the Temple guards, supplementing them with Roman auxiliaries — Samaritans. What's more, he has "prophesied" that your master will die lest Rome take away the religious privilege that Israel already "enjoys" under Roman rule, and the power that the Sadducees enjoy as a result. He has put out an edict that any man with information about your teacher should come inform on him. And so he will make him the scapegoat for us all. Your teacher will die — is even now as good as dead.

Take this warning as proof of my love for you and let your proof be that I never see your face again.

— Nathan

I stared at the message for a very long time, hollow, sick inside.

We had eluded Caiaphas' informants before, but now every man would be obliged by Mosaic law to report Jesus if he saw him. What one of us had not heard the words from youth:

If anyone sins because they do not speak up when they hear a public charge to

345

testify regarding something they have seen or learned about, they will be held responsible.

I showed the message to Simon. When he read it his mouth set as though his jaw had been carved of stone.

"That 'prophecy' of Caiaphas is no more a true prophecy than Caiaphas is the true High Priest," I said. "Except that he has the power to make it come true."

Simon looked at me oddly then. "How do we stay faithful to our master, who said he came not to do away with the law but to fulfill it . . . and to the law that demands we report him?"

I shook my head. It was an impossible situation.

"Even the sages said often that it was better for one life to be risked than for all to certainly die."

That night I made an excuse to go to town. There, I inquired about the nearest mikva. It cost me several prutah to use and I took the coins straight from the money-bag, reasoning that it was better for me to be clean than for us to have coin.

I immersed three times.

Two days later, we retreated to the rugged

hills of Ephraim.

It was five weeks until Passover.

■ ■ ■ ■

PASSION

■ ■ ■ ■

32

The day after Purim, Jesus spoke the words that filled me with hope and dread in toxic measure.

"We will go up to the Holy City. The time is near."

A month ago, we would have cried out for fear.

But now . . . The crowd in Ephraim had swelled with pilgrims come down from as far as Tyre and Damascus and Syria. Fire had reignited in the eyes of our master and only those of us closest to him heard the way weeping hitched the words of his prayers in the middle of the night.

The Pharisees condemned him. The High Priest Caiaphas condemned him. Herod Antipas wanted to kill him. With the growing throng surrounding us, we could no longer hide.

And so our options had dwindled now to two: march on Jerusalem or die.

That was all.

We all knew it, and had suffocated with not speaking it all these days and weeks.

Now, as he said these words, I saw the way Peter sat unmoving as though he had not heard. Only his eyes, darting this way and that, gave him away. James and John glanced at one another. John had aged in these last three years — the rogue curves of his face that made him look young even for a Galilean fisherman beneath sun-dark skin had leaned into the angles of a man constantly vigilant. James, who had always been more boisterous than his brother, had become more and more quiet in these last weeks and months. But now he lifted his head and looked at the master as though he would say something, but then he only nodded.

We had all changed.

Late that evening, I went to the bandit who was also named Jesus.

"We are going to Jerusalem for Passover. The time is nearly here."

He took this in with somber eyes. "How will he do it — how will he make himself known so that they believe? How will he force Caiaphas to proclaim him king?"

"I don't know," I said.

In my dreams I had seen the new Maccabee riding into Jerusalem with an army. I had seen him fighting his way to the Temple. But I knew Jesus would not do it that way; he never did anything the way I thought he would.

The bandit's brows drew together, and I found myself speaking before he could voice his concern.

"He will do as he does. If there is any man who can accomplish this thing, it is he. He raised a man four days dead. Do you think he did it only to bring a friend back to life? You heard what he said: 'So others will believe.' The prophet has said that flesh will be knit back onto the dry bones of the people. What sign do you require?"

I felt an immense peace saying this. It came over me as I spoke, and if I hadn't been aware exactly what I would say at the beginning, I was fully convinced of the truth of the words by the time I finished.

"What should we do?"

"Keep my master safe. Send your men ahead of us into the city to see what they may learn."

They came down, all of them, through the Jordan Valley. The family of James and John including Old Zebedee their father. James and Solome and Little Mary, the siblings of Jesus. And Mary, his mother with the uncanny eyes. Susanna, who cried every time she greeted and every time she left the Magdalene. Chuza, Joanna's husband, who was the steward of Herod, came with new coin for the moneybag, confirming to us that Herod would seize Jesus as soon as the feast was over.

There was a thrum, an unspoken thread of expectation that grew tighter and stronger with each pilgrim or family member who came to join us. Men came down from Galilee — not pilgrims but men from the hills. More bandits, concealing their swords.

We set out two weeks before Passover. We walked as those in a daze, as those who are astonished, caught between dread vigilance and hope. Simon glanced at me once that day as we traveled, not speaking, but I saw the question in his eyes so clearly:

Can it be?

I hadn't dared allow myself to hope. But that day my heart cried out: *Yes! It is! It must be!*

For three years we had flailed at every opportunity — crying out in the storm, or at the lack of food for so many. And we had been rebuked for our lack of faith each time. How could this be any different?

This time we did not travel in obscurity or

quietly. We filled the towns to the roof with our number. We preached by the side of the road, shouting about the coming kingdom. During the day, I felt invincible, tireless.

But at night, the Accuser whispered in my ear.

Tinderbox.

They will kill him.

We went on to the next town, and the next, our numbers increasing as we went, like mud sliding off the side of a mountain in a storm, taking the entire hillside with it.

I tried to gauge the expression of James, Jesus' brother. I saw the way his eyes flickered to Jesus. It was the way one keeps watch on a wild thing, not knowing if it will stay tame or attack those around it.

What if we're wrong? What if we march only to our deaths?

I couldn't withstand this anymore. None of us could. Kingdom or death, one or the other. It was time.

"Master, you must sleep more, and eat, or you will not have the strength to come into your power," I said as the thirteen of us sat together late at night. He was drawn and paler than I had seen him in weeks, but that is not why I said it.

I said it to provoke a response, eager for one small word that I might construe as confirmation of hope.

"Listen to what I'm saying," he said as though he hadn't heard my admonition at all. I almost repeated what I had said, if only to make him acknowledge it, anxiety welling up within me at this small thing as though the fate of the world rested on a single word.

"We're listening," John said. Beside him, Simon, Peter, and James looked between themselves as men who prepare to jump off a cliff, looking for courage, wondering if they will survive the leap.

"The son of man is going to be delivered to the chief priests and teachers of the law." He glanced at me and away. His next words came as though from a distance. "They'll condemn him to death and hand him over to the Gentiles, who will mock and spit on him, flog and kill him."

I blinked at him, barely hearing the words over the frustrated drum of my heart.

No. Not that again! Not now.

Peter's brows drew together, but he did not speak. None of us did.

"Three days later, he will rise."

When he had left us to pray, James stared at us. "I've never understood this parable," he said.

"Perhaps . . ." Matthew licked his lips,

which were parched and peeling. "Perhaps it is not a parable."

"The third day — he means that something will happen on the third day," James said. "Passover is a holiday of seven days. Something will happen in the middle of it."

"He'll be challenged by the chief priests," I said. "But it's a test, as the storm was a test. We all thought we would die, but our master stood up at the last minute and calmed the waters and the wind. How much less is it to calm the mouth of Caiaphas?"

Uneasy laughter.

"Perhaps that's it," Peter said.

"They nearly stoned him the last time we were there," James said.

"And would you have predicted that we would have stayed on as long as we did, and then left with our lives?"

"No. I thought we were dead men."

Quiet, and the nodding of heads.

I was convinced of the truth of my words. Persuaded, too, that though I couldn't conceive of an act greater than raising a man from the grave, I had yet to see his greatest sign.

"We wouldn't believe now what he'll accomplish during Passover if he told us. This, I am certain."

We were gathering a multitude to surpass

that of any that had followed Jesus so far. Soon he would have no choice.

He must announce his kingship success-fully . . .

Or he would die.

33

That night, I penned what would be my last coded message:

You said he should return when he was ready. The time has come. Be ready at Passover.

That same night I fished one of the diminishing coins from the moneybag and sent the message ahead.

There. It was done.

34

There was a ruckus ahead, just outside the gate of Jericho. A man was shouting, grabbing at those that passed closest to him.

"Jesus son of David, have mercy!"

Jesus stopped. "Who is calling me?"

He calls him the son of David, and my master says, "Who is calling me?"

Even a blind man sees.

I stood by as my master bent over him, knowing that he would not stop without healing him, that he could not help but heal him.

We entered the city as triumphantly as Joshua. Even the Pharisees and the elders stood back, starkly amazed at the spectacle of the crowd singing and telling the story of the man who was blind — the same man who was now dancing ahead of us like David himself, yelling and shouting to the sky.

"Isn't that Blind Bartimaeus?" I heard someone say.

I laughed. I threw back my head and laughed, having forgotten the sound, the feel of it vibrating up through my throat like its own kind of honey.

Next to me, Simon was singing in a very loud voice. Peter clasped him around the shoulders, singing with him, and James and John boomed out with them.

I had resented their closeness to my master those days in the northern territory of Philip, but in that moment, I forgave them. I could forgive them anything. I could even give up the seat on the left or right of my master if either had ever been mine to give up — anything, to have him, and them, and all of us near. My heart was filled with gratitude.

I felt the familiar pang; I missed my time alone with Jesus, the way we had it in those early days. But soon there would be time for us to contemplate the evening sky together once more, for me to remark on the strange familiarity on his face when he studied the stars, as one looks at something vaguely remembered from a dream.

For now there were the crowds, and the singing and chanting of "Hosanna, Hosanna!" as something inside me welled and threatened to burst. More than once I had to lower my head, the sun in my eyes too bright, the moment too full, the promises I had wished for, dreamt of, and abandoned in my greatest desperation, too beautiful.

Fall down, Jericho.

The throng bore us all the way to Bethany. We were held aloft by the singing of the hymns, the shouts, the laughter and games of the children darting out and between the pilgrims. It seemed like we hardly walked, our feet never touching dirt or stone, so that at one moment we bobbed in this ocean of pilgrims . . . and the next we looked up to realize that Jericho was far behind us and here were the first houses of Bethany as though they had come to us, rather than we to them.

We entered the house of Mary, Martha, and Lazarus with laughter and kisses. The Sabbath followed us in. I found myself staring at Lazarus, who looked as sun-darkened and hale as ever, as though he had never been sick in his life, let alone in the grave four days. He clasped Jesus, his head bowing against my master's shoulder, his tears falling on my master's neck as Jesus held him close.

"Ah, Lazarus," Jesus said. The look on his face was not one of comfort but of gratitude, as though he were not the one who had delivered him from the grave, but the one who had received him from it as surely as Martha and Mary had.

Mary was kissing the hands of Jesus' mother and Martha told us to come upstairs, our number spilling up onto the roof. That night, beneath a canopy of myrtle and palm, we ate the Sabbath meal with Mary the mother of Jesus, her sons and daughters and their family, Zebedee, the Magdalene, Susanna, Joanna, and her husband. We ate hungrily the simple meal of lentils, figs, and bread, each dish somehow more sumptuous than the delicacies we had eaten just the night before at the home of a Jericho tax collector.

It was my last night of peace ever.

35

A roar went up from the street the moment we came out of the house the next morning.

Hosanna!

The press of bodies. The clamor of the throng pushed past the pilgrims who stopped to stare by the side of the road, obscuring my master from those who craned to see who was at the center of the mob.

Hosanna!

"Come!" I shouted to a group of pilgrims staring dumbly by the side of the road — a bunch of bumpkins from who-knew-where. "Follow us. Here, the son of David!"

"Is this the one?" someone asked me. "Is this the one that raised Lazarus, the brother of Martha?"

"Behold the man," I said.

Others stood back in stupefied awe at the crowd, their gazes going from person to person that passed before them. When I looked back, they had been swallowed by the multitude.

We must have numbers. Zadok was right. Without numbers, we would be put down like dogs. But with enough . . . Pilate did not dare risk a riot this size. Not since the exile of Archelaus or the questionable status of his patron in Rome. He dare not risk unrest, but he dare not risk a massacre, most of all.

And so we drew the pilgrims around us like a dangerous cloak. Like a robe of many teeth. No longer a throng, but a mob. An army.

The tenor of our hymns began to change as someone ahead of us sang:

I have prepared a lamp for my anointed
one.
I will clothe his enemies in disgrace,
while on him his crown shall sparkle.

Soon the entire crowd had taken it up.

We crested the Mount of Olives, the air already warm, the breeze whispering liberation. Ahead of us there was shouting — a group came forward to meet us, and I realized they had been waiting for us on the road. But before we could go out to join them, to tell them "Come!" we stopped to stare — at the hills, blanketed with the tents of pilgrims by the thousands, the gates clogged with those entering the city with their palm fronds and myrtle, the roads bloated with travelers.

Israel's children, returned to her. Next to me, a woman I did not know covered her face and wept.

The group ahead reached us, shouting, waving branches of willow and palm.

Hosanna, son of David!

Hosanna. Save us.

There was an outpost ahead where soldiers kept watch over the road. I saw their faces as we passed by. What could they do against us? They did not move, and they could not come out.

I sang louder. *Hosanna!*

We pressed closer to our master. We had tried to buffer the surge of the crowds — everywhere there were branches poking the eye or hands threatening to tear his clothing in grappling for him so that he could only walk in stunted steps as he clasped the fingers of one hand and then another, as he laid his hand on the head of one baby thrust toward him or this child or that. But now I saw James and Andrew coming through the crowd.

I had not realized that they had gone

ahead — and what was that with them? A donkey. I recognized their cloaks on it.

I added my mantle atop theirs and helped Jesus onto the animal's back. Ahead of us others threw down their mantles and palm fronds before him. I stood back just in time to hear the shout of a woman behind me.

"Rejoice, daughter of Zion!"

I could barely breathe. I knew the words of that prophet. They thrummed in my head like a hammer:

Rejoice greatly, daughter of Zion! Shout, daughter Jerusalem! See, your king comes to you, righteous and victorious, lowly and riding on a donkey . . .

I felt my knees buckle. I fell down to them, dropping to the earth in the middle of the crowd. An instant later, strong hands lifted me beneath the arms.

The bandit Jesus. "This is not the time for falling down. Our brothers are waiting." He was grinning.

I realized then that I didn't know what brothers he was talking about.

To the gate. No one could stop us. We numbered by now in the many thousands. By the time we came to the roads they were filled with pilgrims waving branches and singing, caught up in the frenzy.

Beyond them I could see guards atop the city wall, and beyond them, the Temple guards pacing the length of the royal stoa, their Levite tunics nearly indistinguishable from those of the Romans.

Just then, a cloud passed beneath the sun, and for an instant it seemed I saw shadows, looming like giants on either side of the road. The grotesque and twisting forms of trees draped with men like morbid banners into the city.

Crosses . . .

I blinked and staggered. Someone bumped into me.

"Is this the one, the man from Nazareth?" someone shouted.

"He healed my cousin, this is the man!" came the reply.

A ringing in my ears. Speckling before my eyes. Jesus rode just ahead of me. He turned his head and I imagined I saw him weeping.

We went into the city, borne through the gate by the crowd as the hapless guards stood back and out of the way.

Next to me, someone grabbed my arm, the nails biting through the linen of my sleeve. I looked over to see the Magdalene. She clasped me as one who sees something she has never thought to see, captured between amazement and fear. Her lips were parted, a flush high on her face. I laid my hand over hers and we went on.

We had gone a little farther when the bandit Jesus slipped away toward several men standing within the gate. Perhaps they were going even now ahead of us to the Temple.

And then there, through the crowd, I thought I saw the face of my brother.

Was it possible?

"Nathan!" I shouted. "Nathan!" If he heard me, he did not show it, and after another instant he was gone as the crowd flooded the streets like a river that overflows its banks.

Just ahead of me, Jesus' head was bowed as he sat on that donkey, and though the crowd might take it for humility, I could see that he was indeed weeping.

I tore away from the Magdalene and pushed my way through the crowd, trying to gain him — to shake him and tell him this was the time. We had suffered, worked, and spent ourselves on every sick and starving soul for this very moment. How *dare* he weep? Could he not see the mob — how they welcomed their Messiah?

But the crowd shifted and I fell back as a new group intersected ours, trying to get close to Jesus. They were dragging a litter of some kind, those near it shouting and trying to keep the person on it from getting trampled in the chaos.

I fell back, staring after him.

Beyond the noise, the utter chaos and shouting, there came the slightest distant rolling, back from the direction of the Judean hills. Far thunder, like the rumble of dark laughter.

We came to the Temple's southern steps and held the donkey so that Jesus could dismount. Just as he did, a cluster of Pharisees came to the edge of the mob.

"Make them quiet — send them away!" one of them said. "You're causing a scene, don't you know what could happen?"

I saw the fear in their eyes, the desperate panic.

Let them reap what they sow.

But then the mob was pushing them back and they hurried away.

I glanced in the direction of the mikvot, craving the smell of water, of the bath cut into the stone. It only seemed right on this occasion to be cleansed of road dust, the sweaty hands that had been grappling at us for miles. But my master was already making his way up the steps.

We went after him, hurrying to keep up,

our shouts of "Hosanna!" echoing off the gate, the high arches of the royal porch, ricocheting off the very columns as we emerged into the outer court . . .

Into a marketplace that stank of animals, hay, and manure.

I stopped, dumb, and stared. I had never seen it so full. It was as though the entire market from the Mount of Olives had been relocated here, to the outer court of the Temple — from animal merchants of every kind to the moneychangers, their tables covered with coin and scale.

It might have been all right. We might have salvaged the situation if no one had been so rash, so bold, so mad as to throw away our mission over the indiscretion we saw in the Temple court.

We could have continued with the liberation of our people if someone hadn't cried out in rage and knocked over a cage of doves, sending them into wild flight.

But someone did.

And that someone was Jesus.

I watched in horror as he leapt to the next table, planted his hands against the edge, and threw it over. Coins skittered across the stone courtyard.

His face flushed red above his beard. "Isn't it written that my house will be called

371

a house of prayer?" he shouted.

A moneychanger — a man I recognized from the counting house — leapt back as, with a swipe of his arm, my master swept coin and abacus and scales at once from his table.

"And you've made it a den of robbers!" Jesus cried.

Pilgrims fell to the ground, scrabbling for the coins. Another merchant whisked a stack of coin off his table and into his apron. Someone shouted for help, for the guard.

Jesus surged into a stack of cages. He tore them open, sending more birds into the courtyard, into the faces of the mob, and fluttering up into the air.

Guards ran along the royal porch. Others were coming from the porticoes and gates, but it was too late — more of the mob was swarming through the double and triple gates, into the courtyard, grappling for the birds running between their legs, launching themselves at the money tables, grabbing the choicest lambs.

Another crash — someone had overturned another table. Several goats ran into the middle of the courtyard only to be caught by those who had not stopped to wash but marched right in.

A roar past them — an inhuman roar. My

master. A rope bridle sailed overhead and came down with a crack. I staggered at the sight of him as he drove several merchants like animals toward the porticoes, their hands over their heads.

The clouds had come in, obscuring the sun, throwing the entire scene in shadow. Guards rushed into the fracas, swords drawn. Pilgrims fled for the gates only to be pushed back by the crowd still streaming in from the stair. They clasped their animals, the hands of their children, veering off toward the inner court, if only to get away.

There! The bandit Jesus. I saw him in a flash of motion, sword in his hand, surrounded by those others who had met us inside the gate.

My hands were shaking so violently that when I tried to grapple for my knife I dropped it, unable to hear the clatter of it against the stones over the sound of the fray. Farther ahead of me a man fell down to his knees, his nose bursting crimson. Someone was standing over him, but not for long — he threw his arms up in victory too early. A nearby guard slashed at the back of his leg and he went down. And then my line of sight was abruptly cut off by a wild-eyed cow, hurtling through the riot.

A cheer from the group of bandits. They

were circled around someone down on their knees. Temple guards fringed the edges of the porticoes, swords drawn, but only in self-defense; they were outnumbered.

Overhead the rope whistled and cracked as Jesus dashed another table's worth of coins to the floor. He cried out, "Isn't it written that in that day there will no longer be a merchant in the house of the Lord?"

It was the cry of vendetta.

Of a man with a death wish.

We had come for an anointing, for a king. But we had brought chaos, riot, and unforgivable offense instead. Not to the Romans or to Pilate, or to any Gentile . . . but to our own Temple.

In a flash of clarity, I suddenly saw not a Messiah but a man on the brink of self-destruction, grappling to pull down all that the God of Abraham himself had established.

And as I saw the rage on his face, I finally realized what the Pharisees, priests, and teachers of the law — and yes, the Sons of the Teacher — had seen long before me.

Nathan was right. I had been deceived.

I pushed my way through the southern entrance. It was pumping like an artery, spurting more and more people into the yard.

Shouts outside. Soldiers from the Antonia Fortress streamed along the western wall toward the upper gates.

Hosanna.

Pray save us.

I ran. Down, onto the congested street, into the crowd. A chorus of shouts sounded from the way I had come, a strange and distant cheer.

I had believed him. I had made excuses for him, had pitted myself against the Pharisees and the priests in his name, calling him the son of God.

I spun into a narrow alley and bolted down a side street.

I ran until my lungs burned, until I was as far away from the Temple as I could get. North, to the New City, but I dared not go home.

Behind a line of houses, I fell down against a low wall and covered my face, my hands still trembling. I had lost the others somewhere on the steps, but I knew where they would meet. If I didn't join them, they would think I had been lost in the riot or even killed.

Instead, I stayed there through fits of cramps that seized my legs and questions that seized up my lungs.

What had we done?

How would Rome come down on us now, worse than before? How was Jesus any better than Judas bar Hezekiah, wreaking the havoc that would see us razed to the ground?

I had been a man of God's law once, rededicated after a false messiah had ruined my life. I had thought this messiah would be different, had been seduced by his signs, the way he'd absolved me of my childhood guilt.

By his love.

For love, I had kept myself in the company of sinners. Had spoken alone to a woman improperly, had broken the Sabbath . . .

I had thought it a kind of freedom. An anarchy of the coming kingdom where all men are free from oppression.

But I had let the law leak away like a badly plastered mikva that drains dry the living water within it.

When I finally got up again, it was nearly dusk. But rather than go to join them, I turned my steps to the upper city, sickened and utterly lost.

How could I have been so terribly wrong?

36

This time I was not offered water to wash or wine to drink though my throat was burning and I could barely swallow. I had waited nearly two hours by the back gate. Finally, the steward returned and fetched me upstairs, to this small room.

"Hail, Teacher," I said, rushing forward.

Zadok didn't greet me but merely sighed as I took his hands.

He sat on a bench, not in the robes of a Pharisee but in a simple tunic, the tefillin loose on his forehead and arms as though he had begun to take them off. In that moment, he looked not so much like a teacher as an aging man, the furrows more pronounced around his mouth than the last time I had seen him.

"Very serious charges will be leveled against your master."

"Please, I need your counsel."

"Judas, clearly you love him. But these are

serious charges. You knew that the chief priests put out a call for informers on him, and that they accuse him of blasphemy. But now, after today . . . I don't know that even that will be necessary. He convicts himself." He sighed. "And after all your loyalty."

"No man can convict himself, not in a court," I said. "I, too, know the law!" Jerusalem was not within Herod's jurisdiction — the king couldn't just kill him as he had his cousin, John. It would take a majority to convict him of any charge, unless the mob were allowed to get to him first —

"Judas. Is he so adept at deceiving that you never even saw it?"

"It was the signs! Even I performed signs under him —"

"So did Pharaoh's magicians. Are you so in need of wonders to give you hope? Is the Torah not enough for you?"

I covered my face.

"But that's not all," he said, sounding weary. "I'm told that a Roman auxiliary serving in the Temple was killed today. A Samaritan."

I sat back on my heels. The strange shout, the cheers — that had to be it.

"Now we will all suffer." Zadok shook his head.

"But if it was only a Samaritan . . ."

Even as I said this, I heard the echo of one of my master's stories. Of a Samaritan, a member of that hated people, who helped a man beaten by bandits when a priest and a Pharisee had failed to help him . . .

"Do you think that matters to Pilate? He was wearing the uniform of Rome! He can't let this go unexcused. Anyone associated with your master will suffer. That will include your family, Judas."

"Please, help me to save them!"

"How can I help you? You follow a deceiver!"

"Please. You have influential friends," I said, coming to him on my knees.

He was quiet for a moment, his gaze fixed somewhere in the space between us. Finally, he said, "Judas, an hour will come, I think very soon, when you will have to decide whether it is better for one man, who has repeatedly demonstrated his failure to Israel, to be sacrificed to spare a nation."

The floor fell out from beneath me.

"You would stand up for Caiaphas and his false prophecy?" I said. "He is a Sadducee and not even the legitimate High Priest!"

He looked up at me then and it seemed I saw every line etched on his face. He was worn, tired, but he was also proud. What might a man like Zadok find for himself in the kingdom of God if when that very thing should actually arrive? People looked to him to fill the shoes of his teacher, the militant Shammai. But when God's kingdom finally came into being, what would the world require of men like Zadok?

He was a man whose entire identity was wrapped up in rebellion against Rome, whose very reputation *required* Rome. A man who would not willingly or easily be reduced from visionary to mere policer of the law. And somehow I knew then that he would never lose his life for this cause, but always find a way to survive it.

I exhaled stiffly at this realization, the sound coming out like an abrupt, short laugh.

He needs Rome. He fears Rome.

"Judas, we are not ready for rebellion. Not yet. Your master has placed us all in such straits!"

"*Rome* has placed us in such straits. *We* have. It is *our* sin that has brought about this exile in our own land! Is that not what you teach? How is my master any more to blame for this than me or you?"

His eyes narrowed a warning. His mouth flattened. "Heed me. Your master is soon to die. And I am telling you this as a father to a rebellious son, because I have seen this descent of yours."

A rebellious son? From a man younger than I! My master had told a story, once, of a prodigal son returning to his father. Would Zadok welcome me with a fatted calf and a feast? No. He was that brother standing by, claiming that he had always kept his father's commandments.

"Because of your teacher, Rome will come down to the Temple and wrest away the vestments from Caiaphas for good, and our free religious status with it."

"Perhaps that is what should happen then!"

His face hardened. "Take care, Judas, lest you, too, become a blasphemer! They will close the Temple gates! They will help themselves to the treasury and this time not for an aqueduct. Do you know he was crying out for the destruction of the Temple?"

"He speaks in metaphor," I said. But how could I explain it to him?

"He claims that it must be destroyed — so that he can raise it up. Madness! That Temple took nearly fifty years to build. It is the dwelling place of the Lord, and your master turned against his own people in it — and to turn against us is to turn against God!"

Leave. Get out.

"Do you think Pilate is a lenient man?" he demanded. "Do you think Herod hasn't wanted to kill Jesus since he first took John into custody? He is a dead man, and now you must choose how many others you will consign to death with him."

"There are those who will see him to safety if you will not," I said. "Nicodemus. He was my father's patron. He has powerful friends and his teacher is Gamliel himself, leader of the Sanhedrin."

"Nicodemus can't defend your teacher. Are you so naive? Who do you think controls the Sanhedrin? Not Gamliel but the Sadducees!"

"Even among the Pharisees the school of Shammai has waited for a messiah like my master ever since the days of Judas bar Hezekiah!"

"A messiah yes! But one who rebukes the Pharisees and turns against his own people?" Zadok demanded. "Who forgets the traditions of the elders? Is that a messiah?"

"He's a good man."

"And we might have accepted him. We might have rallied every man to his cause. Don't you see? But you most of all, Judas. You have been wronged more greatly than any of us, you who have lost your dignity and laid down the Torah in your making of excuses for him. And for that, we must call him blasphemer and can render him no love."

But he loves me.

And I love him.

It is the storm. This is the storm. It is only the storm. Soon, he will rise up and calm the wind.

But what if he didn't?

"More pilgrims are coming into the city every day. We will all rise up at once —"

"Yes! More pilgrims are coming into the city every day. Do you think Caiaphas will allow your master to take advantage of that? To cause a real stir in the city at the peak of the Feast? He dare not. Pilate is in the city!"

"Then Caiaphas is acting in accordance with the interests of Rome."

"No," he said, getting to his feet. "Your master is acting in accordance with the interests of Rome. Rome is only strengthened by revolt. At even the hint of sedition, they raise taxes and enforce worship of their emperor. Do you think they haven't looked for any excuse to take away our religious status? That they hadn't had their eye on the riches of our Temple, on the gold dedicated to the Lord? They would take it with any excuse to build their arenas for public spectacle in Rome. Your teacher's rebellion here will feed their empire!"

He paced to his left and turned. "Have you considered that God has placed you in a unique position to salvage this situation in obedience to the law?"

I couldn't breathe. I got up, fumbling with my mantle, torn between reason and love. A love that demanded my master live, no matter how deceived either one of us might be.

Behind me, his voice, deliberate and calm: "Think on what I have said."

I reached the door before the servant could open it. Flung it wide. Drawing my mantle up over my head, I rushed out into the rain.

That night I did not go to join my master, nor did I return home. I begged a place to sleep in the corner of the synagogue, where I curled atop one of the benches in my mantle. Long into the night, I stared at the Seat of Moses, illuminated by a single lamp.

37

Upon rising, I stood outside the Temple and realized I was weeping. Weeping because my heart refused to stir at the sight of it. Because it had become an alien place to me, so that it seemed now ostentatious and made more and more so by the hands of men. Because I didn't know if I would ever pray as fervently as I once had, in the green hills of Galilee.

I was ruined for it. For the Temple and the sacred law. The Israel of my dreams was gone, replaced only by lepers who needed healing, the sick and the hungry. The women put out by husbands only to be caught in the act of survival and hauled before authorities. The boys thrown down in the dirt because they were of questioned birth. The rift between brothers, born of disappointment and bitterness. We had not needed the Romans for any of this to happen, but only cruelty and a code by which to measure our failures.

Jesus had done this to me. With his signs, with his miracles. With his love. All my hopes in the law paled beneath the currency of a love more immediate than Israel itself. And now, standing before the Temple, I felt nothing but the terrible longing for my enigmatic teacher's arm on my shoulders, the fierce desire to kiss him in greeting.

To strike him.

To fall at his feet.

A young man was walking through the rain with his parents. I started at the sight of him. Even from this short distance, the way he walked, as sedately as an adult, the way he carried himself with the seriousness of a young sage, put me in mind of Joshua. Joshua, with his great question of whether the Lord existed with us at all.

And that was the greatest fear of all, wasn't it? The reason we grappled for our laws, and our ways, and our Temple. This fear that without them God did not — would not — remain. And then who would we be? No different than the unwashed Gentiles, and no better.

38

"So . . . Your master is back to bring us all down." Nathan leaned in the doorway as I folded a second mantle around some food. Children's voices sounded from the outer room. Overhead, voices drifted down through the roof.

"Take this," I said, pulling the moneybag from my belt and tossing it to him.

"What? Why?" he said, catching it.

"It's yours."

"Where are you going?"

"You are the one going. I went to Nicodemus. He's promised you a position."

"What do you mean? Where?"

"In Galilee. You will be wealthy and Mother will have slaves. Go to his house tomorrow and leave immediately after you see him. Leave here and cut all ties with the Sons."

He laughed. "You're out of your mind! I'm not leaving the Sons —"

I turned and seized him by the shoulders, shook him.

"Nathan! If you love me, do this. This city is not safe."

"Do you mean that your teacher will —"

"It hasn't been safe for decades. And now you will promise me something. You will take Mother away and you will allow her to die beyond sight of the crosses lining the road to the city."

"What crosses? Judas —"

"No, you listen to me. I have failed you many times. I left you to those who called you a bastard, and I beg your forgiveness. But now, you will do this — not for me, but for our mother. You will take her to Galilee. And you will be free there to do as your conscience and God dictate. I know you have no cause to trust me, but you will do this for her. You will do this thing. Please, Nathan. Brother." My voice cracked.

He blinked at me in the face of my vehemence, and I drew him hard against my chest.

"There are things we must do, you and I. I will do my part, and you will do yours. And yours is to go. The Sons will let you go. Say you are moving to Gamala, and that Nicodemus has sent you. Go, prepare. You will leave the city as one of the pilgrims returning after the Feast, except that you will be leaving it forever."

I became aware of a presence behind us. I let go of Nathan and we both turned.

Mother.

"You are leaving again," she cried. "You have only returned and already you leave!"

I opened my mouth to speak.

"No, Mother," Nathan said, moving toward her.

I braced myself. Shook my head.

"Good news," Nathan said gently, glancing at me. "I've accepted a job. But we will need to leave."

"What?"

"Very good news," I said. "And —" I found the courage within me to summon a lie. "And soon I will join you. We are all going away from this place."

She opened her mouth to protest but it was Nathan who cut her off.

"It is decided, Mother. Isn't it, brother?"

I looked at him, gratitude filling me like sorrow. Like pride.

"Indeed. And so I kiss you now," I said, going to her and embracing her.

How small my mother felt in my arms. How tiny, and fragile. For the first time in years, I thought: *how good and pure.* She was not unclean. She was a mother filled with the courage of love.

"I love you, Mother," I said.

I accepted the embrace of my brother, briefly, fearing that I might weep.

And then I picked up the bundle of food and went out the door, closing it behind me forever.

39

I stopped twice by the side of the road to retch. I could not think. I could not stop thinking.

He was in danger.

They would kill him.

He, himself, *was* danger. He would bring danger to us all.

I would go to my master and beg him to leave, to flee with us to Galilee, and to Syria. Perhaps we would go to Alexandria.

But I knew he would never consent to leave. Whatever he intended, he intended to happen here.

I will show you even greater things, he had said.

At every turn he had saved us. The throng that left returned. The storm that rose was silenced.

But by now I was adrift in the middle of the sea and I could not turn back. The storm had blown to a full-blown squall — a tempest, this time, that not even he could extricate himself from.

40

The chamber at the east end of the royal porch finished in a semicircle, presided over by a lavish gilded arch, its stone dais built with seating enough for seventy.

Seventy-one, to be exact.

Once, I had thought to sit here myself, among the Sanhedrin. But never to stand here like this.

The proceedings happened publicly at the end of the porch where pilgrims regularly came to stare at the members of the high religious court, to gape at the lavish mosaic floors and the carved marble of the upper balcony rail that looked out over those waiting on the benches below the dais.

But today I was the one being stared at. Not by pilgrims, but by those Sadducees from the houses of Phiabi and Hanan, Qathros and Boethus. Caiaphas was not here, but his brother-in-law Jonathan, who was second in command of the Temple, had come in late as soon as the Temple doors had shut for the evening. His younger brother, Theophilus, sat to his left. There was the teacher Joezer, and Jonathan bar Gudgeda, who was a Levite and a teacher of the law and the chief doorkeeper of the Temple.

Malchus, the servant of Caiaphas, offered me wine. It was all I could do to make myself swallow it.

Beside me stood old Elias under whom I had worked so many years, and whom I had begged to bring me to his master so that I might appear here.

"You vouch for this man?" Jonathan, the brother of Caiaphas, said.

"I do. He has served the Temple faithfully," old Elias said in his phlegmy voice. "And now he returns to us, after following the Galilean, Jesus of Nazareth, these last years."

Jonathan leaned forward. "Have you come to inform on your master as the law requires?"

I swallowed, the wine tasting like vinegar in my mouth. "I have come to say that I can take your brother to meet with him. So that he might learn his way. For the sake of peace."

"You're a man of insight. And my brother

is most interested in learning more about your master. But Caiaphas does not go out to meet with renegade teachers," he said, lifting ringed hands. "Surely you realize the risk it poses — especially when the city is full of foreigners and pilgrims."

"The advantage for you is that I will do it at a time that will not cause a scene."

"No. He must come here. Let us send an escort for him — for his safety. We will do it at night, when it won't cause a riot or other excitement." He sat back with a hint of noticeable relief, I thought. "He'll be the guest of my brother, who has many questions for him. Meanwhile, we won't need to worry about how he might further stir up the city, or how Pilate will respond to another incident." His voice hardened on the last word: *incident.*

"You say he'll be the guest of your brother as though your brother never called my master 'blasphemer.' "

"If he's not a blasphemer, he has nothing to fear, does he?"

"You've tried to entrap him every time he's been here," I said.

"Of course. We are concerned. Do you know that he has said he will tear down the Temple?"

"You've no doubt heard many disturbing

things, but hear him for yourself and you'll understand that he speaks in metaphor and parable. Then you'll see that he isn't the threat you believe him to be."

"I have no doubt of that. Some, we hear, have even called him 'Messiah.' Tell us, Judas bar Simon . . . do you who call him 'Master' also call him 'Messiah'?"

My heart hammered. In that one word — Messiah — I heard all my doubts and hopes and fears at once. I saw the hand that healed the leper, the blind man, and the paralytic. That freed a tax collector and prostitute from shame and raised a dead man from the grave.

And I saw the man who offended Pharisee and Sabbath alike and voiced the profane. Who spoke out for the oppressed, but did not condemn the oppressor . . . The man who had risen up in rage in the court of God himself against his own countrymen. How could that be messianic, when by every angle of the law it wasn't even justice?

"Well?" he said, brows lifted.

"No," I said, softly, the word like a spear through my side.

"You see?" Jonathan said, glancing at the others. "Even his own followers don't believe it."

What have I done?

What I must.

I had examined the law and knew that they could not rule without testimony, without a majority, or during Feast days. They could not use anything he said against himself.

He would confound them. They would not know what to do with him. Like the dangerous days in the porticoes, he would live.

He must live.

And so I made my bargain with surety.

"I'll do it, but I require a price."

"Of course you'll be paid."

"Not that." Inside my tunic, sweat rolled down my sides. "If I deliver him to you, I want guarantee that he won't be tried for blasphemy."

They could not kill him for blasphemy, even if they wanted. They didn't have the authority under Rome; only the procurator — Pilate himself — had the power to invoke a death sentence.

But I wanted surety. Surety that would save him.

A few of the others threw up their hands, and one said, "Who are you to demand guarantees of the Sanhedrin?"

"After all these teachings, so many deceived —" Joezer murmured, his hand cradling his head so that his thumb pressed against his forehead. But Jonathan glanced at him with the barest shake of his head as though to say, *No, don't speak of that now.* The teacher lowered his hand, but the thumbprint remained upon his forehead.

Like the mark of Cain, I thought.

Jonathan said, mildly, "That is an obstacle for us. This is a great thing you ask, considering all that your master has said and done to indicate that, indeed, he blasphemes. You all but admit you deliver him to us to keep him alive."

"Yes," I whispered.

"This is great devotion. And such devotion should be rewarded," he said, glancing at Annas. "My brother is a reasonable man, and as you say, he would like very much to speak with your master. And so I believe he will accommodate you."

"I want it in writing, that he will not lay charges of blasphemy against him."

"In writing, then."

Jonathan sat back.

"Well then, Judas bar Simon. To take him into custody, we require a formal charge. Do you lay a formal charge?"

I felt ill.

"Yes." My voice cracked. I cleared my throat. "Yes. I lay a formal charge. He has done the things people say of him."

"There. I think we have what we need," he said, glancing at Joezer and a few others.

Jonathan tilted his head toward a servant who came in and took his dictation of the charge. When it was done, he brought it to me and I signed it.

"What will you give me to broker the deal?"

Without payment, it would not be binding.

Jonathan gestured to the servant, who returned a moment later with a small purse. "There are thirty shekels here."

It was the coin used for paying the Temple tax — Tyrian silver. Thirty silver, the price of a slave. The compensation price of an animal that falls into a hole in a neighbor's land.

Thirty silver. For a man who fed thousands. Who raised the dead and cast out demons.

I watched a hand I did not recognize as my own reach out to take it.

"You have done a service to your people, Judas of Kerioth."

I had done a service. I was absolved.

Why, then, had my hands begun to shake?

I left, those words in my ears. I looked back once as Caiaphas' man, Malchus, escorted me out. But they did not see me, having already leaned in to heated talk between themselves.

In the courtyard, I passed two soldiers playing at knucklebones. There, in the Temple court, beneath the nose of the Sanhedrin, they played at basalinda.

I, too, had played my move.

I had taken an action that would absolve me of guilt under the law but condemned my heart.

Even now I held out hope that he might confound us all. That in direct confrontation with Caiaphas he might work one more mighty act.

Either way, he would live.

But either way, I had forfeited him forever.

41

That evening as we sat down, I felt severed from myself. The dates and the bread on the table seemed both real and not real, as though having coalesced from a waking dream. The faces of the others were familiar and those of strangers at once. And yet Simon sat down next to me with the normal offhanded familiarity.

Did no one see it? Did no one notice?

Simon was silent. He was brooding. Across the table James seemed lost in his own thoughts, glancing up on occasion from under his brows at the others.

And then it came again: the sense that I did not belong here as I once had. That I was as much a stranger here in this company as I had been staring at the white face of the Temple. I had crossed from the familiarity of the Holy City to Galilee, from Temple to wilderness, from the worlds of the learned to the poor and diseased, from the courts of the Sadducees to this upper room here, vacillating between realms like a spirit in an arid place.

What was left to me now?

But it wasn't only me. The entire company was quieter than usual. Even Peter kept his own counsel and I began to look around, the prospect of their silence somehow most disturbing of all.

Jesus had not yet made the prayer for bread, and we were waiting on him when he abruptly got up from the table. My heart stuttered. My pulse was a dizzying drone in my head.

I should tell him what I had done. What to expect. Perhaps he would be glad for the confrontation — but either way, I couldn't bear the burden of my secret. Every moment was torture.

I had to leave, to get out.

"Master," I said, feeling that I was choking as I said it.

I don't know exactly what I said in that moment — something about wanting to procure some special items for the Passover meal from some merchants my brother knew. That I must go before it was too late.

Jesus had not yet reclined at the table, but removed his tunic. Laying it aside, he wrapped a towel around his waist and poured some water into a basin.

I was stymied. After so many meals without washing our hands, would we wash before this one?

He brought the water to the table right before Peter. Setting it down, he reached for Peter's foot — at which Peter jerked back.

What was he doing? It was the posture of a servant ready to wash the feet of his master or of his master's guest! Even Abraham did not stoop to wash the feet of his angelic visitors whom he called "my lord" in the absence of slaves. Even the High Priest washed his own feet on the Day of Atonement. And not one teacher should ever wash the feet of his followers, but the other way around.

Jesus reached for his foot again. This time, Peter leapt up, stumbled several steps away.

"What's this — you wash my feet?"

"You don't realize what I'm doing now, but you'll understand later," Jesus said, his hand outstretched over the bowl. Peter glanced back at us helplessly.

No one moved. No one knew what to say.

"Master, no," Peter said, gently, as one speaks to the confused. "You'll never wash my feet. Let me wash yours," he said, reaching slowly for the towel over Jesus' lap.

"Unless I wash your feet you have no part with me," Jesus said.

It was a moment like a boil. So taut, so full with tension that one breath might lance it.

Peter slowly sat back down. He leaned back, glancing once at James beside him as he extended first one foot and then, as though the water were scalding, a second, into the bowl in this contrarian act of submission.

The first will be last, and the last will be first.

Peter extended his hands. "Then . . . not just my feet, but my hands and my head as well," he said.

An exhaled expression from farther down the table. Heads craned to watch with incredulity.

And then Jesus was smiling, pouring water over Peter's feet. "Those who have had a bath need only wash their feet. Their whole body is clean. And you are clean."

The words stole the breath from my lungs.

How long had I waited to hear words like that?

All my life.

His were no longer the rough hands of a day-worker, but hands to heal. To bless babies. To pray. Murmurs around the table drowned out his next words, so that only those of us closest to him heard him say, "But not every one of you."

I didn't understand him or his topsy-turvy teachings anymore. I saw, too, the confused look of James beside me. His awkward posture as he put his feet into the bowl next.

When Jesus came to me, the water in the bowl was dirty. Clouded since the last time he had emptied it out, and I stared into that water feeling as grimy as it. I put my foot in.

But the moment he began to wash it, I no longer saw the dirty water of a basin, but the waters of the muddy Jordan where I had burst from the surface after that weightless and sublime moment. I closed my eyes as he lifted my foot to his lap to dry it, and something within me cried, *No. Do not finish with me yet.*

I was beside myself. What had happened to me? I began to wonder if I might take back the charge I had filed with the Sanhedrin. I could live out this fellowship, even if it were a charade, for as long as it lasted. Hours. A day. Two days. It didn't matter — I wanted it. Like Peter, bowing to Jesus' insistence that he wash his feet, as one humors a beloved madman.

And what if I urged him to flee? Was it too late? I flailed at the sudden thought that

I had set some great machine in motion. Even now I wanted to beg Jesus to come away, to let us go. I would live without a mikva, without the law, without the Temple, and without my family, if it meant staying with him.

He finished with the last of us and poured out the water. Putting on his tunic, Jesus prayed the blessing of bread, and I lowered my head to hide the tears running into my beard.

"This is the fulfillment of the scripture that he who shared my bread has turned against me."

I glanced up, belatedly, having been lost in my thoughts. His voice had wavered and he covered his face.

Silent glances around the table.

What? What next?

Each thing he said made less sense than the thing before!

"I am telling you," his voice broke, "one of you is going to betray me."

There it was. The weeping I had seen on the donkey the day we had entered the city. The burden that he carried with him. The burden, whatever it was, that he had carried with him now. It broke through the surface so that he was breathing deeply, his breath catching as he covered his face with a hand.

I glanced around the table. Was he speaking of me? Surely not! Was there any man here who loved him more than I? Who would choose his life over even the dream of Messiah?

Had someone gone to the street gangs to tell them where we were then? Was it even now too late, and his life in danger? I glanced sharply at Simon, who looked away. Could he have contacted the Sons after all this time? Had Peter opened his great mouth one time too many — and to the wrong person?

Or was it true that my master's mind had never healed from the grief of John's death, but that he grew more fractured — and paranoid — by the hour?

It wouldn't matter. Soon, he would be in the hands of the guard. He would be safe from death, and we would be safe from the edicts of the law that demanded we turn him in. But more greatly than that, he would be forced at last to rise above this storm and calm it, if he could, once and for all.

He could. He must.

For all our sakes.

"Surely it isn't me?" James blurted, his face, so weathered in this last year especially, near-childlike in the lamplight.

"Or me?" Nathanel said.

Down the table, Thomas stared, stark eyed, not speaking. He glanced at Simon, who was looking from one of us to the other, but said nothing.

Which one of us had not thought at some time of abandoning him, of condemning him, of betraying him in some way?

"One who dips the bread in the bowl with me," Jesus said, his face filled with such pain that I thought he would break down completely.

I looked away, my fists clenching.

We had given up everything, abandoned everyone, for him. Would he accuse us like this? *Us?* Even now, when he went to these mad lengths, didn't he see that we stayed with him, that we played along with his foot-washing and accusations of betrayal?

He gave the blessing for bread, and I was glad for that, eager to get on with this, having no true stomach for food.

We ate in awkward silence, the uneasy brotherhood of confusion, fear, and yes, even anger, on the table between us.

"Listen," he said. "Take this. It is my body."

He passed it to me.

I stared at it. His body. That again.

"And this," he said, lifting a cup of wine.

He gave the blessing for it, and then said, "This is my blood for the covenant for the forgiveness of sins."

Again with the blood. The drinking of blood.

He must stop. But this was not the time for confrontation.

I glanced at him, barely managing a small bite and sip before passing it to Simon beside me. My stomach threatened to revolt.

This was more than not keeping the law. Even to symbolically drink the blood of another was nothing short of abomination. No true Messiah sent by God would make such a claim.

Anxiety was raw on my every nerve.

You follow a blasphemer. Does it matter if he washed your feet?

Unclean. Unclean. It rang through my head.

The sweat that had broken out on my neck was trickling even now down my back. I had to get out. I could not stay. I felt ill, that my bowels would explode at any moment. I would be sick and needed to find the latrine. I was sweating now in earnest.

I started to push back from the table, dizzy, and then jerked at the touch of Jesus, when he leaned over to me. "What you are going to do, do quickly."

I didn't wait to see the way he looked at me.

I got to my feet, my breath expelling in a rush as I hurried down the outside stair.

I ran down the street for a long ways before finally stopping, hauling in a breath, my gut twisting.

Did he think I had to go procure the things for Passover? Or was it possible that he knew what I had done, as he had known in the stern of the boat that we would wake him? And for what — so he could rebuke us afterward for our lack of faith?

Then rebuke me. Better that I should do this now before the one who would betray him — whoever it was — did it indeed.

My bowels stopped churning, twisted into a knot.

Malchus, the High Priest's man, waited.

42

Another Passover I might have listened to the hymns sung from rooftops. Chanted along to the snippets of prayers raised like incense to the wind. Sniffed the smell of food wafting out through open windows.

That night, there was only the stamp of feet making their way down the street. Heads swiveled and anyone near hurried to get out of the way of the Temple guards following me.

"So many?" I had said in some shock when we had assembled near the Antonia Fortress. I rapidly tallied nearly two hundred guards in addition to a contingent of Pharisees and teachers of the law — one of whom I recognized as Joezer from the council chamber — all come to help identify my master in the case that I should turn and flee, no doubt.

"It's Passover," Malchus had said. "You yourself have said that a great crowd follows

411

him everywhere. With a few soldiers, they might be inspired to overtake us, and then we would have the riot that my master has labored to prevent."

Perhaps that is what it will take. Perhaps we have been wrong all these years to try to avoid the very thing.

Ahead of us a group of men were walking with their arms around one another, singing. They might have been Simon and me, or Peter and Andrew, come in from Galilee. But the song flagged as we approached them and I saw the way they looked at me, walking alongside Malchus as we passed.

It is not like that, I wanted to say to them. *I am a Jew, like you, and a patriot.*

I saw the way the guards at the gate let us go by, eyes sliding this way and that. The way the pilgrims camped throughout the Kidron Valley looked up from their fires and gatherings, their conversations cut short. The way they hurried away even from their own belongings.

For one bare moment, it was intoxicating to feel the power of the soldiers behind me, the stamp of their feet, to hear the jingle of their swords and breastplates, their helmets gleaming in the night.

And then I was horrified. Was I seduced so easily? So easily corrupted?

Had I been so easily led astray by my master as well?

Five hours. By now the others would have left the upper room. The fine wine Malchus' steward had given me when I went to his house had worn off. He had not spoken much to me, Malchus. He was a good servant. As was I. A better servant than he. Malchus must only pander to the pageantry and ego of Caiaphas. I must labor to deliver my master. Soon, he would be safe.

But first these anxious pains.

The moon was full, casting the hillside in a light like dusk as we passed through the groves of Gethsemane at the foot of the mount. I knew they would be here — it was where they had always come.

We were just nearing the garden when I took note of the camps, growing thinner out this way. The youths creeping along the trees, watching the soldiers with us, their tunics like ghosting patches of snow in the night.

For a panicked moment, I thought I should have told Jesus and the others to stay someplace closer, and more public. A great sign might happen here, within moments. Or just within the gates of the city.

Either that, or I would soon part from him forever.

My hands began to tremor.

Into the grove, through the trees.

To the cave, where the press was.

"Let me go ahead," I said, turning to them in the descending darkness.

"You laid the charge. You must identify him," Malchus said.

"The one I kiss. He is the one. Now, stay back and wait."

The contingent behind him halted.

I got to the cave in time to see them coming out, several of them looking confused and bleary-eyed — except for Jesus, who looked very alert, having prayed all this time, no doubt. Simon and Peter nodded; it hadn't been unusual for me to come and go this close to the city and my home. But I dared not greet them now. I went directly for Jesus instead.

In the past, he had held out his arms to me. Not tonight.

This time, he waited as I came to stand before him.

"Hail, Teacher," I said.

Suddenly, I wanted to weep. I cupped his face and tilted my forehead against him, felt my expression crumble.

Why this, why like this? Why must I do this? I could smell the warmth of him, the scent that was his, like the smell of sweat and wine and salt and blood. Blood? And then my lungs constricted, and my breath caught in my throat. My hands fell to his shoulders, and for an instant, I thought my knees would fail me again, that I would clasp him as one does while drowning.

His whisper, when he spoke, was warm against my ear. "Do what you came for, friend."

Inexplicable tears — hot tears — coursed down my cheeks.

"Hail," I whispered, and kissed him with trembling lips.

It was greeting and goodbye.

I lifted my head to find him gazing directly at me, something in his wide eyes I had never seen before.

Fear.

And then there was the rush of footsteps, of bodies and the clink of armor.

He was pulled away from me, I wasn't sure by whom, but only that I was jerked back — too soon! — still holding on to him, his tunic pulling askew, his mantle sliding off his shoulders, baring one of them.

I was dragged back as Malchus and several soldiers moved in front of me. And there was Peter and the flash of his sword and then Malchus, who had ducked the arc of it, screaming.

"Put your sword away!"

Jeoʊoı

The soldiers were advancing now — too fast! They would kill him, cut him down, and I was shouting and trying to get between them.

My master threw out his arms. "Don't you think I could call on my father and have twelve legions of angels at my disposal?"

I hadn't known what would happen, but something felt wrong. Malchus was screaming for everyone to put up their swords, his hand clutching at the place his ear had been.

The right ear. Where a man received the oil and blood of his guilt offerings, on the lobe. Without it, a man could never be properly absolved.

My master went to Malchus in the circle of soldiers, silently drew Malchus' shaking hand away from the side of his face.

His ear was whole, and intact — only the fresh blood on his neck and tunic bearing witness that it had ever been removed.

And then the soldiers came all at once.

They grabbed for Jesus, who did not move, but staggered as hands seized him from one direction and then another.

"Master!" I shouted.

Behind him I could see the soldiers seizing one of the young men who had followed us, grabbing his tunic so that the boy spun away, ripping it apart, leaving it in the soldiers' hands.

"Let them go!" Jesus said.

The group scattered in the fading light. Peter turned back, his mouth working, and I realized he was screaming for me to run.

I stood rooted in shock — long enough to see them binding the hands of my master.

And then I turned on my heel and fled.

43

Peter and I pressed ourselves against the gate of the old Hasmonean Palace, calling out to anyone passing through the yard to let us in, to fetch Malchus. It had gone wrong. I had to see Malchus. To demand an explanation. To know that they wouldn't harm my master.

Eventually a slave let us inside the yard. Malchus himself was nowhere to be seen.

Guards passed before the yard's caldron fire — Temple guards, many of whom had come here ahead of us. Overhead, clouds had obscured the moon. We drew our mantles close about ourselves, and waited.

We did not speak. But I glanced often at Peter and thought, *He knows. He knows and disowns me already.*

The hour wore on. At some point, I looked down to see the dirt on my feet — the feet that my master had washed, now covered in grime.

A little while later, the slave came back out. Peter shrank toward the shadows. She didn't seem to notice him — or the lewd looks of the soldiers upon her — as she summoned me.

"What's happening?"

"Malchus sent me to fetch you. They're questioning him."

I glanced back at Peter, his eyes like holes in his face, and then followed her in.

She led me along the corridor of the house I had been so curious to see most my life. But now that I was here, I had no eye for the fine torches or the mosaics, or the great length and breadth of the front room ahead of me as she brought me to a small side gallery tended by a guard. From here I could see only a swath of the larger room beyond.

"You have to stay here."

My heart was in my throat and I nodded, unable to speak. Ahead of me, through the doors, the great room was filled with light and arches . . . and the frowning faces of several Pharisees and Sadducees I recognized. There was Helcias bar Phiabi and several from the house of Boethus, talking amongst themselves. There, Annas, who was High Priest before Caiaphas, and there . . . Caiaphas himself, surrounded by his cronies like a pack of vultures. A group of men known for their scheming and power-lording and corruption, twenty-three in all.

And there, standing in front of them, was my master.

His mantle was gone and his tunic was strangely stained, as though he had bled on it — no, that he had sweated out blood from his very pores.

It was only then I fully understood: He hadn't been brought here for questioning.

He was on trial.

No. I had to be wrong. But there they were: twenty-three. The number of men required to examine or convict a man. But a trial could not be conducted at night, nor on the eve of a holiday! They knew this!

Master!

Through the doors, my master turned his head.

Did he see me? Had he heard the cry in my heart? Did he see me from the corner of his eye — this ant, this termite that I was, crouching in the wall?

But there, on his face. What was that?

A welt.

They had beaten him?

I rushed forward, cried out his name. But they were still on some kind of recess and talking so loudly between themselves that no one heard. The guard standing between the larger room and the gallery gave me a pointed look.

I sat back, chewing the inside of my cheek, telling myself that Jesus had stilled a storm with a word, so surely he could escape them all now.

They came to order. Brought in a man. I thought I might recognize him, that he might be one of the men who picked up a stone during Tabernacles. But how could I know, how could I remember? And what help was it if I did?

"What do you remember of this man's teaching at the Temple?" Caiaphas asked him.

"He said that he would destroy this temple made by human hands. And that in three days, he would make another — not made by human hands."

But that was not it. He spoke in parables!

"What is your answer?" Caiaphas said, looking expectantly at him.

Jesus pitched forward onto the floor and I realized that someone outside my line of vision had struck him from behind. He fell, sprawling, and I could see that his hands were bound.

"You won't answer." It wasn't a question.

The breath went out of me. Where was Nicodemus? Any of his friends — the students of Gamliel? There were none of them here that I could see.

And then a figure I recognized very well came to stand beside Annas.

Zadok.

Cold. A dart through my lungs.

His hair was oiled, and the tefillin seemed to fairly gleam on his arm and forehead, wrapped so tightly that they practically protruded like square, sawed-off horns.

Annas leaned toward Caiaphas, murmuring something too short and too quiet to be heard.

At last, Caiaphas said, "Are you the Messiah? The son of God?"

The words I had longed for him to speak. To hear from his own lips. But now, for the first time in my life, my heart cried out: *No.*

Say no.

Say no and live.

My master was getting to his feet. The form of a soldier stepped into view, a large and thick-shouldered Temple guard. Caiaphas stayed him with a hand.

"I am," Jesus said, his words thick.

Outrage from the gathered council. I staggered back against the wall.

"And you will see the Son of Man sitting on the right hand of the Mighty One," Jesus cried, "coming on the clouds of heaven!"

They rose up in their seats. The High Priest tore his clothes.

Blasphemy.

Death.

They cannot convict him. They swore and put it in writing.

Then why do they continue with this farce?

The trial went on for hours.

It was a charade. Not even legal. It was night. This was the home of the High Priest, not the chamber of the Sanhedrin. It was the eve of a feast. Where was evidence of acquittal? A man could not condemn himself. And even if he could, even guilty, they could not condemn him on the same day. It was the law.

But these thoughts faded away as my master went sprawling again and I covered my ears as the soldiers came to haul him back up.

This time, he was turned away from the council. This time he gazed out past the open doors of the chamber.

This time he looked directly at me.

His face was mottled with darkening bruises. Blood trickled from his lip, already grossly swollen. Despite the blood, the swelling of the side of his face, the look in his eyes was unmistakable.

Love. So much love.

And pity.

I felt my face crumple.

They jerked him to his feet.

"Master!" I shouted. I leapt from the side gallery, threw myself against the guard as my master was led away.

I don't know what I screamed or said after that. I only knew that a part of me was being rent away, taken off by the brutal hands of Caiaphas' men.

Beyond the impenetrable shoulders of the guards, Zadok lifted his head to stare directly at me as the Sadducees buzzed between themselves like a horde of flies.

"You lied!" I screamed. "You swore an oath!"

One word reached me through the fracas then. One word, that chilled my blood.

Mesith.

Leading Israel astray.

I staggered.

It was a charge worse than blasphemy. A killing charge, with no defense, for which they might meet and convict in the same day. For which a man might convict himself with his words. For which they might conduct every aspect of this trial exactly as they were — at night, with only a quorum, on the eve of a holiday, convicted by a majority of only one.

Mesith.

A death knell.

I had bargained for the life of my master, to save him from a charge of blasphemy. I thought I had earned him his safety, his life. But now I knew: They had meant to charge him with mesith all along.

They released me into the yard with a shove. I stumbled toward the fire, tearing at my hair.

What have I done?

The face of my brother Joshua wavered before me. Joshua, the day I spat in his face. The day he fell into Roman hands. Joshua, whom I had loved more than anyone in the world, even Father.

I saw Susanna, dead on the ground. Dead because I had gone to the Temple first, before seeing to her safety.

Father, hung on a cross, because I prayed to stay in Sepphoris.

Someone tugged at my sleeve, and I turned with unseeing eyes. Peter. He was pulling me away. His eyes were swollen. Had he been beaten, too? But no, he had been weeping.

I opened my mouth but I could not say the word.

Mesith.

I had delivered my master to death.

44

They sent him bound and beaten to Pilate in the morning. I followed the guarded escort, trying to catch sight of him. And when I did, I saw that Jesus' face was nearly unrecognizable.

I stopped by the side of the road to vomit. Now who was the dog?

I loitered in the courtyard, watching it fill with Pharisees, pilgrims, and curious onlookers, and then with faces I recognized as those of the bandit Jesus' company. What were they doing here?

Peter was gone; I didn't remember when he left that morning, and did not know where he went. But he had disappeared with the cock's crow, and I had come here alone.

I had been waiting outside through dawn, trying to catch a glimpse of Jesus, to bargain with the guards if they would only let me in to see him.

"What are you doing here?" I said to one

of the bandits now. "Are you waiting for my master?"

One of them, his eyes lighting with recognition when he saw me, said, "We wait on our own. Our leader was arrested in the scuffle your master started."

Someone else shouted, "Give us our Passover release!" They had been shouting this off and on now for an hour, and it took me a moment to remember, dully, that Pilate had once followed in the tradition of Archelaus and released a prisoner at Passover as a sign of goodwill.

I blinked at the man. "Your leader — you mean the bandit Jesus?"

"Yes! He killed a Samaritan that day in the Temple!" There was fire in his eyes.

"He's the one who killed the Samaritan?" I looked around. "But there weren't this many in your company. Why are there so many people clamoring for his release?" The courtyard had steadily filled, not only with those I recognized as priests from the Temple, but common peasants, no doubt come down from Galilee.

"All this time he was with you — don't you know who he is? Or, rather, who his father was?" he said. "He's the youngest son of Judas bar Hezekiah himself."

Jesus the bandit, son of the Teacher himself. Jesus bar Abba.

By the time they escorted my master to the palace, the crowd had quadrupled.

I caught only one more glimpse of Jesus from the courtyard. He had been brutally beaten.

"Master, Master!" I shouted, unable to even hear myself, the cries of "Bar-Abbas!" thick in my ears.

I did not stop to immerse in the mikva. It wouldn't do any good. I hurried through the double gate, shoved my way into the great court. Somewhere within the Middle Court, the Levites sang their morning psalms.

I strode through the columns, the teachers already in the porticoes. Would they pander to the Pharisees and quibble about purity or did they whisper the forbidden challenge of the spirit behind the law? Would they speak the things they should not speak, or mire themselves comfortably in debate forever?

Those shining-faced students, those young boys that would be Pharisees and sages — would they be content with blithe answers and ignore the final *Hosanna* of their hearts?

Did they go into the darkness of their homes and hear the sound of God after so many hours spent studying his law? Did they see their own starlike hands, the lesions on their souls, the adultery of their hearts?

Unclean. Unclean.

We are all white-washed tombs.

With every step, the purse at my side was a jingling liability, the peal of Sheol. Thirty pieces of silver.

I had no need for coin.

"He'll release the bandit to them —" someone was saying as I passed by. "The people love the bandit; he killed that Samaritan in the Temple. One would-be Messiah for another, then."

I saw it then as clearly as though it had played out. They would call for him, the son of Judas bar Hezekiah. For the good of Israel.

And they would turn the king — my king — over to death to placate their Roman masters.

We have no king but Rome.

To the chamber at the end of the portico, the meeting place of the Sanhedrin. Days ago I had waited, sweating, to speak. Now I strode directly to the dais, into the midst of them all. There they were. Jonathan, Joezer, Helcias, and a tired-looking Annas, and there, last of all . . . Zadok.

"You charge the mesith!" I cried, the

words echoing off the sides of the chamber. "That he leads Israel astray?"

Jonathan did not speak, but glanced at Zadok, who sat back. "Ah. Judas." Off to the side, someone snapped for the guard.

"You have played your role. You have done well," Zadok said.

"You promised. You gave your word!"

"That we would not charge him with blasphemy. And we have kept that word," Annas said.

"Blasphemy — or a worse offense!"

"I'm sorry. You did not say that."

The letter of the law. The very word I spoke.

"What can I do to ransom him? What can I give you in exchange? Please." I fell down to my knees. "Any price. Name any price. Give him back to me."

"Get up. This does not behoove you," Zadok said.

"I can give you information on the sons of Judas bar Hezekiah," I said loudly, staring right at him. "On the rebel group who fashion themselves Sons of the Teacher after him. I can tell you all about them!"

Zadok's eyes narrowed at me.

"We have all the information that we require about them," Joezer said lightly.

"Zadok, here, can supply you with far more."

Zadok sat unmoving. Far too unmoving. They all did.

And I realized then I had been played expertly. Right into their hands.

"Judas, be glad. Don't you see? You have your Messiah," Zadok said. "He will die for the people. To stave off the dogs of Rome. For another day, Judas. He saves us. You see? And so you can be content. Hosanna."

Outside, the great court was filling with pilgrims, the strains of their hymns flitting into the chamber.

"I am not content!" I roared, stalking toward them, never caring about the soldiers at the end of the room. "I have betrayed innocent blood!"

I yanked the moneybag from my belt and threw it at the feet of Annas. The fabric split open, the coins spraying out across the foot of the dais.

Would you buy back your master for thirty silver?

"Absolve me of this! I return your money. I have worked in the treasury, I know the law. If you refuse to take it back, then I return it to the Temple. My mind is changed. I want nothing to do with this deal. I undo it! Here is your money — it is invalidated!"

"Judas —"

"I've sinned! I have betrayed innocent blood! Undo it!"

No one moved. Hurrying footsteps, the guard, coming for me.

"He is innocent! No one else has said it, so let me. He is innocent! If the witnesses disagree, then you cannot convict him and your false witness must suffer the condemnation you have put on him. You, yourselves, as false witnesses, must suffer the condemnation you have put on him. I, Judas, son of Simon, condemn you! Undo our agreement!"

No one moved. Desperation flooded my throat, my lungs. I was drowning in it. In bloodguilt.

"I have betrayed a Jew into the hands of the Gentiles!" I screamed.

The eyes of Annas were ice cold. "That is your responsibility."

"It's a dying offense! Such an act invites God's curse — and makes one unfit to dwell in the land. If you follow the letter of the law, you must kill me!"

Annas nodded to the guard, who started toward me. "We do not accuse you," he said, placidly. The guard came, and I struck out at him.

"You!" I cried, stabbing my finger at Annas. "You have turned him over to the

Gentiles as much as I. You are as cursed as I!"

"We? Not we." Annas' eyes narrowed. "We are the children of Abraham. As for you . . . You signed the document. You are the accuser. Blame us all you like, but the decision was yours."

And then the guard's fist found my face and the floor crashed up to meet me. My teeth hit the marble with a crunch that sent my ears ringing. I lashed out at him with a leg, but this time another guard joined him. Together they took me by the shoulders, carried me from the Temple, and threw me down the southern steps.

It hurt to breathe. It hurt to live.

They had turned him over to Rome, because they could not convict a death penalty case themselves.

They would make it seem like a great offering, a sublime submission on their parts, to convict him for them, like a rich man placating his mistress with a gift.

He had called me "friend." But I had played the satan.

I must make restitution. I would make sacrifice.

But how could I bring an offering to the very priests who conspired against my master? How could I take an animal to the Temple to sacrifice ever again? How could I celebrate Passover even as my master was taken out of the city during the killing of the lambs?

Where was the Lord?

Not there with the priests.

No, there was nothing there for me anymore.

The only God I knew was with my master in Pilate's prison and I had accused him and delivered him over to his enemies. I had betrayed the only absolution I had ever hoped to receive in my life.

A faint rumble ran along the horizon like laughter.

I loitered outside the palace, desperate for a glimpse of him. My one tooth had come out and two more were loose. My eye was swelling, and my ribs hurt every time I took a deep breath. I knew all of this, but I did not feel it.

The courtyard was nearly full by mid-morning.

I was weeping, and there were some people staring at me, pulling away in order not to touch me.

"Is he a leper?" someone asked.

"Yes," I said, glancing at them. "I am

unclean." It had been my nightmare all my life.

They fell away from me like water from oil. I gave a faint laugh that sent a shock of pain through my side, tears stinging my eyes.

I wanted him. I wanted him back. It was all I wanted.

I tried to pray. I had not prayed the Shema in nearly a day for the first time I could remember.

Hear, O Israel, the Lord is One . . .

One.

They brought him out, bloodied more even than before. But I knew him. I would have known him anywhere by the way that he moved, the cant of his eyes, swollen as they were.

Let me take his place. Let me die. Let him live.

Get behind me, Satan.

They had dressed him up as the king from the soldiers' basalinda game, this hand-worker from Galilee standing beside the most powerful man in Judea.

When Pilate joined him on the parapet, it was my master who wore the purple of the king.

Pilate washed his hands of it, publicly. One would-be king passively accepting the blood sacrifice of the crowd. How easily he did it. They all did — Zadok, the priests, those members of the Sanhedrin who had convicted him throughout the night.

They led my master away and I fell to the ground, shouts of *Bar-Abbas!* deafening my ears.

It would be my last glance of him.

Last glance. Last kiss.

Too many lasts.

45

The crack team of executioners, those experts in crucifixion, have lined up outside the fortress. Pilate will have his demonstration to quell any further thoughts of uprising.

A part of me says, *Go. Touch him. Be healed.*

I could loiter on the street — hope to catch a word, a glimpse of him. A moment.

It wouldn't be enough.

Does he know that I loved him, that I love him still?

He washed my feet . . .

And I have killed him.

What I wouldn't give to be a tax collector.

A Samaritan.

Even a Roman dog.

46

Near the Hinnom Valley the camps get thinner and thinner, and then there are no tents at all. The trash burns there at all hours, a constant smolder, an eternal fire.

There are trees there, mostly olive, and they are sturdy.

The rope is strong, and I have tied the noose well. I have cinched it with every year of my life.

I gasp but there is no air except that sweeping past me, like water. And I am back at the Jordan, and there is John, pointing from the muddy water.

Behold, the lamb of God.

Hosanna. Pray save.

They will say that I betrayed him, that I reduced his price to thirty silver shekels. They will say that I am greedy. That I turned against my master. They do not know that I die for heartbreak. For regret . . .

For love.

But if they did not know me, neither did they know him. How he shocked us with his compassion. With his unwillingness to restore a nation, preferring to restore individuals instead.

They called him a madman. They called him a liar. But now I know him as the face of God. Who does not save us from the Romans . . .

But saves us from ourselves.

The thought is a jolt and I jerk with it. The rope winds tighter. I would gasp if I could, with amazement. Because ah! I *see*.

I am the leper. The demoniac. I, who was paralyzed by fear, who was blind.

The prostitute, the dead man in the tomb. Me. All me.

I, who denied him and delivered him to his enemies. I, who die with him. My name will be synonymous with "traitor." But he has loved his enemies.

He has loved me.

The sun is setting. It has painted the far rise of the valley gold with the coming in of Sabbath. No one will know to take down my body. My bowels have released, unruly to the end.

Overhead, the clouds have thinned, darkening with dusk. The stars will come, bring-

ing in the Feast. The stars my master loved
to gaze at with the eye of God himself
It is warm for this time of year.
It will be a beautiful Passover.

AUTHOR'S NOTE

I ran away from this story for about a year
before even casually mentioning the possibility of it to author friends and my agent.
Unlike the case with *Havah: The Story of
Eve*, this time I knew what I was getting
myself in to. And so I told them with the
full expectation and slight hope they would
talk me out of it. They didn't. A year later, I
finally admitted it had sprouted in my
writer's brain and rooted in my heart. It
scared me. It fascinated me.

Over the next three years, *Iscariot* became
an intellectual and spiritual quest to discover the life of Judas based on the belief
that we all err in ways that make sense to
us. We do not set out to commit the heinous.
As I wrote in my author's note for *Havah:
The Story of Eve,* there is more — there *must*
be more — to the story than the two-
dimensional account. There always is.

After returning from a research trip to

Israel, I sat down to a library of more than 100 books, documentaries, lectures, commentaries, sermons, and collected articles. Invaluable to me: *The New Complete Works of Josephus,* William Whiston, trans. (Kregel, 1999); *The History of the Jewish People in the Age of Jesus Christ,* Vols. I and II, Emil Schürer (T. & T. Clark, 1979); *Bandits, Prophets and Messiahs,* Richard A. Horsley (Trinity Press International, 1999); and *Judas: Betrayer or Friend of Jesus?,* William Klassen (Fortress Press, 2005).* And of course, the companionship of a team of

* Other invaluable volumes include: *Rabbi Jesus,* Bruce Chilton (Image Books, 2000); *Jerusalem in the Time of Jesus,* Joachim Jeremias (Fortress Press, 1969); *Who Was Jesus?,* N. T. Wright (William B. Eerdmans, 1992); *Judas: A Biography,* Susan Gubar (W. W. Norton & Co., 2009); *Where Christianity Was Born,* Hershel Shanks, ed. (Biblical Archeology Society, 2006); *What Jesus Meant,* Garry Wills (Penguin, 2007); *The Jewish Study Bible* (Oxford University Press, 1999). Also: Amy-Jill Levin's lecture series on Great Figures of the New Testament, Bart Ehrman on the New Testament, Isaiah M. Gafni on the Beginnings of Judaism, and Shai Cherry's Introduction to Judaism (The Teaching Company, 2002, 2000, 2008, and 2004).

scholars — Dr. Joe Cathey and Randy Ingermanson in particular — who walked this
journey with me.

I was fascinated by the context of Jesus —
the Roman occupation and oppression, the
deep groan for national freedom. For salvation. I was intrigued with the increasing
vilification of Judas through the progression
of the gospels. I was caught up in the rich-
ness of Jesus' parables, the historical events
in the scriptural account — in my own need
to be *accurate,* whatever that is, as I chased
vision through the lens of history and
myriad layers of doctrine.

And of course, I was captured by the
person — by the riddle — of Judas himself,
the only disciple Jesus called "friend."

What did his name mean? Could it be at-
tributed to the Hebrew word for "false one"
or is it an allusion to the Sicarii "dagger-
men" — an extremist zealot group active in
the years leading up to the Great Revolt 66–
70AD? Or is it, as I have postulated, a
combination of ish-Kerioth, the "man from
Kerioth"? We know little about his youth or
his family — only that his father's name was
Simon. Was he a zealous patriot? A disciple

A more complete list of my research library can
be found on my website at toscalee.com.

disappointed with the mission of his master? Or a man as confused and prone to failure as the other disciples around him? Was he possibly, as some suggest, a priest with access to the inner court of the Temple — or even a Pharisee?

The gospel of John records that Satan entered Judas. Did the devil possess him literally, or did he become the embodiment of Satan — the "accuser" — as he made his appearance before the Sanhedrin? How was this different from Peter, whom Jesus called Satan in Caesarea Philippi?

What is the significance of the Greek word *paradidōmi,* most often translated as "betray" but more aptly translated "deliver"? When Jesus predicted at the last supper that one of them would betray him, why would Judas, who was knowingly delivering his master to death, openly ask, "Is it me Lord?" and be broken to the point of suicide over it?

What is the significance of the thirty pieces of silver — possibly thirty Tyrian shekels? Is the passage in Zechariah 11 a sarcastic, even ominous, warning of such a betrayal to come?

And was Judas the chief betrayer . . . or merely one among many: priests, Romans, and the mob who handed him over? Is it possible that, as Susan Gubar (*Jesus: A Biography*) suggests, given the benefit of his action we are all accomplices?

The account of his death, in itself, is a riddle. Did he hang himself, as traditionally depicted, by a rope? Or in the way that one "hangs" on a cross or by impalement as throughout biblical times? And what of the account in Acts, in which he fell, breaking open his body so that his intestines spilled out? Are these conflicting or complementary accounts?

Was Judas damned for the act that defined his life? Having no hope for pardon, did he receive none? Can the instrument of divine will be excluded from the outcome he helped enact . . . if so, who has paid the greater price? Or is it possible that grace knows no such limits?

As I wrestled with these questions (anyone who knows me even a little knows I ask too many questions) and the ideas of religious agenda, legalism, personal stymie, and spiritual failure, I could not help but see myself in Judas — at times, too well.

One of the things I looked forward to the most in the writing of this book was the opportunity to slip into the skin of one of those closest to Jesus. To sit, even virtually, at his side. Ultimately, this novel became as much about the person of Jesus as Judas.

I was shocked by and enamored of this Jesus, who concerned himself less with the purity laws of polite society and more with its outcasts. This radical messenger seditiously dared to proclaim another kingdom other than Rome, another "son of God" than its emperor — an action historically treated with swift and decisive action. A man who stood up for the oppressed without condemning the oppressor, more concerned with the restoration of individuals than the salvation of a nation. A man who, through the lens of history, was nothing short of dangerous.

I saw with new eyes this paradox of a man given to emotion. An unpredictable, even scandalous man, nothing like the Jesus of paintings I grew up with. A man who would not be controlled. A man as wild as God.

After a year and a half of research, I collected my notes and began to write. To attempt to capture the tension surrounding Jesus, the historical stage he walked onto the day he began his ministry, the political and theological nuances of his actions, the symbolism of the context lost to us today.

My first draft of this story was nearly three times the length of the book in your hands. But somewhere in those pages filled with intricate detail to delight the history- and theology-minded alike, I lost sight of the most important thing: the heart of Judas' and Jesus' story.

I thought back to my time in Israel. I had stood on the shores of Galilee's lake, sat in Capernaum's synagogue, had seen the theater of history. I had learned so much. But as I entered Jerusalem, I was bereft. Ascending toward the Dome of the Rock that day, steeples and mosques and temples crowding the horizon like so many hands reaching for God, I realized I had not *experienced* one moment of mystery. I fought back tears on my way toward the mosque, distracted myself by stopping to give an old beggar woman a few shekels. The moment I did, she grabbed my hand in both of hers, and I nearly fell to my knees. *Here* was God. And I knew without a doubt I had traveled all the way to Israel just to hold her hand.

In the end, I threw out three theses' worth of historical detail and returned to mystery. One of these days I may make some of those portions available, but for now here is the heart . . . a story of divine and human love — a story of you and me.

Selah,
Tosca

447

ACKNOWLEDGMENTS

My first, biggest thanks goes to my readers who waited so patiently (well, kind of — okay, not at all) for this book. Thank you for your encouragement and love, for keeping me company through the often soul-wrenching hours of this work.

Thank you: Jeff Gerke, who first slid the idea for the Son of Perdition under my skin like a thorn. Robert Liparulo, who told me to write the story. My management team of Steve Laube and Dan Raines, who keep me focused, mostly sane, and off Ramen Noodles. Meredith Efken, and Stephen Parolini, who bravely waded through the behemoth first versions. My co-author in the Books of Mortals, Ted Dekker, you have taught me so much. Kevin Kaiser, Meredith Smith, Denise George and the team at Creative Trust, you are invaluable.

My editor, Becky Nesbit, and publisher, Jonathan Merkh, thank you for taking on this girl and her stories. The entire team at Howard, thank you for your belief and your innovation.

Randy Ingermanson, and Joe Cathy, who kept a running dialogue with me during *Iscariot*'s writing. And the rest of the experts, fellow Smithie Amy-Jill Levine, Darrell Bock, Wave Nunnelly, Joel Kaminsky, Rami Arav, Kim Paffenroth, GB Howell, and Amnon Wallenstein. Thank you for sharing your intellect — and your patience.

Thank you to my family, for still claiming me. My friends — the writers and the Normals — who never shun me for dirty hair. Julie, for your laughter. Jeff Murphy, my favorite secular soldier, for all things military. Eric Wilson, who pointed the way to Kerioth.

And to my God, who shows me great things.

ABOUT THE AUTHOR

Tosca Lee is the author of the critically acclaimed *Demon: A Memoir; Havah: The Story of Eve;* and *Forbidden: The Books of Mortals* series with *New York Times* bestselling author Ted Dekker. She is best known for her exploration of maligned characters, strong prose and solid research. In 2010, Tosca left her position as a Senior Consultant to Fortune 500 companies with the Gallup Organization to write full-time. A former first runner-up to Mrs. United States 1998, Tosca received her BA in English and International Relations from Smith College in Northampton, Massachusetts, with studies at Oxford University. She is a lifelong world adventure traveler whose most recent adventures included piranha fishing on the Amazon. To learn more about Tosca, visit ToscaLee.com.